'Let's hear it, Harris. Just where did you spend your evening AWOL? Out having a malt with your boyfriend?'

It was now or never. 'No, ma'am. I have a permit. A pass.'

'A pass. What kind of pass? I give out the passes around here and I don't recall you having one.'

My heart was pounding as I handed it to her. The secret would be out any moment.

She would know about me, and she might guess that I knew about her.

Sergeant Roster took the paper from me and opened it, a sceptical look on her face. As she glanced at it, her colour deepened, the pink seeping into her cheeks. She looked at me, her eyes locking with mine.

'As you were, cadet. Get on to the showers. Look sharp!'

She turned on her heel and left. A sense of elation rushed through me as I realised I'd gotten off scot-free.

Hard Corps

CLAIRE THOMPSON

BLACK
lace

Black Lace novels contain sexual fantasies.
In real life, make sure you practise safe sex.

First published in 2000 by
Black Lace
Thames Wharf Studios,
Rainville Road, London W6 9HA

Typeset by SetSystems Ltd, Saffron Walden, Essex
Printed and bound by Mackays of Chatham PLC

ISBN 0 352 33491 6

Contents

Chapter One

Hell Week

There was mud everywhere. Mud in my nostrils, mud in my hair, mud in my panties. Before I could wipe away the ooze dripping into my eyes, Brady was on me again. We wrestled, gripping and holding each other, trying to find a weakness as we fell, in slow motion, back into the pit. We twisted as we fell, and he landed with a thwack on top of me, knocking the wind from my body. We were in what they call the demolition pit. It's an oblong pit, about one hundred feet long and maybe fifteen feet deep, filled regularly with water to create a slimy mud-bath in the bottom. Strung across it were two heavy, three-inch-thick ropes anchored by poles on both sides.

'All right, toads! You've had your fun. Get out and make room for the next two victims,' Sergeant Sinclair, our drill instructor, barked through his bullhorn. His voice blasted through the pit and I resisted the impulse to cover my ears. We scrambled up, gripping the ropes, and hauled our mud-soaked bodies out of the muck. As I manoeuvred to the side rope, Brady had already managed to climb out of the pit. He extended a hand to me which, naturally, I ignored. I'm no pussy.

Well, technically, I suppose I am. I'm a girl, you see. A woman, I guess I should say. I was eighteen then, and a freshman at Stewart Military Academy. I had signed on for this. I had worked my ass off in ROTC in high school to get to the Academy. This was my second week here. We'd had an easy first week, getting to know our way around the campus, finding our classes and getting settled in our barracks. They have barracks here, at least for the underclassmen. Makes it more authentic, I guess.

But this week was Hell Week and the name was apt. It wasn't boot camp. We'd already had six weeks of that in the summer prior to school starting. Compared to this, boot camp was summer vacation at the lake. This was one week of pure, unadulterated hell. To top it off, I was one of thirty entering female freshmen who were contributing to 'ruining' the Academy. Stewart had been co-ed for just five years and, though the standards are higher than ever, try telling that to the male contingency. To them, we weren't just toads, as they fondly referred to the incoming cadets. We were 'bitch toads', an unofficial but much-used title, though no one would have admitted it to the outside world. And we were going to pay for our impudence in infiltrating the system.

As two more cadets hurled themselves into the pit, I ran to the barracks to shower and change. My body was aching from the day's arduous events. We had gotten up at 5.00 that morning to the

2

deceptively sweet voice of Sergeant Roster, our 'den mother', as she liked to call herself.

'Wake up, Remy, darling,' she'd said, leaning her head close to mine. 'Five minutes to shower and dress, dear.'

I've never been very good at getting conscious in the morning and today was no exception. She sounded like my mother, who used to wheedle and cajole me into rising for school each day. I think I was actually confused for a moment and thought I was back home, because I said, 'In five minutes, mom.'

'Mom?' Roster's laugh rang out. I came fully awake at that laugh. Suddenly, she pulled out some kind of plastic gun with a large reservoir on top. She yanked back my covers and sprayed me with ice-cold water. I screamed, scrambling to my feet, trying to avoid volleys of spray that were soaking me to the skin.

'Next time,' she hissed, her face right up in mine, 'I won't be so easy on you, toad. When I say wake up, I mean it. Got that?'

'Ma'am, yes ma'am!' I managed to croak, shivering. For a moment, I hugged myself, covering my wet form with my arms. A glare from Sergeant Roster, and I quickly dropped my arms to my side and thrust out my chest, standing at attention. I could feel her eyes raking my body. I didn't dare make eye contact: that would have had me on the ground, doing fifty. I stared straight ahead, trying to keep my teeth from chattering. My nipples were stiff from the cold. The sergeant stood so close to me that I could smell the sour coffee on her breath. Her starched uniform brushed my soaked nightshirt: I could feel the rough fabric against my breasts. I wanted to pull back, to cover myself.

As the sergeant leaned forward, I suddenly felt a sharp pain; she had reached up, her body covering her action from the others, and savagely twisted my right nipple. Shocked, I let out a small scream.

'That's for failing to stand at attention, slime-bucket. Next time show some respect,' she hissed in my ear. No one else had seen what happened, or, if they had, they certainly weren't going to draw attention to themselves.

I was too stunned to respond, but just stood there, my nipple on fire, my face red with humiliation. Roster grinned and then stood back to address the group. 'Five minutes, children. And then five more to clean up this mess. I'll be back in ten.' She swept out of the room, while everyone rushed to the showers. I followed after some seconds, still in a mild state of shock from her actions.

Sergeant Roster came back in precisely ten minutes. I was dressed in the Hell Week uniform. White undershirt, dark-green fatigues and an orange baseball cap with the initials PMI emblazoned on it in black. My hair was tucked up with bobby pins and, of course, I wore no make-up. As Roster passed my bunk, she suddenly jerked back the covers, pulling out my perfect military corners as she did.

'Remake it, slob. Those sheets are all wrinkled up. Then hit the floor and give me twenty.'

Quickly, I remade the bed, though I didn't see any wrinkles. I'd gotten on her bad side this morning, and I was determined to get back on the good side, if I could. Done with the bed, I dropped and executed the push-ups quickly. Twenty was nothing for me: I could do forty without working up too

4

much of a sweat. Then I jumped up and stood at attention. She ignored me, which I guess was a good thing.

'Breakfast, and then report to your assigned stations. As you know, today begins your week of hell.' Sergeant Roster laughed a low, almost musical laugh that seemed incongruous with her words. 'You all worked hard to get here. Well, look to the left of you. Look to the right. By the end of this week, some of you won't be here. This is a tough course, and they aren't planning on making it any easier for you, just because you're female. I know your records, and you are a good group. Make me proud today, girls. Don't let me down.'

I wouldn't, not if I could help it. Though I wasn't doing this for her. My father was army, my mother was army, and I was an army brat. I was their only child, and it just seemed natural to me to choose this path. I had always wanted to be an officer and Stewart was an excellent school. If I could make it through this week, the rest would be easy sailing. Or so I thought.

After breakfast, we stood in the large asphalt-covered courtyard they call, simply, the Yard. Silently standing at attention, there were 135 of us, scrubbed, uniformed, nervous but eager. The rest of the class, which totalled 540, was scattered about the campus at different locations for obstacle training, distance swimming, and other tortures.

While we were waiting for the drill instructor to show, I noticed a tall, lanky upperclassman standing in the shadow of the building next to the Yard. He was dressed in an upperclassman's service dress uniform. The starched pants and blazer outlined his long, lean form. His face was in shadow, but something about him struck me as sure, somehow; as confident without being cocky. Mr Cool, I thought to myself, wondering who he was. For a moment he leaned out of the shadow and I saw his face. He seemed to be looking right at me. I cocked my head a bit, trying to see him better, but he leaned back into the obscuring shadows.

Before I could even wonder about it, though, the drill instructor, Sergeant Sinclair, strode out of the building and stood in front of us, hands behind his back. Sinclair explained the day's schedule and then blew his whistle for the first whistle drill of the day. If an instructor blew his whistle once, the students had to dive to the ground, cover the back of their heads with their hands, and cross their legs to simulate the position they would take with an incoming artillery round. Two blows of the whistle, the students would begin crawling toward the sound. Three blows of the whistle, they would stand.

We dove to the ground and waited. Two blows and we were off, crawling along the asphalt toward the sergeant. Three blows and up we jumped. I thought we had done pretty well, it being our first time since the summer.

'That sucked!' the instructor screamed. 'Do it again, toads. Do it right this time!' He blew and down we went. For what seemed like hours, but was probably more like thirty minutes, he blew and we jumped, fell, crawled and jumped up again. Up. Down. Crawl. Up. Down. Crawl. My knees were scraped and my joints were aching, but on we went. Finally, he seemed satisfied, and we ran to the obstacle course. Hell Week had begun.

For the rest of the day, with brief breaks to eat

and five-minute 'rest breaks', we clawed walls, balanced on beams and ran, ducked and dragged ourselves through mazes of wire and mud, poles and concrete until we were dripping in sweat and panting with exertion. At each new obstacle another drill instructor, fresh and rested, stood ready to torment and humiliate us for our pathetic attempts to run the drills. Panting, and soaked with sweat and caked-on dirt, we ran, slithered and jumped through the various hoops invented to test our endurance and our character.

The sun was already low on the horizon when it came time for the pit. At first the cool mud was a relief from the heat and dust of the day. But when Brady tackled me, and my muscles turned to jelly with the effort of wrestling in the thick slime, I considered giving up for a moment and letting him win without a fight. Then I heard a hiss from above. One of the other cadet's remarks reached my ears just as I was about to sink down in defeat.

'That bitch toad can't even wrestle. What the fuck is she doing here, anyway?'

The derision, the disdain, made my blood boil. I would show him – and all the assholes who didn't think women had what it took to make it here – that not only could I wrestle, I could beat the shit out of any cadet there. My bravado gave me just enough energy to put up a good fight. Mercifully, Sinclair called it quits just before I gave out completely.

On my way back to the barracks, I noticed Mr Cool again. He seemed to be watching me, which was disconcerting, but somehow exciting. I toyed for a moment with the daydream of walking over and saying 'Hi', but of course, as an underclassman,

I wasn't permitted to do that. When I looked up again, he was gone.

Back in the barracks, someone was already in one of the shower stalls, covered with soap. The whole bathroom was steamy. I pulled off my filthy fatigues, my whole body aching for that hot water.

'How'd you make out?' a voice called out, as she turned off her shower. Out stepped Jean Dillon from behind the plastic curtain. Her compact, little body was wrapped in a large, white towel, her thick, dark hair hanging wetly down her shoulders.

She smiled at me, but somehow it came out as a grimace. Jean seemed like a girl with a chip on her shoulder. From the moment we had arrived at school, she had been finding things to complain about and ways to insult the people around her. She always seemed to be looking for the worst in everyone. But then, I tended, and still do, to jump to conclusions about people, so I decided to try to be friendly, and to quell my own suspicions that she was trouble.

'Great,' I lied, never wanting to admit defeat. 'I whipped his sorry little ass.'

'Oh,' Jean said, her mouth twisting into an unpleasant smile. 'Well, you saw how I did. I think that asshole Graham broke my arm, for God's sake. I don't think it's fair that they put us with the guys. They should put us with each other, even up the score a little.'

For the moment I forgot my well-intentioned plan to give her the benefit of the doubt. 'Oh, grow up, Jean. This is Stewart Military Academy, not Miss Priss University. If you want to compete with other girls, go to a girls' school. Be glad they're treating us like equals.' I was naked now, and standing under the luke-warm tap, trying to scrub the mud from hidden cracks and crevices in my body.

'Fuck you,' Jean hurled back at me, her voice changing from whine to snarl. 'I've been watching you, Harris. You think you're so tough because you can fight like a guy and do the drills like a guy. I think you're just a big dyke, if you want to know. So do the other girls.'

I flushed at her remark. Not that it's true. I'm not a lesbian, though I certainly have nothing against them. But the vehemence of her response caught me off guard. I turned away from her, with no smart response of my own to put her in her place. I don't know why her remark stung so much. I'd been called a dyke, a lesbian, a pussy-lapper; every name in the book, ever since I'd hit puberty and failed to trade in the baseball for the hair ribbons. But I guess I didn't expect it from her, an entering freshman woman in one of the most sexist institutions in the country. She knew what it took to get in here, and to stay in without going insane.

I felt anger start to overtake the hurt feelings. 'Why don't you go to hell,' I shot back, finally. It was lame, I admit it. I couldn't believe I was fighting with this girl over nothing.

'Dyke bitch,' she snarled back. I turned away and stuck my head under the shower. My first enemy and it was only the second week of school. This was going to be a long year.

I didn't have much of an appetite that night: I had over-exerted and felt nauseated. When lights-out came, I thought I would have a hard time falling asleep on the thin, hard mattress, but all too soon we were being screamed at to rise and shine, as a trash-can lid was banged on the floor for emphasis.

9

At breakfast I realised that I was ravenous. I heaped my plate with scrambled eggs, stacks of pancakes, ham, bacon, grits, a cup of milk, a mug of hot cocoa, and some coffee. Along with the rest of the cadets, I hurried to the table and began to wolf down my meal. Brady, my mudwrestling partner, sat down next to me, his tray as laden as mine. He smiled at me and I smiled back. He crossed his wrists on the table for a moment and looked at me. It was almost as if he expected me to respond somehow. There was no talking in the dining room, so of course I didn't.

What was that about? I wondered, as we jogged to the Yard for day two of hell. But I had no chance to ask. Students in green fatigues and orange caps poured on to the concrete. Sinclair was there, whistle in hand.

'Oh, God,' Brady moaned softly, next to me. As the veins bulged in Sinclair's neck from blowing so hard on the damn whistle, down we went. Day Two had begun.

Time became meaningless as we stretched ourselves to our physical and emotional limits. My entire goal became to make it through without collapsing. I didn't care if I finished with honours, or even with dignity. I just wanted to get through it alive.

It was now midnight on the final night of Hell Week, and the whole lot of dishevelled, exhausted freshmen sat slumped on benches in the mess hall, nursing hot cocoa and eating cookies. Except for those who didn't make it through the programme. Several had been disqualified as a result of broken bones or sprained joints. They would be allowed to return to classes, of course, but there was a certain honour inherent in completing the week that they would never know. One fellow really lost it; he sat down smack in the middle of an obstacle course on the fourth day and just started crying. Nothing, not the sergeant's threats, or cajoling, or the encouragement or scorn of his classmates could stop the poor guy from sobbing. He was assisted off the field and was never seen again. Notably, not one of the dropouts was a woman.

We'd just finished a two-hour forced march with full gear. Hell Week was over and thank God for that. Brady was next to me again; I'd begun to notice that he always seemed to be near me. About five-feet nine, with a wiry, though muscular frame, Sam Brady wasn't really my type. He had carrot-red hair and pale skin scattered with freckles. He wore glasses that were forever slipping down the bridge of his nose. We walked out of the dining room together and he turned to me.

'So, Harris. We did it. We're full-fledged toadies now.' He grinned happily and I grinned back at him. A lot of the freshmen boys had taken their cue from the upperclassmen, and treated us girls as if we were intruders who didn't belong. At least Brady treated me as an equal.

'Yep. Now we get the honour of being treated like shit for the rest of the year by a bunch of asshole upperclassmen. But at least we get to sleep all day tomorrow.'

'Yeah, well, not me. I've got more important things to do.' Without further explanation, he said 'good night' and headed toward his dorm. I did the same, wondering what could be so important for a

11

toad to do during his one Sunday off since we'd arrived.

Despite my best intentions, I couldn't sleep the day away. I did sleep in until 10.00, rising slowly, feeling the ache in every muscle from the gruelling week that had passed. I stood in the shower until there was no more hot water; that took about seven minutes. Towelling off, I thought about how to spend my first free day. It was a perfect, breezy day, slightly overcast: just right for a bike ride. And I figured that would stretch my sore muscles, too. We had been given the whole day off, and that was not likely to happen again for a long time. We were even permitted to wear 'civvies' for the day, and go about on our own, rather than marching in tight, little groups of two or four, as we did on our way to classes and drills. So, donning my favourite faded T-shirt and bike shorts, I headed for the bike racks.

I decided on a ride through the park near the school. There was a long, winding bicycle path through the tall pine trees. Even though it was September, autumn had yet to arrive in Georgia that day. I rode slowly, watching the path, not thinking about much of anything. After about 45 minutes, I stopped to rest near a little stream. I sat against a tall pine and leaned back, closing my eyes.

'A cyclist. That explains those long, perfect legs.'

My eyes flew open. There he was, right in front of me. Mr Cool, also dressed in civvies: a white, button-down shirt and black slacks. He still looked rather formal, but it was certainly better than olive drab. I noticed he was holding a bottle of Coke, which made me realise I was thirsty.

'Oh! Excuse me. I didn't realise there was anyone here.' I started to get up; toads aren't supposed to

12

sit in the presence of upperclassmen without express permission.

'Oh, please. Sit down. It's Sunday and we're not even on the campus. Take it easy.' As he spoke, he eased himself down next to me. I wrapped my arms around my knees, waiting to see what came next.

'So, how's it going?' he asked, his voice low and pleasing. 'You survived Hell Week, I see. No permanent scars?'

Mr Cool looked at me then, his eyes raking my body, making me feel very self-conscious. I huddled to myself even more as I mumbled something about still being intact. I blushed then, as his grin made me conscious of the double meaning of my remark.

What was going on here? I'm usually very self-assured around guys, even older ones, mainly because I don't give a damn. My tastes at the time, at least in theory, ran to older men, men who had been around a bit, who had experienced something of life. I looked for someone who could take control, someone who wasn't too easy to wrap around your finger. Even upperclassmen like Mr Cool usually left me indifferent.

But there was something about this guy. It wasn't just that he was very handsome, with dark, wavy hair and blue, almost violet eyes. There was something about his expression, his bearing, that I couldn't quite pinpoint. Something intriguing; something dangerous.

'What's your name, toad?' His tone was suddenly formal, demanding. I sat up straighter, reminded again of his status.

'Harris, sir. Remy Harris.'

'Remy, huh? Unusual name.' He relaxed back into

informality, stretching his long, lean form out on the grass.

'My mother is a Francophile. She loves everything French. It's a French name.'

'I know. It's derived from the town of Reims. I've been there. My dad was stationed in France when I was in high school.' No one had ever heard of the name before, much less known its derivation. I was suitably impressed, but said nothing. He smiled again and held out the bottle.

'Like a swig?' he offered.

I started to say no but, for some reason, held out my hand and took it. As I drank the cold soda, I was reminded that I hadn't eaten since the midnight rations of the night before.

'Hey. Don't drink it all.'

I stopped at once, looking over to see if he was angry, but he was still grinning. Mr Cool looked at his watch and said, 'It's about lunch time. Wanna come with me to the pub for a bite to eat?' The pub was for seniors only, unless by invitation. It was a place for them to meet for lunch or dinner, or just to hang out.

I was surprised at his invitation. I didn't dare refuse. Not that I wanted to. 'Well, thanks! That would be great, I guess. Maybe I should know your name first?'

He stood, his smile like a sunburst across his features, and said, 'Jacob. Jacob Stewart, at your service.' He held out his hand to help me up but, of course, I didn't take it. Jacob had ridden his bike too, which I now saw leaning against a nearby tree. He retrieved it and together we rode back to the campus.

Over a lunch of cheeseburgers and onion rings, I

finally asked the question that had popped into my head the minute he had introduced himself. 'So, are you related to "old cannonball Stewart" himself?'

He laughed, throwing back his head as he did so as if the question were hilarious to him. 'I admit it, though I had nothing to do with it. He was my great-great uncle. Real whacko, so the family lore has it. Stone-cold crazy. But I hope to follow in his hallowed footsteps, or at least make it through graduation at this damn place. Then my army stint, and I am a free man.'

'Sounds like you aren't really into this, then. Did your family force you along the military path?'

'You could put it like that. Let's just say that I chose the lesser of two evils. Or so I thought at the time.' He grinned at me, but said nothing else. Of course, I was dying to ask more, but I didn't dare. As friendly as he was, he was still a senior and, as such, my superior officer.

'Well, well, well.' Another upperclassman sauntered over to our table. He was a short, heavy-set guy, with dark, curly hair and a jutting browline that was positively Neanderthal in proportion. There was a sneer on his face and I was at once on my guard. 'What have we here, Stewart? Slumming for toadies again?' I looked down, controlling my impulse to slap him.

He focused directly on me then. 'Stand up, toad! You are before two senior upperclassmen! Where are your manners, cadet?'

I jumped up, my hand automatically finding my forehead for a quick salute, my eyes straight ahead. I was cursing myself for having dropped my guard around Jacob. He had seemed so friendly and

15

relaxed that I had forgotten my position as a toad in senior territory.

'Excuse me, sir,' I mumbled. I stood a good two inches taller than the Neanderthal as he edged in close to me. He pressed in so that my breasts were touching his chest. I resisted my urge to pull back.

'No. I won't excuse you. Hit the floor and give me thirty, bitch toad.'

I thought of appealing to Jacob, but I didn't dare look at him. There was nothing he could do anyway: to question the orders of another senior would be decidedly bad form. I hit the floor. Technically I could report the Neanderthal for using foul language, but I wasn't about to make trouble. As I rose from the floor, palms flat and body straight, I felt his shoe against my ass. He pushed down and I lowered myself to the floor. Each time I rose to complete a push-up, his foot was there to press me back. I was flushed with exertion and fury by the time I completed the thirty.

When I stood up, breathing hard, the Neanderthal laughed cruelly. 'Not bad, bitch toad. Not bad for a stupid bitch.' He turned to Jacob. 'At least you picked one that can pass muster this time, Stewart.' His eyes were small and close together. He reminded me of a police artist's recreation of a criminal. He was bad news.

Jacob made no reaction; it was as if the Neanderthal didn't exist. 'Get up, Remy,' he said softly.

I stood shakily, wishing I could disappear. Dazed, I saw that quite a little crowd had gathered around us. They all seemed to be staring at my body as if I were a slice of beef that they needed for their sandwich. Jacob was the only one sitting. He was looking at me, his face impassive. Then he stood slowly, and held his hand out to me.

'Come on, Remy. Let's get out of this dump.' Not sure what else to do, and hoping desperately to escape the leering eyes around me, I took the offered hand. He led me from the pub, still seemingly oblivious of the Neanderthal, who was glaring at us both with pure hatred. Enemy number two. What next?

Chapter Two

Jacob

We walked back in the direction of the senior quarters. He hadn't even asked me if I wanted to go with him. I followed numbly, still dazed from the incident at the pub. I don't know why I let it get to me so much. During the two weeks I had been at the Academy, and the six weeks in boot camp the summer before, I had been treated worse and spoken to in even cruder language. It went with the territory of being a toad. It was expected and accepted as part of one's initiation into the Academy and the service. I knew that going in and, until now, it hadn't really fazed me. I knew it wasn't personal.

Maybe that was it. This had felt personal. Perhaps because Jacob was there, and he had sort of invited me on a date. So for a moment, I hadn't been Harris, freshman toad, I had been Remy, just Remy. I had let down my guard. I made a mental note not to let it happen again. Not even with Jacob. He was my superior and I wouldn't forget it again.

Because he was a senior, Jacob had his own room. It was military perfect. Everything was ship shape, as they say, with nothing out of place. Though a small room by civilian standards, it seemed spacious to me. I sighed a little as I thought of two more years sharing everything, including the shower, with nine other women. Juniors were allowed two to a room. But that was the drill and you weren't allowed to live off campus at all.

Jacob gestured to a chair and I sat, still feeling shaken by the incident in the pub.

'Listen,' he said, getting two Cokes from the little refrigerator in the corner of the room. 'Don't let Decker bother you. He's an asshole. He is ranked at the bottom of the class. He was too stupid to make it into Officer Training and is going to land some bureaucratic nobody desk job somewhere in the bowels of the military establishment. This is his last chance to lord it over someone. And he always picks the easy target. So a freshman girl is perfect fodder for his sadistic, creepy little games. Just ignore him.'

'Well, I can't ignore him. Asshole or not, he is my superior officer, just like you are. This isn't just any college, you know. This is the Army, for all intents and purposes, and I am lowest ranked private scum there is.'

'Fuck that, Remy. This place isn't the army. This is some trumped-up bunch of kids playing at soldiers. Most of the guys here are insufferable frat-boy types or nerds who generally have little or no understanding of the real army or the essence of leadership, setting an example.

'Sure, you can learn a lot here. It's a good school academically and we have some great teachers. And

I'm even willing to admit that you can learn a little about discipline and honour from the warmongering bullshit exercises they put you through during your tenure. But this isn't "real life". It's school. Just get through it, and don't get brainwashed by all the military trappings. It's bullshit. There is a lot more this place has to offer, anyway.'

I just stared at him. Jacob had reduced everything I thought I admired in my parents and my country to bullshit in just a few sentences. I was too stunned to even be insulted. Jacob sat quietly, gazing back at me. He had a smile on his lips but his eyes seemed flecked with intensity, as if he had much more to say. His skin looked to be naturally fair, but was tanned by the sun. His nose was just slightly asymmetrical, as if it had been broken once.

He moved from the chair to the end of his bed, so that his knees were almost touching mine. 'Let's not talk about it anymore. I know you're "regular army". You have that expression, that "don't fuck with me" face that so many of these eager-beaver cadets come in with. I'm willing to forgive you that.'

I bristled at this remark, at once pleased to be 'regular army' but also insulted because of his obvious distaste for that particular distinction. Basically, I was confused, which was something new for me at the time. I started to protest, not even sure which part I was protesting, when he leaned forward and stopped my argument with an exquisite attack by his lips to my surprised mouth.

Oh, that kiss. His lips crushed mine. His tongue raped my mouth. It wasn't exploratory, tentative, groping, the way it was with boys I had kissed until that point. It was a claiming, a victory, an establish-

20

ment of ownership. I didn't know it at the time; I wouldn't have described it that way then. But that is what it was. As he kissed me, he pulled me forward on to him. I felt his hard-muscled chest against my breasts. My nipples stiffened against him and I felt pleasure coursing through me, heating my blood.

The kiss continued, but now his hands were on me as well. I felt those large, strong hands moving down my sides and up again, leaving an electric path of sensation and desire. I moaned into his mouth, feeling a familiar ache in my loins that no man had yet satisfied. His hands responded, moving down to my belly, and further down.

I tried to pull away – things were moving too fast for me – but Jacob wouldn't let me go. His kiss kept me mute as his hands roamed and explored my body. I felt his fingers slipping under my cotton shorts. I was struggling in earnest now; I was afraid.

Jacob at last seemed to notice my protestations. He stopped and pulled away from me. I lay on the bed, panting and still, trying to process what was happening to me. While my mind was trying to analyse and assess the situation, my body already knew just what it wanted. It wanted Jacob. I could feel the familiar tug at my sex as my clit throbbed.

Still, a part of me didn't trust Jacob. Not yet anyway. We had only known each other a few hours! The struggle must have registered on my face, because Jacob leaned over me and whispered in a hoarse voice, 'Come on, Remy. You want this as bad as I do. Don't go all coy on me. What's wrong?'

'I don't know. I'm scared. I've never, that is, I . . .' I trailed away, terribly embarrassed to admit that I was a virgin. I turned my head from him, wishing I were older, braver, surer. It wasn't that I was a prude, or had any moral quandary about 'losing my virginity'. In fact, that very term seems absurd to me. It would be no loss to me: I regarded my virginity as a liability. But it was humiliating to admit to this older guy, who was obviously experienced, that I didn't know what the hell I was doing.

He seemed to understand, though. Gently, he said, as he stroked my hair, 'Remy, I want you. I want to claim you.'

Claim me. That's what he said. I found it rather romantic, in a Gothic sort of way. At the time, of course, I had no idea that that was exactly what he intended to do. I nodded up to him, no longer caring that I had known him only for an afternoon. The time seemed right and I felt a strange attraction to him that I had never felt toward another person before. It was almost as if we had known one another at another time, as if we were old lovers finding each other again. I let him pull my shorts down and lift my T-shirt. I didn't protest as he unclasped my bra and pulled down my panties.

His weight was on me, pinning me down, as his knee edged my thighs apart, roughly. A renewed moment of panic gripped me as I realised just how completely at his mercy I was at that moment. I was naked, with his full weight on me, his strong knee pressing my legs apart, opening me to his invasion. I started to whimper, to struggle, despite my rising desire. One hand came firmly across my mouth, while the other hand cupped my pussy. My breathing was harsh and fast, my breasts rising with fear and desire. As his fingers entered my tight, slick opening, I felt the panic begin to ebb away. Desire overtook the fear as he inserted first one, and then two, fingers inside of me. As he pulled them out, they grazed against my already hard clit, and I moaned with pleasure, my legs falling open. For a minute or so his fingers pulled and rubbed my clit, sliding down to enter my sopping, wet pussy, and sliding back up to tease my throbbing button. A little sigh escaped me as he withdrew and left me open, naked and exposed before him.

He stood up before lifting his shirt over his head and tossing it aside. He pushed his slacks down, and kicked out of them. I watched in wanton fascination as he peeled his underwear down, causing his fully erect cock to bob there just a few feet from my face.

It wasn't the first cock I had seen. The other times had been in the back of my high school boyfriend's car, late at night after one too many beers. We would jerk each other off with our fingers, and once or twice I tried to suck his cock, but could never quite manage to take the whole thing in.

But this was different. I was with a man at last. Not a boy. And neither of us was drunk. I knew Jacob expected more than a hand job. His penis was long and thick. It had one long throbbing vein from base to tip. The head was rosy and a drop of pre-cum glistened from the tip. He was so erect that his cock was perpendicular to his hard stomach.

I licked my lips as I stared at his gorgeous body. Grinning at me, Jacob lay across my naked body and pulled my underwear all the way down till it caught at my ankles. His fingers found my clit again as his mouth covered mine.

I was ready. I was aching for what he offered. I barely cried out as his hard, rigid cock pressed its way into my tight opening. I wanted it. I was ready to receive him. I couldn't believe how good it felt; it filled me up completely. I barely noticed the little rip of pain at the entrance as he began to fuck me, hard and sure. It felt so good, so good that I cried out like a petulant little girl when he suddenly withdrew, moaning.

He came in hot little streams of pearly, grey come, aiming his cock to shoot over my belly, my pussy, my breasts. I felt shocked, stunned. He had withdrawn the pleasure and then come all over me like I was some kind of whore. I felt my face flush with anger and shame. But at the same time something in me, something perverse perhaps, made me even wetter. I was on fire for this man who had just used my body for his own pleasure, disregarding my own needs.

Spent at last, he scooped me into his arms, ignoring the sticky mess that pressed between our sweating bodies. Then he held me, kissing my neck and throat as I lay still, legs clasped together, feeling fully now the pain of the intrusion coupled with my still-intense arousal.

He lay still, his eyes closed, one hand idly massaging my impossibly erect nipple. I didn't dare say a word. I was way out of my league. But in only a few minutes, Jacob was erect and ready again.

'This time,' he said, kissing my breasts, lingering to pull and suck each nipple until I moaned in pleasure, 'this time is for you.'

Inspection was at 1700 hours. I met the other girls an hour and a half beforehand so we could get the barracks ready. We scrubbed down the place, changed the sheets, and organised our footlockers

24

and closets for a military inspection. I realised as I crouched next to the toilets, scrubbing the tiles with a rag, that I was still sore. Along with my stiff muscles from the week that had just passed, I could feel a dull ache in my pussy that wasn't entirely unpleasant.

Thoughts of Jacob, naked and strong, making love to me in his room just an hour before, streamed through my mind like a silent movie. I was startled by the sound of Amelia's voice right next to me.

'You look like the cat that just ate the canary,' she said, grinning at me, her head cocked to one side in an unspoken question.

Amelia had a lovely face, with skin like porcelain and large, innocent blue eyes. She had light-brown hair, cut with bangs that gave her a little-girl quality. With a dumpy body and short legs, however, Amelia was our 'fat girl'. I wasn't sure how she had gotten through the rigorous physical exam that all cadets are required to pass to enter the programme. Of course, when I say fat, it is a relative term. She wasn't obese, just maybe twenty or twenty-five pounds over the ideal weight for her height, which was about five-four. But presumably she was able to surmount her weight problem, because she had made it through Hell Week with the rest of us. I was glad, actually, to see that she was still here. There had been snickering that Hell Week would be the end of Amelia. I was glad she'd proved them wrong.

When I didn't offer an explanation, she asked, 'What happened to you? You are positively beaming! There's talk that you were seen with an upper-classman. Might that have something to do with it?'

Talk that I had been seen? Didn't people have better things to do with their time, I wondered?

But to Amelia I simply said, 'Oh, I guess I'm just glad that Hell Week is over. Today was so relaxing, riding my bike, enjoying the sunshine –'

'And getting reamed by a senior at the pub for not obeying protocol.' Jean's voiced poured over me like acid. She was standing just behind Amelia with a mop and bucket in her hand. I stared up at her in horror as she continued.

'That's right,' she said loudly, in a voice designed to carry through the barracks. 'She sucked her way into the good graces of some horny senior, and got him to buy her a burger. But she thought she was above standing when another senior came to the table. She forgot she was at the Academy; she thought she was back in high school on a date with the football captain.'

I stood then, easily five inches taller than Jean, who was dark and compact, but deceptively strong. She leaned forward, staring up at me, daring me with her expression to throw the first punch. I controlled my fury and embarrassment. I refused to give her the satisfaction.

'Jean, shut up. You don't know what you're talking about.'

'Oh, don't I? So you deny that you were told to drop and do thirty push-ups? And that he kicked your ass each time you lifted up? And then you left with your new guy and went back to his room? Do you deny it?'

'How the fuck do you know all that?' I exploded, completely taken aback by her total knowledge of my whereabouts and behaviour. Did she peep

26

through Jacob's window, too? Jean laughed derisively.

'I have my sources,' was all she said, grinning smugly. I felt my right fist curling into itself, as my body tensed in pleasurable anticipation of knocking her flat on her ass.

'Move it, girls. This isn't time for chit-chat.' Joan, the assigned cadet company officer of our barracks for the month, was all business. She insinuated herself between us, breaking up any possible fight as she folded her arms, each elbow pushing us apart. She was the one responsible if Sergeant Roster decided there were any problems at inspection.

I realised how stupid it was as I made myself take a deep breath. I forced my body to unwind, to relax its fighting stance. I would deal with Cadet Dillon another day. Jean turned away, but not before I heard her hiss, 'Coward.' I bit my lip; she wasn't worth it.

Inspection went reasonably well. Roster seemed preoccupied and in a hurry to get it over with. She found a few things to fault, just to keep us on our toes, but in a matter of minutes she had swept out of the room with her usual theatrical flourish.

'Maybe she's got a date,' one of the girls suggested, as we congratulated ourselves on getting off so easy this time.

'A date?' said Joan. 'I didn't even know she was a woman. I thought she was an army-issue robot.' We all laughed, but I was still badly shaken by Jean's spying on me. It was study period, so I grabbed my books and headed for the computer rooms.

The days passed quickly after that. My classes took a lot of my time and I enjoyed the challenge of

27

college studies. With a major in computer science and a minor in English Literature, I was plenty busy. I got into the habit of rising very early, just as the sun was spilling over the windowsill each morning, so that I could study before PT (physical training) and classes, leaving me more free time after school for Jacob.

After that first time together, I had raised the obvious concern of birth control. Jacob said he despised condoms. They ruined the spontaneity, he said. At his strong suggestion, I went to the university clinic and got birth control pills. I was embarrassed when I was called in to see the examining doctor. He was a heavy-set man with a double chin. I was subjected to a perfunctory and unpleasant gynaecological exam, attended by a sour-faced, middle-aged nurse who glared disapprovingly at me throughout. I was then told to dress and come to his office to ask any questions I might have.

I decided to cut to the chase; this whole thing was wearing on my nerves. 'I'd like to get birth control pills, sir.'

'So.' The doctor leaned back, ducking his head so that the two chins became at least four. 'I presume you are sexually active?' He waited, looking bored, his eyebrows raised in an imitation of interest.

The question, which I felt was unnecessary, embarrassed me. But dutifully I answered, 'Yes, sir,' half expecting him to launch into a lecture about promiscuity. Instead, to my vast relief, he simply pulled a pen from his lab coat and scribbled something on a prescription pad. Tearing it off with something of a flourish, he pushed it across the desk to me.

I reached forward and took the little piece of

paper, half feeling it might disintegrate if I didn't grab hold of it right away. I stood, thanking the doctor. He nodded, adding a final warning not to skip a day.

I told Jacob that night that I had gotten the contraception. He was pleased, though his remark was something less than romantic. 'Thank God for that. Last fucking thing I need is a kid!'

Still, Jacob's magnetism was undeniable. He wasn't like any boyfriend I had ever had. We didn't talk much about our lives or our dreams. Really, we didn't talk much at all. Whenever I had free time, I would come to his room and knock softly on the door. After a moment, he would open it just enough to let me slip through. Sometimes, before even saying hello, he would press me up against the door and, taking my head in his hands, roughly kiss me until I was panting and ready for more.

Often he would stay fully clothed, or almost so, but I was always naked. I would stand in the middle of his room, arms loose at my sides, as he unbuttoned my uniform. I would stay still as he slid the heavy, cotton clothing from my body, leaving only my T-shirt, bra, and panties. He would lift my arms above my head, smiling at me as he pulled the T-shirt up and off, and then unhooked my bra.

For a girl who had spent her life to that point denying or at least hiding her femininity, Jacob's domineering treatment of me had a curiously freeing affect. Somehow he made me feel beautiful, feminine, sexy, in a way no boy I had been with had ever managed. I felt completely sexual, completely vulnerable and open to him. It was electrifying. It was almost terrifying, but too much fun to be really scary.

At first he made gentle, careful love to me, taking his time and making sure I was completely satisfied. I was no longer even the slightest bit shy: I wanted to be fucked. I craved to be used and sated and spent like someone's fuck-toy.

As the days passed, he started adding some twists to the game. Sometimes he would hold my wrists over my head while he forced my thighs apart with his knee. Then he would take me, sometimes roughly, making me cry out. I found it oddly thrilling when he did this, like he was some medieval knight claiming his prize. It never occurred to me to protest: he was my mentor, my teacher, my experienced lover. I accepted everything he did without question. I didn't want to think about it, really. I just wanted it, all of it.

Though it seemed in some ways as if we had always been together, really it had only been a few months, with meetings taking place only several times a week. A cadet's time is not her own, for the most part. I thought I was falling in love with Jacob, and assumed he was with me, though neither of us ever said as much. Then one day, things changed.

We had just spent an idle first few minutes, getting naked and snuggling together. Suddenly Jacob covered my mouth with one hand, grabbing my wrists in the other. Then, without warning or provocation, he slapped my cheek, hard. I gasped from the sting and the shock of his action. Twisting under him, I pulled away and managed to get free of him. Jacob was on me, all at once. He threw me back on the bed and pinned me flat with his body.

'Going to fight me, are you?' he said in a low voice, breathing hard from his exertions.

'Jacob, stop it! You're scaring me. I don't like this.

Let me go.' My heart was pounding. I felt a rush of adrenaline not unlike the feeling I get when competitively cycling or wrestling, but with a definite sexual overlay.

'You don't like this? I think you do.' Jacob's voice was insistent, harsh. As he spoke, I felt his fingers entering and opening my pussy. He brought his fingers to my face then, smearing my juices along the cheek still hot from his slap, and on to my lips. I turned my head away, humiliated and embarrassed, yet, at the same time, secretly and intensely thrilled.

'Jacob! No! Stop it!' I started to struggle again, as much to distract him and myself from my own arousal at this treatment, as to escape.

'No, Remy. You stop. I want you to stop resisting me. I want you to submit. Enough of these games. I've given you time. I know what you're made of, slut girl. You can handle this. Don't offer the coy little virgin shit anymore. We both know better. I want you to let go, to surrender all your inhibitions. To take it for me. To suffer. For me.'

As he spoke, he gripped my wrists tightly, while his other hand found my pussy and began to tease and caress me until I was moaning with desire. I didn't understand what he was saying at the moment. This certainly wasn't suffering. It was surrender, of that there was no doubt. And even though at the time I refused to focus on the meaning of his words, I understood the intent. He wanted to drive me wild with lust, and he was doing just that. And because I was held captive (though I admit now I could have probably gotten away if I had really wanted to), I was suddenly free to feel it all, without worrying about how I appeared to him.

'Spread your legs, whore.' His voice was low, insistent.

I felt a curious mixture of embarrassment and lust. It was stronger than anything I had ever experienced. Obediently I spread my legs, my naked pussy pouting and opening. I could smell my own musty desire.

'That's right, slut. You want it, don't you? You need it, don't you? You need what I give you?' When I didn't answer, he took my chin in his hand, forcing me to look at him. 'Answer me, slut.'

Part of me hated him, but most of me adored what was happening. 'Yes, sir, yes!' I admitted it, not understanding what magic he was weaving, but just giving in finally and totally to what he offered. I was rewarded with his fingers again, opening my pussy, leaving lines of swirling, aching pleasure over my body. Liquid fire was pumping through my veins. I was falling into a perfect darkness, waiting and desperate for the shock of stars that would be my release. I was so close to coming and so intent on doing so that I cried out with a little whimper of dismay when, suddenly, his hands were gone from my body.

I felt the sting on my cheek; Jacob had slapped me again! My eyes, which had been shut in blissful sexual abandon, flew open with shock and surprise. He was sitting back on his heels, straddling my still-spread legs, looking intently at me.

His expression wasn't loving, or even lustful. It seemed distant, even angry. 'What? What is it? Why did you slap me? What's wrong with you?' I asked, trying to close my legs, suddenly self-conscious of my lewd and wanton display.

'I don't want you to come, slut. Not yet.' He held

me in position, hands over my head, my naked body completely exposed to him. I could still feel the heat pulsing through my swollen, needy sex. My wrists were still caught in his grip so I couldn't even touch the heated folds and offer myself some relief.

'What?' Anger was beginning to take over the confusion and arousal I had felt.

'You heard me, Remy. I don't want you to come. I want you to learn some self-control. I want you to learn what it is to wait, to suffer.'

I stared at him, refusing to comprehend.

With a sigh he let go of my wrists and pulled away from me. 'Remy, we have been making love for over a month now. You come to my room and let me fuck you every day.' I blushed and ducked my head, but he didn't seem to notice. 'And I have enjoyed it, and enjoyed teaching you the pleasures of the body. But there is so much more, Remy. There is so much more we can experience together if you let me take you there. I like you. I see enormous potential in you. I want to claim you.'

I sat up, hugging my knees, still confused and still flushed with my unrequited desire. More than anything, I was terribly hurt by his little phrase, 'I like you', which he seemed to throw in almost as an afterthought. I had thought we were in love; in my eighteen-year-old mind, when you became lovers, it meant you were in love. But he only 'liked' me, maybe only because I 'let him fuck me'.

I tried to mask my confusion with bravado. 'What the hell are you trying to say, Jacob? What more is there? What do you mean, claim me? This isn't the Dark Ages, you know. People don't just go around claiming other people, for crying out loud.'

'Don't they? Are you sure you know so much about it?' He was smiling as he spoke, but his eyes had a steely expression that I hadn't seen before. I felt a shiver go through me; this was a side of Jacob I hadn't seen and didn't understand. He continued, his voice quiet, though his eyes were blazing.

'I want to explore with you. There is something about you – I sensed it from the moment we met – something ready to yield, ready to taste a new world. You are almost all potential right now, untapped. I want to exploit that potential. I want to mould you, to use you, to create you.' He was staring at me as he spoke, his voice suddenly husky with intensity.

'Remy,' he said, leaning toward me, grabbing me by the throat so I could barely breathe. 'I want to teach you to submit.'

Now he was scaring me. I pulled at his hands, trying to get up and away from him. As I twisted and pushed at him, he let me go suddenly, and I fell back on the bed, panting to catch my breath.

I couldn't understand what was happening to me. I lashed out. 'What are you, some kind of pervert? What the fuck are you talking about? Me, submit? Oh, you think you have me all figured out. It's always been my dream to be someone's sex object, sir.' My voice was heavy with sarcasm. He was scaring me, though not only because of what he was saying and doing. It was my own reaction that scared me most. Here I was, feminist tomboy cadet who had made it into one of the most rigorous programmes in the country, and I was turned on by a guy who wanted me to be his sex slave, for God's sake! It was really more to deny myself than him that made me respond so harshly. But Jacob didn't know that, couldn't see how much of my response was generated by fear. He recoiled at my words, at my biting tone. There was to be no second chance.

'Get out, Remy. I must have been wrong. You're not ready yet. This is my fault. Maybe I thought you were something you're not. Maybe I want something you aren't able to give.' His voice was cold. He was standing, already pulling up his khakis, his face averted from me.

My heart was pounding. At the time I chalked it up totally to anger at his cruel treatment of me, but in truth there was more to it. I wasn't ready to know that yet, though. I focused instead on my bruised ego. He had told me to go. Tears were threatening to erupt but I wasn't going to give the crazy bastard the satisfaction.

'Listen,' I said through clenched teeth, pulling on my clothes as fast as I could. 'I don't know what the fuck you're talking about, or what's going on here, but I don't think I want to be a part of it. Anyway, I've got to get to PT.' It was a stupid parting statement, but I hadn't had much time to rehearse. I ran out the door, still buttoning my uniform blouse. Jacob didn't try to stop me; he didn't say another word.

I thought he would come find me later that night. During free time I waited near the fountain where we sometimes sat and talked, pretending to read my book. No Jacob. I fell asleep that night, the tears I hadn't allowed him to see staining my pillow.

By the morning I had managed to convert the sadness to anger, a classic trick of mine. Grimly I decided to put the bastard out of my mind. Forget that prick. Who needed him anyway? I was here to become an officer, not have an affair with a control freak.

But it didn't work. I couldn't get Jacob or what had happened that last day out of my head. I was numb, still stunned by the whole affair; I had been 'dumped' and I didn't really know what had happened. I alternated between abject hatred and utter misery and confusion. How could he have seemed so involved with me at one moment, and so cold and rejecting the next? What was his deal, anyway, with all this bending-to-his-will crap? Who needed that weirdo?

Then I would remember his kiss, or the thrill when he would fuck me till I cried out for release, and the tears would spill down my cheeks. I drifted through classes and PT, barely noticing when instructors hurled insults at me for not performing up to their standards. I was angry with myself for it, but couldn't help missing Jacob. I remembered our passionate love-making, and the way he made me feel so completely feminine and vulnerable. I yearned for that kind of release again. But he had told me to go and my pride wouldn't allow me to return.

Days passed and turned into weeks and still I didn't seek out Jacob. I saw him now and then: in the mess hall, in the Yard, walking between classes. I avoided him; I hid from him. If he saw me, he gave no indication. Finally one day he was standing with a group of seniors as I passed by on the way to the library. I saluted the group, trying to behave normally though I was afraid my heart would pound right through my shirt.

They all saluted back, casually, indifferently, including Jacob. It was as if I didn't exist, as if none of it had ever happened. To Jacob I was once again a toad, nothing more.

Once in the library, I signed up for a private cell and, pressing the door shut with a click, I collapsed in the single, straight-backed wooden chair. Laying my head on the table, I sobbed until there were no tears left. I missed Jacob. I missed the sex; I missed the closeness.

Later that evening I took a shower just before lights-out. There was no one else in the shower stalls at that moment and I had a little privacy for a change. As hot water streamed over my upturned face, images flashed in my mind of Jacob, naked and strong, towering over me in the bed. Behind the flimsy screen of the plastic shower curtain, I raised my arms high over my head and clasped my hands together, in my mind's eye his large hand gripping my wrists. I pretended for a moment to myself that I was just rinsing off the soap, but I knew better.

There alone in that shower stall I could almost feel his hands on my body, his lips crushing mine, his cock forcing its way into my pussy. Listening for a moment, gauging if anyone were nearby, I let my hands fall and then touched my breasts, cupping them gently, letting them fall, rolling the hard, fat little nipples between my own fingers, imagining they were his, wishing they were his. I felt the sweet ache in my pussy and let my fingers find the swollen bud already throbbing between my thighs.

It had been a long time since I'd allowed myself to come. I had been too engaged in mourning, I suppose, in feeling sorry for myself that Jacob had let me go just like that. But now, as need and lust took over any thought of sadness or loss, I let two fingers slide up into my wet entrance. It felt so good. I rubbed and finger-fucked myself as fast as I could, hoping no one was there to hear my barely suppressed sighs and moans.

The words he had used kept whirling through my brain. 'There is so much more we can experience.' 'I want to claim you.' 'You are still untapped potential.' 'I want to use you, to create you, to control you, to own you.' They were what I heard as I stole that little orgasm in the shower stall.

As I towelled off, my lust sated for the moment, I thought hard about Mr Stewart. Was he just a pompous, controlling asshole, or was there something to what he was saying? For the first time since he had let me go, I really pondered the question.

After lights-out – well after, when I was sure that all the other girls were asleep – I again dared to slip a hand into my panties. The little episode in the shower had only scratched the surface of my need. As my fingers found their target, I opened myself to the lovely sensations. I was taken back to the last time, when I had been so close to orgasm, and he had slapped me away from the brink. You must learn self-control, he had said. For him. For Jacob. To suffer for him, to yield to him. The words aroused me as much as my fingers rubbing and swirling on my clit. As I remembered his hands on my wrists, his lips taking mine, his cock claiming me with its thrust, I exploded in another silent spasm of release.

Funny how sex, even all by yourself, can make you feel so much better the next morning. Just the physical release of the orgasms must have calmed me down somewhat. Something that had been left wound up tight when Jacob and I had our last fight seemed to be unwinding, unbending, at last. But, even though I was perhaps through the 'mourning phase', I couldn't seem to stop thinking about the bastard.

As we were jogging around the perimeter of the Yard, warming up for the obstacle courses that were scheduled for that morning, my thoughts inevitably turned to what was becoming my obsession. Why had I run from him? What was I so afraid of? And why could I now not put him or what he had said out of my mind? Part of me knew, even then, what I was afraid of. I was afraid of my own desire. I wanted to submit, but I didn't dare. Looking back on it now, I can almost laugh. But back then I was eighteen and considered myself a staunch feminist who didn't put up with anything from anyone. For me, that manifested itself as physical strength and endurance. Which extended in my mind by defini-tion to the bedroom.

One reason I had chosen a military school was precisely because I knew I could excel in the physical arena. I wouldn't make it on a pretty face and a nice ass, but on my own grit and determination. What better place to prove my worth – which at that point I still felt I had to prove – than at a military academy where physical prowess and endurance were valued even above academic excellence?

On some level that I couldn't articulate yet, I think I was terrified that Jacob was trying to take that away from me. That he would strip me of my cover, my tough-girl exterior that no one, not a soul, had ever penetrated before. But he was gone, of his own accord. I kept on with the birth control pills, though. Don't ask me why. Maybe I was hoping to get lucky.

Chapter Three
The Bell Tower

*S*ergeant Ellen Roster was a woman of medium build, about five-six, with dark-auburn hair and squinting, green eyes. Her jaw was heavy, almost masculine. Her skin was pale, with hints of teenage acne still scarring her cheeks. She wasn't what I would consider a pretty woman, but there were times, like when she smiled, that a sweetness came to her features, belying the 'tough man' image she liked to portray. She cut a neat figure in her perfectly starched dress uniform. Her torso was slim but her hips flared out wide and feminine, rounding to an ample bottom.

For the past few months, I had managed to avoid her wrath, and had begun to relax a little around her. That was a mistake. Sometimes she was all sweetness, really acting like the 'den mother' she said she was to all of us. But then, without warning, she could turn into a viperous snake, all hiss and fang. If you were her chosen target, watch out: you didn't stand a chance.

40

We were already up, preparing quickly for the morning. That day's uniform was dress: a pale-green blouse tucked into a closely cut skirt that flared slightly just below the knees. It reminded me of the soldier girls in the 1940s. We had just been issued these new uniforms, and the fabric felt stiff and scratchy against my skin. I was buttoning myself in front of the bathroom mirror when I felt her behind me, just before I saw her. She leaned in, startling me, as her reflection suddenly appeared next to mine in the glass.

'Morning, Harris. Getting all sexy for the upperclassmen?'

I felt a sudden cold finger of fear in my belly. Her voice was low and tight, no trace of the honey overlay that identified the 'den mother' persona.

'Excuse me, ma'am?' I turned to her, standing at attention, eyes focused in the middle distance, chin jutting, waiting for whatever her latest excuse to torture me would be.

'Don't play coy, cadet. Your uniform. It's a disgrace.' Sergeant Roster stood at ease, her hands behind her back, bouncing slightly on the balls of her feet. She held a black, leather-covered baton in her hand. The stick resembled a riding crop, except there was no loop at the end of it. It definitely wasn't army issue.

As she spoke, she stuck the long, thin stick at my chest in a small gap between the buttons. 'First your blouse. I can see your tits through that gap. Who are you trying to impress, Harris?' As she spoke, she let the cane smack down on my left breast. I flinched, more from shock than pain. There was no way this was regulation, but I stood still, not certain if I should try to defend myself. She knew that my

41

uniform blouse had been issued to me based on my measurements. We hadn't gotten the chance to try them on beforehand.

'What are you anyway, Harris? A double D? Bet those babies sag without that industrial strength bra. You'll have to show us next time you shower, cadet.' Her face was now twisted into a crude leer, her eyes little slits of hatred. Heat flooded my face and unconsciously my hand clenched into a fist at my side. The incongruity of a tomboy with tits had been the focus of taunting in the past, usually by girls with flat chests and slim hips, or skinny boys too afraid of rejection to be polite.

Roster had small, high breasts that she made a point of jutting out as she stood ramrod straight before me. Several girls had gathered to watch the little scene. Suddenly she leaned in, her face close to mine. 'I asked you a question, Harris.'

'Ma'am, 36C, ma'am,' I managed, trying to keep my voice from trembling, whether from fear or rage, I couldn't tell you. She pulled back, grinning. Then, slowly, she moved the leather baton down my body to the hem of my skirt. I felt the stick slide under a few inches and brush my bare thigh. The girls who had gathered behind us were silent now. I didn't dare to look at them. I stared straight ahead, lips compressed, hands clenched. I couldn't have reacted at that moment, even if I had chosen to. I was paralysed with fear and anger. Roster's back was to the girls, and I don't think they could see precisely what she was doing. The sergeant had a strangely trancelike look on her face, as if she had forgotten where she was, or who I was. Her long, thin tongue darted out over her lips, licking them shiny with her spittle. Her eyes were still narrowed,

42

as if she were concentrating very hard. A few girls giggled nervously. I remained at attention.

Suddenly, the stick was lifted from my thigh and pressed up firmly against my panty-clad pussy. Forgetting my position, I jumped back, startled. Heat flooded my face and I was close to hitting my commanding officer, very close.

Some movement and murmuring from the girls behind her must have snapped Roster out of her peculiar reverie. Abruptly she withdrew her baton and stepped back, coming to attention in front of me.

'Fix yourself up, Harris. Your blouse gapes; your skirt is too short. Report to KP this afternoon. There are a few thousand potatoes with your name on them. Maybe that will help you remember not to dress like a slut. If there isn't improvement by tomorrow, I might have to spank you.' She laughed then, a light, trilling giggle that seemed incongruous with her threatening, insulting words.

Before I could respond, she had whirled about in her own perfectly fitted, dark-green skirt and marched from the room. The entire event had taken less than a minute, but during that minute, something in me had snapped. As I stood there, deflated and humiliated, I realised with a small shock that I hated this woman. Even though I understood her tactics were designed to break me down and remould me into something useful to the army, I hated the process. I hated her obvious relish in devising plans to humiliate and insult me, and I hated her.

Amelia rushed over to me. 'Remy, are you okay? You look so pale. Don't let that bitch get to you. She always picks one, you know. That's what I've heard. You just happen to be the one.'

'Lucky me,' I muttered, choking back my rage and humiliation. The knot of nervous cadets had dissolved back into young women preening and rushing about to get ready for their day.

That evening found me out of the barracks on a library pass. I had just spent several hours researching my paper topic for English and was on my way back. The Georgian sky was dark, sprinkled with illuminating silver. The air was moist and cool. I still don't know what made me do it. Until then I had never broken a single rule as far as I knew. And it was a rule that, if you were out for library after dark, you returned directly to your dorm when you signed out. Theoretically I could get caught, if anyone ever bothered to check the sign-out sheet and compare it with the sign-in sheet at my dorm.

But something about the crisp, November night made me swerve in the direction of the Campanile tower. The campus, built in the late 1800s, boasted a beautiful old bell tower on the southern edge of the campus that they called the Campanile. There was a large, cracked bell in the tower that no longer rang. As far as I knew, the tower wasn't used at all these days. There was a small copse of trees near its base. This wasn't my first trip to the tower; I loved the peaceful feeling it gave me to be near it. But this was my first time at night.

Feeling like a little kid sneaking out at Girl Scout camp, I edged my way silently over to the tower. Just as I drew near, something rustled in the trees. I crouched down instinctively, and froze, cursing the bright stars that surely illuminated my huddled form. I stayed still, listening with ears sharpened by fear of discovery. I heard something that sounded

44

like a moan. Startled, I listened harder. It must have been a trick of the wind. But there was no wind that night.

After a moment I heard it again, a long, low moan. There was a rustling and a strange swishing sound whistling through the air. Curiosity outweighed trepidation as I got up and tried to follow the memory of the sound. It seemed to be coming from the trees to the left of the tower. I edged closer, holding my breath, wishing I wasn't weighed down by the heavy backpack full of schoolbooks on my shoulders. Slowly, I crawled until I was so close to the source of the sound that I could hear someone breathing heavily. Carefully, holding my breath, I lifted my head until I was peeking over a thicket of small bushes.

What I saw wrenched a gasp from me before I realised I was making a sound. My hand flew up to silence my mouth, which remained open in surprise. None of the three figures standing there seemed to have heard me. They were only a few feet away. I realised with another start that I knew the boy in the middle. It was Brady! Sam Brady and two older guys, both dressed in black. Sam was naked! His lean, muscled frame was stretched taut between two trees, coils of soft rope wound tight around his wrists and ankles. I stared, my mouth open. My eyes fell to his naked sex. His cock was rigid, long and thin, the balls heavy beneath, covered in dark-auburn curls. His cock was erect! So, whatever the hell was going on seemed to suit him, apparently.

In the light of the stars I could see that his body was crisscrossed with thin, pink lines. Each man on either side of him wielded a long, thin rod, perhaps of bamboo. I realised they were beating him with the switches! This went past any hazing that I had ever heard of on this campus. My impulse was to leap into the group and fight both men, while simultaneously freeing Sam from his bonds (even as a kid I always identified with the hero, not the damsel in distress). But something kept me back.

It was Sam's expression. It wasn't one of fear, or even pain. As I eyed his naked body, again fixing on the erect cock with its tip glistening, I could see that he was enjoying their harsh treatment of him. I watched in fascination as they took turns marking his pale flesh with their bamboo whips. After several minutes they stopped. Sam remained bound, eyes shut, his mouth open, breathing hard.

No one had said a word, but on some silent signal, one of the men dropped to his knees in front of Sam. They were at such an angle that I could clearly see him open his mouth wide and lower his head on to Sam's still-rigid member. I watched, transfixed, as he took Sam's long, rigid cock in as far as it would go. He started to pull back, but the second man was behind him now. He pressed the kneeling man's head forward, forcing him to take Sam's cock until his face was pressed against Sam's pubic bone. Sam moaned and moved his hips slightly. For the first time, the man still standing spoke.

'Don't move, slave! Who told you to move?'

Sam's eyes flew open and I ducked. If he had turned his head slightly, he might have seen me.

The man continued to speak. 'You stay perfectly still while this slut sucks you off. Don't come until I tell you, but make sure you come when you are told. And you –' I presumed he was now addressing the kneeling man, though I hadn't dared to lift my head again '– you suck that cock like your life depended on it. Because guess what, boy? It does.'

There was silence, except the small, slurping sounds as the guy continued to suck Sam's cock. Slowly, I angled myself until I could see through a chink in the bushes. My vision was now somewhat obscured by branches and bracken, but I could still make them out. The standing man had dropped his pants and was masturbating furiously over the back of the kneeling boy, whose shirt he had pulled up. After a few minutes he cried, 'OK, slave. Come! Come now and make sure he doesn't spill a drop. Now!'

Semen gushed in little spurts over the back of the kneeling guy, while I saw Sam arch forward, his eyes clenched tight, as he moaned and jerked in evident orgasm. It was silent and still for a moment as they all collected themselves.

Then, at a signal from the man in charge, he and his 'assistant' untied Sam, letting him fall forward as the ropes were released. He slumped, naked, to their feet and pressed his head against the hard ground. They looked at him for a moment, naked and prostrate at their black-booted feet. Then, without another word, they disappeared into the darkness, leaving Sam, still naked, kneeling, his head touching the ground, his thin back rising and falling with his still-ragged breathing.

I stayed very still, my heart thudding in my ears. Should I go to him? Was he hurt? Before I had a chance to make any decisions, Sam was up. He walked over to a little pile of what I saw were his clothes, and gingerly he pulled them on over his marked body. Then he too was gone, having slipped through the trees as silently as a night animal. I was left alone with the stars still sparkling overhead.

I realised with a small shock that my panties were soaking. Watching Sam be whipped and then sucked off by another man had aroused my body, even while my mind was busy with its virtuous outrage. Knowing I should be getting back to the dorm, but too horny to care, I sat back on my heels and let my fingers find my throbbing clit. Images of Sam, naked and at the mercy of those two strange men, were overlain with memories of Jacob, holding me down, fucking me hard. Fast and furious, I fucked myself with my hand, alone in the dark, until I came with a little gasp of my own.

Standing, heart still pounding from the whole experience, I quickly retrieved my backpack, which had slipped off during my play. As I turned back toward the centre of campus, I thought I heard a sound. I looked in the direction of the sound, standing as still as I could for some seconds. I didn't want to get caught out without a pass, my face flushed from the recent bizarre events I had witnessed, and my own little solo adventure in the dark. When I heard nothing further, I decided it must have been a squirrel or a bird. I headed back to the barracks, full of curiosity about what I had witnessed.

The next afternoon, Amelia and I were eating lunch in the dining hall. We were just about finished when Sam Brady joined us at the table. Setting down his tray, he nodded toward us, silently asking permission to join us. Amelia smiled, nodding her assent. I stared at this fresh-faced boy, his glasses slightly askew. Could he possibly be the same guy I had seen strung up and naked the night before? I looked down, hoping the heat I felt in my face wasn't translating itself into a bright-red blush. But Sam seemed perfectly at ease, smiling as he sat down next to us at the table. I couldn't help but sneak glances at him as we ate. He seemed oblivious of my scrutiny, as he stuffed fried chicken and corn bread into his mouth like a man with a mission.

'Well,' Amelia whispered, defying the no-talking rule in the dining room, 'I have Special Calisthenics at 1300 hours. I'd better not be late. See ya'll later.'

We both watched her walk away. Sam seemed to stare at her with a special intensity. He looked back at me, as if he were about to speak, to ask something, but he reconsidered and looked down thoughtfully at his plate. I picked at the last of my apple pie while Sam finished off his meal with slurping gulps of milk from his carton. I was wondering what Special Calisthenics were, anyway. I realised that I never did see Amelia in any of my gym classes. Maybe she got to be in a special class because she wasn't as physically fit as the rest of us. I made a mental note to ask her, albeit delicately, so as not to offend.

Just then an upperclassman strolled by our table. We both sat up straighter, ready to stand and salute if he came any closer. He didn't, but he looked over at us and, as he did, Brady laid his hands on the table. Slowly, he crossed his wrists in that peculiar fashion, one bony wrist resting on the other, just as I had seen him do once before. I looked at him but he was looking down, head bowed, back very straight. Once the guy was out of sight, Brady relaxed and resumed the last of his meal.

When he stood to put away his tray and leave, I stood with him. I hadn't decided yet whether to confront him about what I had seen. I had, after all, been out without permission when I spied him. And how did one bring it up? Oh, by the way, why were you naked and tied between two trees while some guys whipped you and then sucked you off? As I followed him out of the mess hall, I decided on a safer tactic.

'Sam,' I ventured, 'I just have to ask. What the hell is that wrist thing you keep doing?' He didn't answer but he looked uncomfortable. 'Come on, Brady, is it some secret hand signal for some Mickey-Mouse secret club you're in, or what?'

Sam flushed suddenly.

'I'm too obvious,' he said. 'I don't know how to be subtle. There are ways of doing it without drawing attention, but I'm too theatrical.' He turned from me, still not answering my question.

'Are you going to tell me? Or speak in riddles all day? Because I have a class to get to, too, you know. You don't have to tell me if you don't want to. It's none of my business.' I started to walk away, pretending to give up on mysterious Mr Brady.

'I have to go, Remy. Maybe later.' Maybe never, from the sound of his voice. Some devil got into me as I watched him walk away, and I said, quietly, 'And it's none of my business if you like to hang around the bell tower after hours with mysterious upperclassmen in black.'

Sam stopped dead in his tracks. For a long moment he stood perfectly still. He turned slowly toward me then, and his face was ashen. He reached

50

out suddenly and grabbed my arm. His grip was tight; he was hurting me, his fingers digging into my arm. Turning my wrist, I bent his thumb back, forcing him to let go.

His voice was pitched too high as he said, 'What. Did. You. Say?' It came out like that. Like separate sentences. He was obviously terrified and I didn't have the heart to make him suffer anymore.

'Relax, Brady. Your secret is safe with me.'

He stared at me intensely, as if gauging how much he could rely on those words. Then he seemed to collapse in on himself, though from relief or fear I couldn't tell.

Finally, he whispered, 'What do you know, Remy? Who told you? Who else knows? Oh, God,' he ended with a little whimper. It was embarrassing.

'No one told me. I saw you. I was there.'

'You were there? Oh, Jesus God, I'm a dead man. They'll throw me out. Oh, God, it's over.' His face was pale, the freckles standing out, and tears filled his eyes.

I moved in closer to him, grabbing him by the shoulders. 'Sam! Stop it! Get a hold of yourself! Who are they? What are you talking about? I haven't told anyone. I just want to know what is going on. Are you OK? Are you in something over your head? What's going on? Do you need help?'

'OK, OK. I'll tell you.' He was trying to get control of himself, and I waited. He made several false starts, but kept lapsing back into silence. I glanced at my watch and realised that I didn't have time for this right now, even though I was dying to hear what he had to say.

'Listen, Sam. I have to get to class. Meet me at the

fountain during free time. Get yourself together. And relax. I won't give you away.'

He looked at me with a mixture of gratitude and terror. I hurried away, wondering if he would meet me or not.

I waited by the fountain, having arrived just in time. No Brady. Five minutes passed, then ten, and I was almost ready to give up and leave when I saw him running toward me.

'Sorry I'm late,' he said breathlessly. 'I couldn't get away right away. I had, um, duties to perform.'

I waited, without saying anything, for him to catch his breath. After a minute he said, 'Let's get out of here. Too public. Let's go over there.' He gestured toward a little path away from the main buildings of the campus. I followed, expectant about what he was going to tell me, but biting my tongue. I didn't want to scare him off. I wanted him to feel safe enough to tell me everything.

We came to a wrought-iron bench where Sam sat, looking around as he did so to make sure we were alone. He fidgeted and wriggled until he finally tucked his legs up under himself, which made him look like a little kid, all freckles and knees.

'OK,' he said after a moment, 'what do you want to know? You caught me. If I confide in you, will you promise not to tell anyone? Please, Remy, promise.'

'Of course I promise, Sam. Who would I tell, anyway? Who would even believe me? I half don't believe it myself, except that I saw it with my own eyes. And why the hell were you guys out practically in the open if you didn't want to get caught? At first I thought it was some hazing thing, but then

I saw your reaction. Sam, you loved what they were doing to you, didn't you?'

He turned away, but not before I saw the colour again creep into his cheeks. His skin was the sort that showed every mark, every flush, with painful clarity. It was barely a whisper as he said, 'It's more than that. I live for it.' I heard the drama starting to creep in; Sam was histrionic in the extreme.

'Tell me,' I whispered back, my curiosity raging.

'You promise –' Again the hesitation.

'Yes, yes,' I shot back impatiently. 'Come on, Sam. Tell me before I beat the shit out of you. I mean –' Here I broke off, stammering, suddenly confused as I realised that beating was what he craved, though surely not what I had in mind. To clarify I said, 'And not the good way!'

We both laughed then. It sounded so silly. Somehow that changed the mood and Sam relaxed a little, uncurling his legs and sitting back against the cold iron.

'Well. What you saw was part of my training. I am a novice. A novice slave.' As he said the word something jolted inside of me. I realised I was holding my breath, waiting for more. 'When I cross my wrists like that, like you saw, it's part of my training too. It is a gesture of submission. I'm in this club. It's a special kind of club. You know?'

He looked at me appealingly, as if willing me to say, 'Ah, yes, I see now,' and leave it at that. But instead I said, 'What kind of club? A slave club? For real? What do you mean?'

Sam sighed and ruffled his short, red hair with a gesture that made me think it must have been much longer before his cadet-short military cut. 'OK, let me try to explain.' Again he paused, trying to

53

compose himself. I resisted my strong urge to scream at him to tell me already. Finally he started again, and this time kept going.

'Well, you know maybe that some people are just naturally dominant, right? And some are just naturally submissive. I don't mean men versus women: it's something deeper than that. I think you're born to it, really. Most people tend one way or another. I personally think people that are drawn to the military have more pronounced tendencies, either dominant or submissive, but that's just my opinion.

'Because here you are either a soldier – a follower – or you are the leader. There is no in-between. Well, I am a follower, no question about that. I like the order and discipline of military life. I like knowing exactly where I stand, and what is expected of me. I like –' he hesitated, as if trying to find the word, or the courage to say it '– to serve,' he finally finished.

I was still waiting for the real story. So far he hadn't said anything particularly novel. I mean, I understood the dynamics of a military hierarchy that naturally had leaders and followers. But I let him go at his own pace. He continued, relaxing a little as he warmed to his subject.

'Some people were born to serve, and to submit; others to control, to use and to claim.' My hands suddenly felt sweaty, and my throat was dry. Of course, I knew where I had heard these words before. Thoughts of Jacob flooded through me, causing me to draw in my breath to keep from moaning at the vivid memories of our last time together. Sam continued calmly, unaware of my discomfiture.

'Normally in this society there is very little opportunity to explore these feelings in a controlled, safe environment. Well, here you can. It's like heaven on earth for someone like me.' He paused again, and looked at me slowly, a little smile now curling on his lips. I realised I was holding myself very still and tense. Feeling suddenly self-conscious, I leaned back into the unyielding bench, trying to look nonchalant. Inside, I was coiled, as if ready for something I had always been waiting to hear.

'Well –' he leaned very close to me, so that his nose was almost touching mine '– it's called the Slave Corps. It's been around since the Academy was established, maybe longer. It's a formalised SM club.' I must have looked puzzled. He defined it. 'Sadomasochism. You know. Whips and chains. Masters and slaves. OK, Remy, you can close your mouth now.' I realised with a shock that it had actually fallen open and I shut it, biting my lips.

He went on, now clearly warming to his topic, fear of betrayal behind him, or just accepted. 'But the Hard Corps isn't just a sex-play group.'

I interrupted him, confused. 'The Hard Corps? Didn't you just say the Slave Corps?'

'Oh,' he laughed. 'The Hard Corps is a joke, a nickname. I suppose I really should show more respect, but everyone calls it that. You know, like hard core.' He laughed again, and then went on. 'Anyway, as I was saying, it isn't just a bunch of horny people getting together to get their rocks off in some kinky way. It's a real life choice that we have made. If you join, you make a commitment to serve or to lead, as we say, with all your heart and all your soul. There are lots more submissives, or slaves, than real masters.'

'Wow, Sam. This is too much. Who is in this group? How did you find out about it?' How do I join? I didn't say that, but somehow it came, unbidden into my head. I ignored it, focusing on Sam.

'Of course, the group is mostly men, since this place is 85 per cent male, after all,' he continued. But there are women, too. And not just students. Staff and professors are involved, too. If you join, you take a pledge to serve them all, or lead them all, depending on your position.'

I listened in stunned silence. Staff and professors too. Slaves, masters, serving, obeying, submitting. Sam tilted his head to one side, as if he were listening in on my thoughts. I shook my head, again to clear it, and said, 'We've only been here for two months. How did you get so involved in all of this?'

'My brother was here before me. He's a senior now and very high up in the ruling echelons. He, unlike me, is dominant. I've known about this place for three years. It's why I'm here. I could have gone to West Point; I have the grades. But they don't have the Slave Corps. I've dreamed of submitting since I found my brother's magazines and books on SM when I was fifteen. I read it all, inhaling it, needing it, craving it. It gave voice to something that had always been inside of me. When I finally got up the courage to tell my brother, he told me about the Slave Corps. He was a freshman here at the time, and he told me I would be able to join, at his recommendation, once I got here. It's everything I dreamed it would be, and more.'

We sat for a while, both of us quiet. I kept wanting to say something, preferably something scathing and smart-assed about his being a pussy slave boy, but somehow it wouldn't come out. Nor did I believe it. What I was really feeling was intense excitement. A club! Somewhere where you could explore the feelings safely, in a controlled environment. Not in the arms of a lover. But it was that lover, it was Jacob, who had awakened these feelings in me. And now Sam had put words to them. I understood him far better than I would have admitted to anyone, even myself, at that moment.

'So,' I finally said. 'So there are whole groups of people into this stuff? And you "serve"? What does that mean, really? Do you call letting guys whip you and suck you off "serving"? Or is it more like you mostly wash their cars and lick their feet and stuff?'

'Remy, I know you're joking around, and I know you're kind of shocked about all this. I haven't really explained anything at all. Everyone's experience is different. It's a very individual process. Like the wrist thing: that's just between me and a particular master.'

I flashed back to the upperclassman who had passed in the cafeteria. So he was a master! Who else was in the club? Two people walked by at that moment and I found myself staring at them, wondering, were they in the club? Who did I know who was in the club already? My mind was brimming with questions. The one uppermost in my mind popped out. Neither of us was expecting it, most especially not me!

'How do you sign up?' At last, I asked the question I had really wanted to ask.

'Interested?' he asked, his freckled face split into a grin, his expression at once surprised and pleased.

'Well, no! I mean, I just –' Now it was my turn to blush, and as I did so, I turned my face, feeling the heat in my cheeks and neck.

'It's all right, Remy. Don't feel ashamed. It's a

natural curiosity. Even if you aren't dominant or submissive yourself, you probably have some tendency, some basic interest. It's just a part of human nature. I'll tell you what!' His voice was suddenly enthusiastic, almost pleading. 'I can invite you to a stage show. We're allowed to invite a guest, if we think that guest is ripe for recruitment. Always looking for a few good men.' He laughed at his own reference to the Marine slogan.

'On Thursday there will be a showing of some of the novice slaves. We've been training in some military exercises with a, um, twist. It's going to be pretty intense. But if you're interested . . .' He trailed off, his hands twisting in his lap. I realised I had been holding my breath as I listened to him, my eyes as wide as plates.

'Man.' I finally let out a long breath that ended in a sigh. 'Will you be in the show?'

'Yes,' he said quietly, 'I will.'

I looked at him, appraising his lean, wiry frame, his tousled, red hair, his fair, freckled skin. He didn't look like a 'slave', whatever a slave looked like. It must have taken enormous courage to share all of this with me, I realised, as he looked down, waiting for some response. When none was forthcoming, he reached around his neck and unclasped what seemed to be a necklace chain.

Holding his hand out to me, he said, 'This is my key. My key to the bell tower. You can't get in without it. You keep it. Just till Thursday. You keep it and think about all this. If you decide you don't want to go, just give it back to me, or put it in my mailbox. If you want to go, meet me at the fountain on Thursday, at 1900 hours. I'll take you. I'll introduce you to the right people. Then, you know, I'll

58

have to leave you, because I'm in the show.' He was standing now, no longer nervous. He even seemed defiant, daring me silently to put down his submissive status. I realised I liked him.

'OK, Sam. I'll keep the key. I have to admit that you've got me way curious. But I don't have to do anything if I go, do I? I mean, I'll check it out, but no one better mess with me. They'll know I'm just a, um, an observer, right?'

'Oh, no one will "mess with you", don't you worry. Not unless you give them express permission to do so.'

I took the key. It was curiously heavy and thick; it felt like real gold. It was hung on a fine, pinkish-gold chain. I put it in my pocket, still fingering it as we walked back to the barracks, both of us silent with our own thoughts.

Chapter Four
The Stage Show

Thursday evening found me at the fountain, all right. I had the key in my hand and it felt so smooth and heavy, so right, somehow. Sam sauntered toward me in his olive drab fatigues, same as me. He smiled at me, looking a little nervous, as I'm sure I did too.

'I'm supposed to be at the library,' I whispered. 'I could get killed for this.'

'I'm supposed to be right here,' he grinned back at me. 'One of the perks of membership. The rules change. You become part of an elite. You get freedoms, so to speak, that you don't have as a regular cadet.' As he spoke, Sam held out his hand, and I was actually reluctant to part with the key I had had for two days. I had grown fond of it, somehow. I found myself wishing it were mine. Instead, of course, I handed it to him, feeling his cool palm against my hot one as the key passed back to him.

'Let's go.' he said. 'I don't want to be late.' We walked toward the bell tower. As we approached the old vine-covered building, I saw the little door in its side. Sam walked right up to the door. After inserting the key into the lock, he pulled the little door open and gestured for me to enter before him. As I walked ahead, he pulled the door closed behind us and it shut with a click.

We were in a little corridor, at the head of a curving staircase. Sam took the lead, and I followed behind him, anxious with trepidation and excitement. What was I getting myself into? At the bottom of the stairs there was a long hall. Sam and I walked, still silently, toward one of the doors. The hallway was thickly carpeted, luxuriously so. It was lit by frosted glass sconces set at intervals of a few feet along the wall. The walls were painted a dark-cream colour and I was reminded of a grand old hotel. It was hard to believe this was the basement of some broken-down bell tower on a college campus.

Sam stopped in front of a door and knocked softly. After a moment, the door silently opened and a young woman dressed in a sheer, black bodysuit ushered us in. It was as if it were painted on her flesh: I could see her nipples, her pubic hair, the shape of her breasts and thighs. She looked down as we entered and I couldn't really see her face. Ignoring her, Sam pulled me along with him, wending his way between tables closely placed to one another. The place had the atmosphere of a small jazz bar, with low lighting and white table-cloths covering maybe ten round tables which seated only three or four at most. Sam led me to a table near the stage, where three people were already sitting.

Sam kneeled suddenly, as if we were in the

presence of royalty. As he went down, he pressed my shoulder so that I fell into a sort of ungraceful crouch next to him.

'Ah, Sam. What have you brought for us today? A new recruit?' The woman who spoke had a deep, almost masculine voice, but that was the only masculine thing about her. She was small, with delicate features. Her little mouth was curved up in a smile as she looked at me. She looked familiar to me but I couldn't place her at the moment. Her large, brown eyes seemed to look right through me, and I had to look down to keep from blushing. She was dressed in a dark-blue dress of what seemed to be soft leather. As she stood, pushing her chair back from the table, her dress clung to her small breasts and cinched in at her impossibly small waist.

'Stand up, girl,' she said to me gently, her hand lightly touching the top of my head. I did so, feeling awkward and huge next to the petite woman. She moved in very close to me, so that I moved back, uncomfortable with her closeness. She stiffened then and started to speak, but Sam interrupted her.

'Oh! Excuse me, ma'am! This is my guest, ma'am. She isn't a recruit, um, not yet, anyway.'

I shot him a look but he ignored it.

'Is that so? Well, you would do well to teach her some manners, novice. I will forgive you because you are new. And you –' she turned to me, no longer smiling '– you are here to watch the show, eh? Well, you can look, but keep your mouth shut. This isn't a peep show. Do you understand?'

'Yes, ma'am,' I whispered, angry with myself for already making a mess of things. I realised that I must have angered her by moving back. I guessed a 'slave' or 'new recruit' wouldn't have dared to do such a thing.

'Well, then,' she said, softening a little. 'You may sit with us.' Suddenly I knew where I had seen her. This was Dr Wellington, a chemistry professor at the Academy. She wasn't regular army; several professors on campus weren't. I wasn't sure whether to salute or not, so I kept my hands at my sides, standing military straight.

'Novice, go get ready for the show. I know you've been practising hard and I can't wait to see the results.'

Sam melted away and I saw that there was an extra chair at the little table, which Dr Wellington gestured for me to take. I sidled into it, feeling very uncertain and insecure. As I sat, she said, 'And what may we call you?'

'My name is Harris, ma'am. Cadet Remy Harris.'

'Ah, you are Harris? Ellen Roster is your sergeant, isn't she?'

'Yes, ma'am,' I answered, wondering how she could possibly know this.

'Yes, Ellen has mentioned you, though I don't quite see what caught her attention. But then, in those awful fatigues, who can tell anything.' I wasn't sure what she was getting at, but didn't feel free to inquire. I realised she was gently putting me down in some way and I didn't like it. But I didn't dare question her.

She continued. 'Allow me to introduce you, Remy. I am Dr Wellington and these are my friends, Mr Jordan and Sergeant Sinclair.'

I looked at the two men with her. Mr Jordan had wavy, blond hair, ruddy skin and blue eyes. He might have been in his mid-thirties. I had never seen him before, as far as I knew. But, of course, I recognised Sergeant Sinclair at once. I wasn't quite sure which of us should be more embarrassed by this meeting in such strange circumstances.

Sergeant Sinclair was dark-skinned with tightly curled hair and a cruel-looking mouth that curved up slightly with a natural look of disdain. He stared at me, his dark eyes flashing with amusement and something else. 'Cadet Harris. Who would have expected to find you here? Tough girl cadet that runs rings around half those pussy wimp freshmen during PT? But maybe you are a leader, a would-be mistress? Though at the moment you look quite submissive, I must say.'

I looked down, confused and very embarrassed. If I could have gone back in time to the minute before I entered that tower, I would never have come here, never have put myself in this awkward confusing position.

'Ah, you know her, I see?' Dr Wellington smiled at Sergeant Sinclair.

'Oh yes, she is one of our more promising toads, er, cadets,' he amended unconvincingly. In spite of my embarrassment, I felt a hot flush of pride course through me at his remark. He had never given any indication that he even knew who I was, much less that he approved of me. 'But I wonder what she is really made of?' he mused.

'Well, sir,' I felt I had to say, 'I am only visiting, sir.'

'We'll see about that, won't we?' He seemed to leer toward me.

'Don't press her, George,' Dr Wellington interjected. 'She is here to visit, as she says. Let's just watch the show. It should be starting soon. We'll show Ms Harris how PT is done around here, right George?' Mr Jordan, the other man at the table, laughed nervously, perhaps a little too loudly for the small space. Sergeant Sinclair was silent, but he kept staring at me, so that I was forced to look away, pretending his eyes weren't boring holes through me.

The lights dimmed and the stage lights brightened. Their attention diverted, the three turned their faces toward the stage, which was a little raised dais on one side of the room. With relief I also looked over, glad their scrutiny was no longer focused on me. The stage lights were blue, casting an eerie light across the room. The stage was empty, save for a chin-up bar supported by two poles. In the back corner I also noticed a small table that had some things on it, but I couldn't see what. The audience grew quiet as music began to filter through small speakers that I now noticed on the walls. The music was unusual. At first it seemed repetitive but became soothing, almost hypnotic. I learned later that it was Brian Eno's *Music for Airports*.

After a minute, a young woman dressed in all black glided out on to the stage. She wore the same gauzy, soft fabric that the girl who had let us into the room had been wearing. It covered her arms, her body, her legs, like a dancer's leotard and tights. She was barefoot, her white, slim ankles and feet in striking contrast to the black of her outfit. She curtseyed deeply to the audience, and remained in that bowed position as two more people came on to the stage. One was Sam, stripped of his army-issue fatigues. He was now dressed only in black leather shorts that seemed moulded to his body. Hanging from his chest was a long chain, which I saw was held in place by clamps, one on each nipple. I stared in fascination at the chain. God, that must hurt! But he looked so calm, like it was nothing. I wondered how he could tolerate those pinching teeth, feeling my own nipples stiffen perversely at the thought.

Following Sam was another young woman, dressed as the first, in sheer black to the ankle. Her feet were also bare. She was built similarly to the other girl, with smallish breasts and slim hips. They both had their hair pulled back, reminding me again of ballet dancers. The second girl curtseyed deeply, as the first had. Sam, in the centre, dropped to his knees and touched his forehead to the ground, as I had seen him do that night by the tower. They all stayed very still until, at some silent signal, both women rose up gracefully and each faced the still-kneeling Sam. Leaning forward, both women took Sam's arms and then pulled him up. Silently the young women led Sam to the chin-up bar. He took hold of the bar, his body now an X below it.

Bringing his hands together on the bar, Sam executed several chin-ups in very good form. This was something one saw and did everyday on the campus. But suddenly, one of the women was behind Sam, standing just to the side. I saw that she had something in her hand that she had gotten from the table. It looked like a whip! The whip had long, unbraided tresses, too many to count. As Sam continued to pull himself up, the woman began to whip his ass and back with long, heavy strokes. The room was silent, save for the cracking sound of the whip and Sam's grunts. It wasn't clear if he was grunting from effort or pain.

The second woman approached him now with an identical whip in her hand. They beat him, alternating the lashes as he pulled himself up and let himself down, keeping a steady rhythm.

I was riveted to the scene. It seemed surreal as the music pulsed around us. I realised I had forgotten the people I was sitting with, and I had forgotten myself as I watched the choreographed little torture scene take place. Just when it seemed Sam would collapse, the two women stopped whipping him. They each presented their whip to the sweating Sam, who kissed each leather offering, his eyes closed as if in worship.

Then the women kneeled, one on either side of Sam. They were each faced away from him, so that their heads faced offstage, their backsides toward the audience. He left them there, walking back to the table to get his designated instruments of torture. It was their turn to suffer, it seemed.

Taking a small knife, Sam then drew the blade down the back of the first girl. I leaned forward, actually making a little sound as I strained to see what he was doing. I soon saw that he wasn't actually touching her skin. Instead, the gauzy, black fabric fell away from her body, leaving her white back, bent like a swan's. With a prod of his foot, she raised her ass high in the air so we could all see her naked globes. With his other hand, Sam brought down a large, black object that I saw was a phallus.

We were sitting at a table slightly at an angle from the stage, which afforded us a view of a side of her face. I watched in horrified fascination as he held the dildo in front of the girl's mouth. Though her eyes remained shut, her little pink tongue darted out to lick and suckle the rubber cock. Once

Sam was satisfied that it was slick enough, he pulled it from her eager lips, and walked around to her bottom, which was still appealingly raised up. Slowly Sam inserted the dildo into her little asshole, and the girl moaned and pushed back against the huge phallus now impaling her. In and out Sam drew the cock, while I blushed for the naked girl on the stage.

I looked down, feeling my own heart pound as if it were me up there. How could that girl possibly allow such a thing to happen to her? And, forget the public humiliation, didn't it hurt? I was again confused by my own rising desire. My clit was pulsing with need, even as I felt ashamed at what I was witnessing. I had been affected watching Sam that night by the tower, but this was even more intense, perhaps because now there were witnesses to my own voyeurism. I was no longer hiding in a bush, my panties getting damp. I was sitting in a room full of people who were turned on by this show, who had maybe done all the things we had seen and were about to see. I was here with them! I was guilty by association. I looked down, embarrassed, my face burning, my panties perversely wet.

After just a moment, I looked up again, not able to resist. Sam had stopped fucking the first girl with the play-cock and was now using his knife on the second girl's outfit. She had remained perfectly still, waiting her turn to be raped by the dildo. As I looked back at the first girl, I saw that Sam had left the dildo sticking lewdly out of her ass.

From where we were sitting, I couldn't see this one's face. After she had made oral love to another rubber dildo, Sam came around to her firm little ass. He spread the cheeks for a moment, so that we could all see the puckered little asshole waiting to be violated. She shivered slightly, and seemed to tense up somewhat. There was a slight murmuring in the audience. Sam paused a moment, as if giving her time to collect herself. Then he began to press the second dildo into her ass. As the tip penetrated and he began to push harder, the girl suddenly flinched and fell forward with a little cry. Sam jerked her back by the hair and she struggled to get back into position. I realised I wasn't breathing as I waited to see what would happen. She seemed desperate in her efforts to control herself, to resume her still and submissive position, so he could fuck her for all of us to see.

Again Sam used the dildo, pressing slowly but forcefully until the poor girl had the whole thing shoved up her ass. I could see her body trembling slightly but, to her credit, she remained still and in position. Mercifully for her, the lights dimmed and Sam left the girl, dildo sticking from her body, and kneeled in the centre of the stage, again in his subservient position. As the curtains fell, the lights went up in the room. The music stopped and it took me a moment to come back to myself.

I realised that all three at the table were looking at me, staring at me. I wasn't sure what was expected. My mind was still reeling from the wild events I had witnessed. Then Dr Wellington spoke.

'Well, what did you think? Other than the fact that novice M. fell out of position, I think the show was nicely executed. Your Sam did very well indeed.'

'What will –' I stopped, not sure I should speak.

'What? You have a question?' It was Sergeant Sinclair. I turned to him. I had to know.

'What will happen to her, sir?'

'Oh, she'll be punished, to be sure. But not too severely. After all, she is still learning. Have you ever had a huge dildo shoved up your ass, cadet? Not so easy to take.'

I looked down, acutely embarrassed by his question.

'Answer the master, cadet. He asked you a direct question.'

I looked up to see Mr Jordan speaking to me. His voice was high and had a slight nasal twang to it. I noticed that his eyes were too small for his face, and too closely spaced. I took an instant dislike to him. 'Well? Even as a "visitor" you are still addressing your commanding officer, toad. Speak up. Have you ever had your ass fucked with a rubber cock?' They were quiet, waiting for me to respond.

'No, sir,' I managed to say, but it came out as a squeak. They all three laughed and I felt a burning humiliation rising in me.

'Relax, Remy. Mr Jordan has an unusual sense of humour. He is teasing you.' Dr Wellington put her cool hand over mine and looked at me with a small smile on her lips. I looked over at Mr Jordan, who was glaring at me through squinting eyes. He didn't seem at all amused.

Just then Sam came over to the table. He was dressed again in his fatigues. He kneeled by the table until Dr Wellington tapped him lightly on the shoulder. Then he stood and said, 'Excuse me, ma'am. I have to take Remy back. She is AWOL.'

'Oh, is she?' Here Sergeant Sinclair spoke up and I realised with horror that I was caught. But he was smiling as he scribbled something on a piece of paper. 'Here,' he said, extending his hand to me. 'If

Roster gives you trouble, just give her this. She'll leave you alone.'

'Thank you, sir,' I said, taking the folded sheet. I stood with Sam, not sure what to say. How does one thank such hosts? So I said nothing.

Again he bowed low before them. After just a moment's hesitation, I did the same. I realised even as I was doing it that I should feel stupid, bowing like that, but somehow I didn't. Somehow it felt natural, there in that darkened room, with Sam by my side. He stood and we waited a moment until Dr Wellington said imperiously, 'You may go.'

As we left the tower, stepping into the cool night air, I turned toward Sam. 'That was incredible!' I looked at him with awe. 'You seemed so calm, so brave.'

Sam looked down and muttered, 'Thanks.' Looking up, he said, 'Not exactly the image you have of me, eh?'

It was my turn to be embarrassed. Sam's image so far in school was of a kind of nervous, geeky guy. Nothing like the submissive but courageous man on stage.

I still clutched the piece of paper the sergeant had given me. To change the subject, I said, 'Oh, I haven't looked at what she gave me yet.' I opened it up, trying to see the words under the dim lights of the streetlamps along the walkway.

'SC Pass. Approved by G. Sinclair.' That was all, plus the day's date.

'SC pass, right?' asked Sam, as though certain of the answer.

'Yep,' I said, impressed. 'What does that stand for?'

71

'Slave Corps, of course. Roster will know what it means. She's in the Corps too. She's a slave.'

I was too stunned to respond for a minute. Roster was a slave! And she treated me so harshly, so dominantly! It confused me.

'Weird, right? To find out your commanding officer is just another naked slave girl after hours.'

'Wow. Man. That is so bizarre. Especially because she is so tough. I mean, she is constantly putting me through my paces. She goes around with that little leather baton like some crazed little Napoleon. If I had to pick, I would have definitely said she was a, um, a mistress.' As I said the word it felt silly on my tongue. Mistress, master, slave. But then I looked over at Sam, a self-professed slave. And I recalled Dr Wellington looking right through me with those rich, dark-brown eyes. I bit my bottom lip, feeling a confusing jumble of unresolved conflict and desire.

'Oh, you'd be surprised just who is in this little organisation. On this campus, I'd say well over a third of the population is involved one way or another in the Slave Corps. And others must know about it. I can't believe it hasn't made it outside the grounds, you know, in the media or whatever.'

'Yeah, why hasn't it? Something like this couldn't remain secret forever. Just one slighted slave or rejected master –'

'I guess it's a code of honour. I don't know. I do know that you swear some pretty heavy stuff when you join. And there are some very powerful people involved. Not just at the Academy, but way high up, in positions of power, all the way to the Pentagon. Maybe it just isn't worth the risk. I know I don't plan to find out.'

'You really are into this, aren't you, Sam?' We were getting close to my dorm and I spoke faster. 'I mean, I was watching you up there. You enjoyed being whipped. You get off on it. And you liked fucking those girls, too. I saw it in your face, in your whole body language. You were having a blast.'

Sam laughed. 'You're on to me, huh? Yes, I love it. I adore it. I breathe it. I am it. Don't you see? This is what I was born for: to exhibit myself, to expose myself, to allow myself to submit and to serve.' Suddenly he leaned toward me, so close I could smell his citrus cologne.

'And you, Remy. What about you? You came to the show. You stayed. You bowed to the masters. You blushed like a sweet little novice. Admit it, Remy. It's in your blood, too. You know it is.'

I didn't answer, but my facial features were suddenly defined by heat. I felt the flush and I knew he was right. Something in me had been awakened by Jacob and it wouldn't go quietly back to sleep, no matter how I ignored it or denied it.

We stood at my dorm entrance now.

'You better get your ass in there, Remy. No point in pushing your luck. Save that piece of paper: you might need it sooner than you think.'

And he was gone. I had been waiting for what I was sure was coming. I thought he was going to invite me to join the Corps. To become a 'novice', like him. I found that I was actually disappointed that he hadn't. Even though I had been planning to refuse. To be interested is one thing; to join some slave ring was another! Then again, perhaps he didn't have the authority to invite me. Perhaps only a master could do that. That would make sense. I consoled myself with this thought, though I felt ridiculous for even considering it.

Slipping into the darkened room, I quickly undressed. As I climbed between the cold sheets someone hissed at me.

'Your ass is fried, Harris. You're dead meat. I was at the library tonight, cadet. Where the fuck were you? I'm sure Sergeant Roster will be very interested.' It was my nemesis, Cadet Jean Dillon. Why did she hate me so much?

'Fuck off,' I snarled back at her. I shut out whatever else she had to say with a pillow pressed down over my head. Closing my eyes, I let the events of this most amazing evening play again and again in my mind. I must have been more tired than I thought, because next thing I knew, dawn was creeping over the windowsill.

Chapter Five
The Initiation

*H*ow did morning get here so fast? As I jumped out of bed and rushed to the shower, Jean sneered, 'Say your prayers, Harris.' I felt a cold rush of fear as Sergeant Roster came toward us.

'Having a little morning chat, girls?'

'Ma'am, yes ma'am.' Jean stood straight as a little arrow, saluting smartly. I stood at attention as well, waiting for the axe to fall, still not believing that the pass in my pants pocket would save me.

'Do tell.' Roster leaned in toward us, smiling sweetly, though her eyes were hard.

'I was just wondering where Cadet Harris was last night when she was signed up for library. She must have got lost on the way.' Jean looked intently at Roster, ignoring me completely. I glared at Jean. If looks could kill, she would have been dead on the spot.

'Oh, is that so? What do you have to say about that, Harris? How many more demerits do you want this term? Haven't you done enough push-ups and peeled enough potatoes for one lifetime? Speak up, cadet.'

I glanced over at Jean, willing Sergeant Roster to dismiss her. To my amazement, she snapped, 'Thanks for the report, Dillon. Now go shower. You stink.' Jean shot a poisonous glance at me, as if I had been the one to insult her, and skulked off to the showers.

'Now, let's hear it, Harris. Just where did you spend your evening AWOL? Out having a malt with your boyfriend?'

It was now or never. 'No, ma'am. I, um, I have a permit. A pass.'

'A pass? What kind of pass? I give out the passes around here, and I don't recall giving you one lately.'

'Please, ma'am. It's in my footlocker. May I get it for you?'

'Get it. And this better be good, Harris. You have stepped over the line one too many times.' I rushed back to my bunk and pulled my pants out of my footlocker. Inside the pocket was the little folded piece of paper. My heart was pounding as I presented the pass to her. The secret would be out then. She would know about me, and she might guess that I knew about her. I didn't see any way around it though. Thanks to Jean, my hand was being called before I was ready to make the play.

Sergeant Roster took the paper from me and opened it, a sceptical look on her face. I waited, terrified that it was all a horrible mistake and that the pass was some worthless hoax. As she glanced at it, her colour deepened, the pink seeping into her cheeks. Slowly she looked up, her eyes locking with

76

mine. After what seemed a lifetime, but surely was just a few seconds, she spoke.

'As you were, cadet. Get on to the showers. You have PT this morning. Look sharp!' She turned on her heel and left. I stood for a moment, as if I had been glued to the floor. Jean snapped me out of it.

'What was that about?' She was sneering, ready to launch into some diatribe, no doubt, about my attempts to curry favour with the sergeant. I was in no mood to listen.

As elation rushed through me with the realisation that I had gotten off scot-free, I whirled toward Dillon, feeling the power of victory. Grabbing her by the throat, I pressed her against the wall.

'Mind your own business, Dillon. You made your trouble. Now go back to your slime hole.' I dropped my hold then, and swept past her. I was tired of taking her shit. I had a pass.

After classes that evening, an upperclassman by the name of Charles Smith came over to where I was sitting at the library. Leaning down, he said, in a quiet voice, 'Excuse me.' I knew his name because he was on the basketball team, and a good player at that.

'Yes?' I looked up, wondering why he was talking to a toad, and so politely to boot. I started to get up, not wanting to remain seated against protocol.

'No, no, don't get up.' He sat across from me, leaning forward conspiratorially. 'I'm here on different business. SC business.'

I looked around quickly, as if we might be overheard. SC business! I didn't say anything, but I was listening with every fibre of my being.

'Interested?'

I nodded, not even daring to speak.

'This is an invitation. This will be your only invitation, so pay attention. If you choose to accept, be at the tower at twenty-one hundred hours. Be prompt. There is no consequence for choosing not to come. However, be advised that if you break ranks on this, if you say a word to any of the uninitiated, you will regret it.' His veiled threat bothered me a little, but I was too curious to hear what he had to say to focus on that.

'If you choose to accept . . .' It sounded so secret-agent, so James Bond.

He went on, leaning toward me, speaking barely above a whisper. 'You are to wear nothing under your daily uniform except the ankle bracelet you will find in your mailbox this evening. Be prepared to strip. Be prepared to suffer. We have chosen you.'

I almost laughed at his pompous words. Chosen me, indeed! But even as I tried to dismiss it as so much nonsense, my heart was racing. I had trouble catching my breath. Be prepared to suffer. Oh, my God. Just the words set off something inside of me. I knew before I admitted it aloud in my thoughts: I would go. I had to go. I had to know at last if this was for me.

I couldn't manage much more than an 'I'll be there, at the tower, at twenty-one hundred hours.' Smith nodded, stood and strode away.

That evening I found a little packet in my mail slot. I went to the bathroom, closing the door to a stall for privacy. With fingers almost trembling with impatience, I ripped open the package. Inside were three things: a little velvet box, a piece of paper, and a key. A key just like the one Sam had. My fingers slid up and down the smooth metal. I pressed the key to my cheek, enjoying its cool, hard feel against my skin. I would need to get a chain, like Sam had, so I wouldn't lose it. For now, I slipped it into my pocket and turned my attention to the other items.

Inside the little velvet box lay a pretty little gold chain. After unlacing my boot and pushing down my sock, I secured it around my left ankle. It felt cold but quickly warmed against my flesh. I shivered in spite of myself, remembering the direction to wear it, and only it, under my uniform.

Next the piece of paper. It was a pass, just like the other one, only this one was typed and more specific. 'SC Pass for 2100–2400 hours, Friday, November 5, Bell Tower, 2B.' Three hours! And here it was, already only an hour until I had to be there! I jumped up and went to the showers. I'd better make myself presentable for whatever the hell I was letting myself in for.

And so 2100 hours found me at the tower. Just as I pressed my key into the lock, the door was pulled open, startling me for a moment. It was Sam! I felt so relieved to see someone I knew that I almost hugged him. 'Sam! I didn't expect to see you! I'm so glad you're here. I –'

'Ssh! Don't talk. I was sent up to escort you to the chamber. We aren't supposed to talk.'

'God. The chamber. It sounds so Gothic. I can't believe I'm doing this.'

'I remember how scared I was. I wish I could warn you, advise you, but everyone's test is different. Just be honest. Be brave and be yourself. Don't fake something you don't feel, because this isn't a game, Remy. If it isn't for you, this is definitely the time to find out. You won't be the first one to back out, and no one will hold it against you.'

There were so many questions I wanted to ask, but Sam put his fingers to his lips as we reached the bottom of the steps. The lush atmosphere of the thick carpets and muted lighting reminded me sharply where I was. Pressing my lips together, I followed Sam. We went past the door where the stage show had taken place and stopped a few doors down. Sam knocked and, as he did, my stomach flip-flopped. Silently he moved back and stood to the side, so that I was alone in front of the door. A part of me wanted to bolt, to turn around and run back the way I came. But I stayed rooted to the spot. I had come too far to back out now.

The door opened on silent hinges. Dr Wellington was there, smiling at me. I glanced toward Sam but he was gone. 'Come in, Remy. We've been expecting you.' For a second I imagined I was entering her home for a small get-together. She pulled the door open and I saw three people, one woman and two men, sitting on chairs arranged in a half circle. One of the men was very young, most probably an upperclassman. There was one empty chair, that presumably Dr Wellington had recently occupied. None of them was anyone I had met, which relieved me. It would be hard enough to pass whatever tests they had in mind without the more personal aspect of someone I knew well being there.

Dr Wellington led me to the area in front of the chairs. 'May I present Remy Harris? She has agreed to submit to this initiation. She is a complete novice, without any training either in or out of the Corps. Please bear that in mind as you choose your test. I will start, since I extended the invitation.' Before I had time to dwell on that, she said, 'Now, Cadet Harris. Are you here of your own free will?'

'Yes, ma'am,' I said in a voice so low I had to repeat myself.

'You are about to undergo a series of tests, devised by each of us on this committee, to determine your suitability as a member of the Corps. If you pass, then from that moment forward you will become a novice in the Corps. Eventually you may earn the rank of slave. It is not inconceivable that you might even earn the rank of mistress, but that is unlikely. Not many slaves have what it requires to lead others. But we will speak of this later.' I noticed that she didn't introduce the other people in the room to me, as she had the night of the stage show. Maybe now that I was 'auditioning' for a position as a novice in the 'Hard Corps', it was no longer necessary to extend such courtesies. She continued. 'For right now, you can start by removing your uniform. Then kneel in front of us, head touching the floor, arms extended in front of you.' As she spoke, she gracefully lowered herself into the fourth chair. The test had begun.

I stood, staring at her, willing my mind to process what she had just said. Her eyes flashed as she watched me and I realised they were all staring, waiting to see what I would do. Shit. I could strip. We saw each other naked all the time in those lousy shower stalls with the flimsy curtains that wouldn't stay put. But there were no men in the showers.

Well, first the boots. That was easy. I removed my boots and socks, automatically folding the socks per army regulation. Then I stood again, consciously avoiding the eyes of these people watching me so intently. Taking a deep breath, I began to unbutton my uniform shirt, willing my hands not to shake. As I reached the bottom button, I had to exert all my willpower not to pull the olive drab fabric tight against my naked torso. Instead, I let it fall open, wriggling my shoulders to allow the shirt to fall. As always, I was uncomfortably aware of my breasts. I wished for the thousandth time that they were small and high, instead of full and large. I felt my nipples tingle and harden under the gaze of these strangers.

I realised with a small rush of triumph that I had managed to remove my shirt without passing out. I was breathing hard and knew I was flushed with embarrassment, but I could do this. I was as tough as Sam and those girls on the stage. Now came the panties. I opened them and pushed them down, wondering briefly how to remove them while still standing up without looking like a clown. I don't think I succeeded too well in the grace department, but somehow I got them off. I kneeled quickly, relieved at the chance to be able to cover myself by crouching on the floor. With my forehead touching the ground, I didn't have to look at anyone. I closed my eyes.

I could hear my own breathing as I waited for whatever might happen next. My heart thumped painfully in my chest, and I had to consciously keep my body from rising and falling as I struggled to control my laboured breathing. If only I could slow my heart just a little, calm myself enough to relax. I heard a sound, and felt someone near me.

'Stay in position. I am going to blindfold you.' It was Dr Wellington. She spoke softly into my ear and I was so startled that I jumped and let out a gasp.

'Nervous little slut, isn't she?' It was one of the men, and I bristled at his remark. But I did as she asked, hoping I was doing what she wanted. I felt the soft blindfold cover my eyes, resting snugly on my face. It seemed to be held in place by an elastic band, and I later saw that it looked like a sleeping mask, but it was of deep-crimson satin.

'You may stand now, novice. And lift your arms, hands behind your head, elbows out.'

Slowly I stood, slightly off balance from being blindfolded. As I stood and assumed the ordered position, something strange seemed to come over me. I was still breathing hard, and as nervous as a cat, but there was an overlay of excitement that I couldn't deny. I stood quietly, keenly aware that three strangers were staring at me, at my naked body, at the blindfold on my face, at the anklet on my leg.

And along with the shame was an undeniable surge of desire. I was bared before them, and it turned me on! I was glad of my strong body, my firm stomach. And with my arms raised, I was even almost proud of my breasts, whose tips I could feel stiffening, engorging further, both from the cool air and from my awareness that these strangers were staring at my naked body.

'Very nice,' murmured an unfamiliar female voice, which must have belonged to the other woman. 'Such strength in her body, but still very feminine. And all that gorgeous blonde hair. Shame how she pulls it back like that. I'd like to see it down, hanging over her luscious tits.'

Part of me wanted to sink into the floor. I was never comfortable being looked at, even in the most innocent of circumstances. But naked in front of

83

strangers, who proposed to 'use' me in whatever fashion they chose! Thank God for the blindfold, I thought.

'She looks good,' interjected one of the men, 'but let's see what she's made of. I'm going to whip her pert little ass for my test. I want to see how her flesh responds to the lash.'

I bit my lip, fighting my impulse to run out of there. And yet, even then, I couldn't deny the little pulse of desire that surged through my body at the mention of a whip.

I felt a hand on my elbow.

'Let me guide you to the whipping table, novice. I will only whip your ass, since you are new. Bend over and grip the table. And don't move, or I will start over.' He led me a few steps and then pressed me forward until my hands made contact with what felt like smooth wood. It was just the right height to allow me to bend forward at the waist, keeping my legs straight. I felt a gentle kick to the inside of my ankle that sent my legs wide apart.

I gripped the table hard, trying not to focus on the fact that my ass was now spread and bare for all to see. They were probably behind me, with a good view of my pussy and asshole showing between my spread legs. I felt an almost unbearable heat creep into my cheeks and spread down to my chest. I must have been blushing a bright red. But somehow I stayed still, my skin prickling in anticipation of the whipping.

There was a slight whistle and then I felt it. The whip was a heavy one, and I felt many licks of soft leather against my flesh. It must have been like the one the girls had used on Sam during the stage show. It really didn't hurt much. I could take this, I thought. I had endured far worse just in the course of regular army training. Again and again the lash fell, and while it stung, it was nothing I couldn't easily tolerate.

After several minutes, the beating stopped, and I stood, still bent over, my body now covered in a thin sheen of sweat. My ass felt hot, but I had made it through without moving.

'Not bad, not bad for a first time,' murmured the man, as I felt his large hands stroke the heated flesh he had just whipped. He seemed to linger, his hands smoothing my ass, straying closer to the open cleft between the cheeks, until he pulled back suddenly, seemingly startled by Dr Wellington, who cleared her throat theatrically.

As he stepped away, I stayed in position, my mind swirling with confusion and excitement, my ass hot from the whipping and the stranger's hands.

'Well, she did all right on that one.' The disembodied male voice seemed grudgingly impressed. His voice was a tenor, and I was pretty sure it was the upperclassman. For some reason I felt less submissive to him than to the other older members of the 'committee'. I guess it was because he was my 'peer'; I might have a class with him one day, or sit next to him in the cafeteria. The thought was sobering and I realised I was more nervous than ever. He brought me back to the moment by continuing. 'Though with such soft strips, and so many, it was probably more like a massage than a whipping. We'll see how still she stays with the stinger.'

That didn't sound good. The stinger. I didn't have much time to worry about it, because suddenly there was a stinging cut across my ass cheeks. I jumped and cried out with the pain and surprise.

'Stay still, novice!' As he spoke, he grabbed my hair and pulled my head back, forcing my face up toward the ceiling for a moment. He was very close, so that I could feel his hot breath on my cheek.

He held my head back for a moment, then released my hair. Roughly, he pressed my head back toward the table. I was still so stunned from the cut of the lash that I didn't even think of disobeying. I bent my head down, trying not to tense my ass cheeks in anticipation, trying not to cry aloud.

Again the single lash fell, and again, despite my best intentions, I jumped and yelped. Four more times the little lines of heat seared across my flesh. I felt my knees about to buckle and the blood rushing to my head left me dizzy. Mercifully, he was done.

I felt another hand on my back. 'Come with me, novice. So far you have done reasonably well, for a beginner. And you do mark in such a lovely fashion.' As the second woman spoke, I felt her smooth fingers graze my heated flesh. Then her nails dragged across the tender skin, causing me to gasp from the pain. 'But now I want to see you really submit. You can take a beating, but can you give yourself on command?' I had no idea what she meant, but didn't think she was actually asking a question that required response. At any rate, I remained silent as she led me, still blind, away from the table.

I felt her hands reach up and release the clasp that held the blindfold in place. As she removed it, I squinted for a moment in the light. I was facing the group, who were now all sitting in their chairs, staring up at me.

'OK, novice. Get on the floor and come for us. And make sure we can see your hot little pussy while you do it. That's my test.'

No. I couldn't have heard that right. Come for them? I could take beatings. I could assume embarrassing positions. But masturbate in front of these gawking strangers? Oh God. Then I realised, in a flash, that this was really submitting. This wasn't about exhibitionism, or proving some secret macho thing to myself that I could 'take it'. This was the first 'test' that actually involved real submission, because it was so personal, so revealing.

Trembling, I lowered myself to the floor. I no longer had any thoughts about being as tough as the next guy. This was totally about me. I kneeled in front of them, spreading my legs so that my knees were almost at right angles with my body. My naked pussy was wide open, covered only by dark-blonde little curls. I couldn't quite summon the nerve to look up, but slowly I dropped my hand to my sex.

As I touched the soft, hot flesh, I was momentarily shocked by how wet I was. I was soaking! Another defence dropped as I realised, or at last really admitted, that my body loved what was happening to me. Beyond the beatings and the discipline, this was what had reached me at last. To be naked on the floor, rubbing my clit in front of these strangers: this excited me beyond any experience I had ever had in my life.

The heat of my welted ass against the rough fibres of the carpet, the slight tension of my leg muscles as they stretched to accommodate the unusual position, the wet silkiness of my aching pussy all combined to make me dizzy with need. My eyes fluttered shut and I felt a deep heat welling up from inside my belly. I was close, very close to the edge.

'Yes,' hissed the other woman. 'Yes, do it, novice. Come for us.'

It was as if I had been waiting for her command. On her order I came. I came and came with such a rage of heat that I fell back, no longer aware of my surroundings or my situation.

I don't know how long I lay there, lost in a fog of perfect release. I had never come like that before. Even with Jacob. With him it had been intense, but somehow I had always held something back. Not this time though.

Slowly I sat up, unsure what I was supposed to do next. As the haze of the endorphin rush started to lift, I became self-conscious. I hugged my knees together, looking up at my judges. Had I passed? They ignored me for the moment, leaning toward each other, speaking so softly that I couldn't hear what they were saying. This must be the reckoning, the 'tallying' of my scores. They were deciding whether they would allow me to join the ranks of the Slave Corps. As I waited on tenterhooks, I realised I wanted it very much. I wanted more. I wanted to find out what it meant to submit. I held my breath. At last they sat back, the other three demurring silently to Dr Wellington.

'Cadet Remy Harris, stand and come forward.' She beckoned me with a finger, looking as imperious as a queen. There was a trace of a smile on her lips, which gave me hope. I pulled myself up, and stood with my arms loose at my sides, not daring to cover my nakedness, even though the test seemed to be over. I looked down at the floor, still feeling caught in a sexual trance, still feeling like their slave girl.

'Remy, would you like to become a novice? To be trained to be a true slave? You have potential. We are pleased.'

I nodded and then, feeling I should speak, managed to say, 'Yes, mistress, yes please.' I hoped my yearning wasn't too palpable, too obvious, but I couldn't help it.

'You were born to this, weren't you, slut?' The older man spoke. Even as I blushed at his directness, I nodded again. He was right. He was so very right. I was born to this. I felt more at ease, at peace than I could ever remember feeling. And over it, on top of the peace, was a furious excitement. I was starting a new adventure. Something I had never planned for but, somewhere secretly inside of me, I had always been waiting for.

I struggled to focus on Dr Wellington's next words. 'You must swear never to reveal our existence to anyone outside of the Corps, unless you are given direct permission to recruit. You must promise to obey all the rules of our organisation as long as you are a member. If you accept temporary membership, you will be assigned a guide, who will explain all the rules and duties of a novice. Once everything is explained to you, and if you agree to abide by the terms and regulations, you will be inducted into the Slave Corps.'

She stood and walked over to me. When she was so close her clad breasts almost brushed my bare ones, she said, 'This Corps is not only a chance to serve, a chance to explore your own sexual submissiveness. It is also a gateway to a very powerful community that has influence in all levels of military and civilian life throughout this country and beyond. You are being offered a gift of membership. Never betray that gift, Remy, and the Corps will never betray you. That much I can promise. Do you accept?'

Feeling pride mixing with fear of the unknown, I decided to follow my instinct.

'Yes, mistress. I accept.'

Wellington smiled at me. 'You're a natural, Remy. Welcome to the Corps.'

Chapter Six
Captain Rather

When I got back to the barracks, lights were out and only the moon illuminated the sleeping forms of the girls in their bunks. Quietly I stripped off my uniform, automatically folding it neatly and placing it in my footlocker. Slipping on the under-shirt I should have been wearing underneath, and a pair of white cotton panties, I tiptoed to the bath-room to brush my teeth.

The moon was splashing a pale, white light through the bathroom windows. I was almost done, just drying my face, when a sound behind me startled me. I turned and there was Amelia, smiling quizzically at me.

'Welcome home, Remy,' she said. I knew she wouldn't tell on me for being out after lights-out. But she seemed to want something.

'Oh, hi, Amelia. I'm sorry. Did I wake you?'

'Not at all. I've been waiting for you.'

'What?' I looked at her sharply.

'I'm your guide.'

No words came to me at that moment. I just gawked at her. Amelia was my guide? The one to introduce me into the Slave Corps? Dumpy, quiet, little unassuming Amelia was my guide? She smiled at me and I hope I smiled back.

'Get some rest now, Remy. We'll talk tomorrow. You've been reassigned to SC – Special Calisthenics – starting first thing tomorrow. I'll show you where to report. Again, welcome, and good night.'

Amelia stepped away, hidden now by the shadows of the darkening room. The moon was setting as she climbed into her bunk and settled down to sleep. I stood there a moment longer, my mind reeling with this latest bit of information. The initials SC. Of course. Special Calisthenics: Slave Corps. How convenient.

I was grinning as I climbed into my own bed. Life was certainly getting interesting!

In the morning as I dressed for PT, Amelia handed me a slip of paper. 'Your new orders, as promised,' she said, her face giving nothing away. I nodded and took the piece of paper. It wasn't unusual to get assigned to different training units. I didn't bother to keep track of where the other girls in my barracks were assigned, and they, I figured, were equally as uninterested in me.

I continued to dress, and was on my way out, reading the slip of paper to see where I should head, when Amelia appeared next to me. 'We'll walk together,' she said. I started to speak, to ask her a million questions that had been gathering, when she stopped me with a hand to her lips. 'Not yet, Remy. Wait till we get there. There will be time. You and I are excused from basic training this morning. We have been assigned to a private cell at the Special Calisthenics Unit. We can talk freely there.'

'But, Amelia! You are my guide? No way! How come you never said anything? Are you a –'

I was stopped abruptly by her sharp 'Hush!' and a warning hand on my arm. I heard footsteps behind us and, just then, none other than Cadet Jean Dillon joined us, walking briskly, her arms swinging.

'Well, well. So, it's come to this. What a pleasant surprise.' Her tone was flat and decidedly unpleasant. 'New meat, eh, Amelia? I wouldn't have thought she had it in her.'

While trying to process that Jean was walking with us and seemed to know where we were going, I also felt compelled to respond. My gut reaction was to snarl back some insult at the cocky, arrogant bitch but, before I could open my mouth, Amelia's grip tightened on my arm and slowly, almost imperceptibly, she shook her head. She looked afraid, and I didn't want to upset her, so I shut up. Time enough later to deal with Cadet Dillon.

As we arrived at the training area, Jean swerved off to join the small knot of cadets milling around the courtyard waiting to begin the day's training. 'Later, Harris. Your worst nightmare is just beginning.' Jean laughed as she spoke, and suddenly I felt a vague pang of fear, mixing in with the anger.

I followed Amelia into a small building that I had never been in before. Still not speaking, she led me down a hall to a series of doors, spaced closely together. Each door had a number on it. When we came to Number 5, Amelia stopped, unlocked the door, and pushed it open. We stepped inside a musty little room that had only enough space to accommodate two chairs and a small table. The place had a decidedly Depression-era feel about it.

Amelia shut the door and indicated one of the chairs as she sat in the other. 'OK, we can talk now. This room is secure. Before you ask a million questions, and I know you have them – I did last month when I was initiated – let me talk for a minute. I might answer some before you even ask.'

I waited expectantly. Dillon could wait. The Corps came first. 'Well,' she said, smiling at me, her round, blue eyes sparkling. 'First, welcome to the Corps, Remy. I had no idea when I first saw you that you were slave material. But when you got hooked up with Jacob, I thought you had potential, till he dropped you due to your lack of submission –'

'Whoa! Hold on here, Amelia. Just how do you know the details of our breakup? I mean, I know it was no secret I was seeing him, but how do you know the intimate details?' Even as I asked I instantly knew. Jacob must have told her. Or someone in the Corps. He was in the Corps. Of course. It made sense now. Jacob was in the Corps, and Jean was in the Corps. That was how she knew all about my movements all the time. They were friends, for God's sake. Or at least colleagues, or whatever the hell you would call it in the Corps. Amelia looked at me, her expression gentle.

'I know this is a lot to absorb. The Corps is a very close-knit community. There are few secrets here. When you sign on as a novice, you give up your right to your own privacy, basically. You become the property of the group at large. Sort of like the Army, really, but on a far more intimate level. Jacob saw potential in you as a possible recruit. He was hoping to invite you to join the Corps, but then he decided you didn't really have what it took.'

I sat up, my face burning with indignation but Amelia silenced me with a wave of her hand.

'Please, Remy. Let me finish. You'll have a chance to ask me everything, I promise.' I sat back and she continued. 'Jean was following the progress, because she is a mistress-in-training. She was assigned to learn technique from Jacob, among others. She is dominant.'

'Dillon is a fucking mistress!?' I yelled it, louder than I meant to. I was horrified that someone like Jean Dillon could actually be considered mistress material. She was nothing like Dr Wellington, who had been so refined, so delicate in her control. Jean was so obvious, so coarse. Maybe I had overestimated this Slave Corps, if they accepted creeps like her into the programme.

As if reading my mind, Amelia responded, 'I know, I was quite surprised myself. She doesn't seem to have the control necessary to effectively dominate with grace. But then, her uncle is General Dillon. I presume you've heard of him?'

'I think so. He isn't involved with the Academy, is he?'

'No, but he is involved in the Slave Corps. I don't know it for sure, but maybe he had something to do with getting Jean into the Corps.'

'That would sure explain it! No way that bitch could make it in on her own.'

'Well, we don't know that. But you know, we aren't really in a position to judge. She must have had to pass whatever tests and initiation they come up with for dominants. If she passed muster with the Corps, maybe she has some potential that we just don't see yet. From what I've observed to date, the Corps has enough integrity and class to keep her tightly under control, but still, she has some power, at least enough to make your life miserable. So watch out, Remy. Just keep away from her, if you can.'

I sat still, trying to take it all in. So Jean not only knew about me, she was in a position where she might have some power over me. I had to understand more, and quick. Maybe this wasn't the place for me, sexual fantasies notwithstanding. Amelia continued to talk, and I struggled to concentrate on her words.

'I am your guide, as you know. They like to pick new slaves to guide the novices, because we've just been there. We know exactly what you are going through and can anticipate some of your questions and fears. I was so glad I got you, Remy. You're my first assignment.' She sat back and smiled at me.

'So what does that mean, exactly? How do you "guide" me?' Images of plump Amelia bending over and showing me how to take a whipping leaped unbidden to my mind. I shifted uncomfortably and waited for her reply.

'What that means is, for the first month, I will be available for your questions and concerns on an informal basis. If something doesn't seem right, or you don't understand your duties, or just have questions, I am here. You can withdraw at any time from the Corps, Remy. All you have to do is sign a contract swearing never to reveal our existence to the outside world in any way, and you are free to go. Nothing said, no hard feelings. And there are people who find out this really isn't for them.

Wannabe's who thought playing at sex slave would be cool, but then couldn't cut it. And some who simply found out it wasn't right for them. It isn't for everyone, of course.

'We can always talk and remain friends, whether you choose to stay or not. I've always liked you, Remy. You have character.' Here she smiled again, that angelic smile that made her look absolutely beautiful. I couldn't help but smile back. 'Let me start by telling you what to expect these next few weeks. You will begin with a series of meetings with masters and mistresses. Not any new or still in-training dominants. Don't worry. They only get to practise on well-trained submissives. About once a week for the next month or so you will have a new assignment, which you will find in your mailbox the night before. You will be given instructions, and Remy, be sure to follow them to the letter. Remember, this is serious business. They expect you to behave as professionally as if you were applying for Officers' Training.

'Your mentor – that's the dominant who will kind of take you under their wing – will meet with you, either as one of your assignments, or after you've had a few, to discuss your novice status, and decide if you are slave material or not. The mentor will have had input from the other masters who have met with you, and input from me and other Corps sources.

'Once you get accepted into the Corps as a slave –'

'If I do, you mean,' I interjected.

Amelia smiled softly at me and said, 'Don't you want this, Remy? No one is forcing you to be here,

97

surely you understand that. This is an honour, a gift.'

I looked down, contrite. I did want it. I had to find out, to explore these wild sexual feelings just budding inside of me. I nodded, and she continued.

'You will receive a sort of basic slave training. Things like how to walk, how to bow and curtsey, how to take a whipping with grace. There are trainers who do nothing but train us would-be slave girls and boys so we can become worthy of our masters and mistresses. You will be bound and taken to limits you never dreamed of, Remy. You will learn what it is to suffer, and to exalt.'

Amelia was speaking very softly, her voice dreamy, mesmerising. I had to lean over to hear her. Clearly she was speaking from experience. She went on, seeming to snap back to the moment. 'For this month though, you will just meet with several masters or mistresses, or perhaps the same one several times in a row. You will spend from forty-five minutes to four hours with each, serving them in whatever manner they wish. You will be expected to perform sexually, to be used sexually, to accept whatever torture or punishment they deem appropriate. In short, you will be their personal property for the time you are with them.

'No sexual intercourse, though. We are all tested regularly, but still, we don't want any pregnancy or disease gumming things up. We can't rely on over-eager masters who might forget their condoms and over-eager-to-please slaves who let them. So they've made it easy. No vaginal fucking. Period. But everything else goes.

'And what do you get from this? I don't need to tell you, do I, Remy? You get the chance to serve.

To realise at last what has always lain dormant or secretly alive inside of you. You get the chance to become what you really are. Do you understand, slave girl?'

The room suddenly seemed too close. I realised I hadn't been breathing as I listened to her. Yes, oh yes. I did understand. There was no reward required. It was something one was born to. I knew it in my bones, even as she explained it aloud. I was one of a secret elite now. I had been given the chance to serve. I couldn't wait to begin.

I was lying in my bunk, staring at the metal slats of the bunk above me, wondering what the dawn would bring. It was my first day as a full-fledged novice and I had found the long envelope in my mailbox the night before. My first assignment during what would have been PT, in the pre-Corps days, was to report to Captain Rather, professor of biology.

I was to wear my daily uniform, as if it were any other day of classes and training. I had awoken at around 3a.m., from troubled, vaguely erotic dreams. What would Captain Rather be like? What would he have in mind for my first 'assignment'? Amelia had filled me in on what to expect, basically. She warned me that some masters really did want to train you – to teach you discipline and grace – while others were really only there to get their rocks off. But, she advised, even submitting to them was a worthy submission, perhaps even more so than with 'true' masters, since you gave of yourself with grace, no matter the circumstance.

I imagined myself kneeling at Captain Rather's feet, waiting for his touch. He would reach down and I would feel a gentle tap on my shoulder. I would stand and see a tall, handsome man, with strong, commanding features. His violet eyes would flash as he leaned forward to kiss me with those red lips. Oh, my God! I was imagining Jacob! How absurd. I realised I had barely thought of him these past few days, but here he was, popping up again in my fantasies.

Annoyed with myself, I got up and showered before anyone else had stirred. Finally it was time to go to my first assignment. I made my way to the science building through the fine drizzle of a grey day.

A middle-aged woman with a heavy, rather masculine face looked up from her secretary's desk as I stepped out of the elevator on the second floor. I couldn't help wondering if she was in on this, if she knew just why I was there.

'Hello,' she said pleasantly. 'You must be Cadet Harris. Captain Rather is expecting you. You may go right in.'

I thanked her, my voice coming out like a little kid's, as I approached the door she indicated. It was slightly ajar and, as I pushed it open, Captain Rather hailed me in a jovial voice.

'Come in, come in, cadet. Close the door behind you and we can talk about your biology project without interruption. I've already advised Miss Martin not to disturb us for the forty-five minutes I have allotted for you.' I shut the door as he spoke, aware that his little performance was entirely for the secretary's sake, and whoever else might be wandering about the hall.

Seated behind a desk was a plump, little man with curly, short grey hair and small, bright eyes set in a ruddy face. He looked more like someone's doting grandfather than a master, as far as I could see.

Once the door was shut, he gestured for me to follow him as he walked to the corner of his small office and opened a little door that led to an even smaller private bathroom. As we squeezed in together, I realised my heart was pounding and that I had no idea what to expect from this man.

As if reading my mind, he said, 'Now then, novice. I understand I am your first assignment. For the next forty-five minutes you belong to me completely. You will not speak unless I ask you a specific question. You will strip at once. I can't stand that damn uniform on a woman.

'Instead, you will wear this.' He handed me a skimpy black sort of bathing-suit thing, with no crotch. He also handed me long, black gloves like the kind I had for my Barbie when I was a little girl. My distaste must have registered on my face, because suddenly he barked at me, 'Strip, bitch! I didn't ask you if you liked it, whore. I just said put it on.' Grandpa was gone. Master was here, and what an asshole he was.

Still, I didn't want to mess up my very first assignment, so I struggled out of my things and pulled up the little black garment. Captain Rather watched from his perch on the toilet seat as I wrestled with the lingerie. It was too small for me, and the bra cups forced my breasts up and together, spilling over the tops and sides. I pulled on the gloves and stood before the little man, easily five inches taller than he, even in my bare feet. I felt absolutely ridiculous in my little whore get-up, but apparently I passed muster.

'Oh my, my, my.' His voice was low and husky and he licked his lips several times, looking as if he were about to bite into a big piece of cake. 'Very nice, very nice. Too bad I don't have heels for you. That would definitely complete the look. What size shoe are you anyway?'

A direct question. 'Size nine, sir.'

'You're a big girl, huh? How tall are you?'

'Five-ten, sir.'

'Hmm, a bit tall for a girl. Ever been a pony?'

'Excuse me, sir?' I was completely puzzled by the question.

'A pony girl. You know, horse tail, carry your master on all fours, a bit in your mouth.' He stopped talking suddenly and slapped me, hard, on my right cheek. Stunned, I fell back against a wall. Tears involuntarily welled up in my eyes.

'You need to get control of your face, novice. You are too open. I could read your disgust as I described a pony girl to you. If you want to make it as a slave, you keep your goddamned feelings to yourself. If your master asks you something, you answer, without editorialising with your expression. I don't give a fuck if you like being a pony girl. I don't give a fuck about you, period. I just wanted to know if you ever did it.'

As he spoke, he pushed my shoulder down so I was kneeling, and he pressed my head so I was forced to look at the floor. I was humiliated and afraid. Why was everything so difficult? This was nothing like the dream master I had foolishly fantasised about this morning in the safety of my bunk.

'No, I haven't, sir,' I managed to say.

'Well, you would make a good pony, slut. Bend over like a horse and let's see.'

I was blushing fiercely, the heat in my face palpable, but I bent over just the same, until I was on all fours.

'First we'll let your reins down.' I didn't understand what he meant at first, as he pulled out the few bobby pins holding my French braid in place. He pulled my hair free and grasped it firmly in his two hands. As he jerked slightly, I understood. The 'reins' were my hair: I was to be his pony girl.

Captain Rather jerked my hair, forcing my head up and back. I couldn't help the sharp intake of breath at the unexpected pressure. Thankfully, he ignored me as he came around behind me and put his pudgy hands on my ass. 'Ah. Yes. This is more like it. Imagine a tail right here.' As he spoke, he pressed a finger against my asshole, causing me to flinch.

Then he seemed to lose his temper again. In a harsh voice, he barked, 'You are pathetic. You have absolutely no discipline whatsoever. How did you even get into this academy, cadet?'

As he spoke, his hands continued to caress my ass and thighs. Occasionally his fingers would stray precariously close to my exposed sex. I felt at once aroused by his touch and insulted by his words. It was confusing, to say the least. I wasn't sure if I was expected to answer. When he began to speak again I realised it was probably just a rhetorical question.

'I have decided on your training. First I am going to spank your ass just like the bratty little girl you are, to teach you manners. Would you like that, pony girl?' When I didn't answer he jerked my head back again by the hair. 'Answer me when I speak to you, girl, or suffer the consequences.'

I didn't know what to say. I blurted out the truth. 'I – I don't know, sir. I've never been spanked.'

He began to smack my bared cheeks, little smacks at first, then progressively harder. As he spanked me, he punctuated each blow with a stinging comment. 'This smack is for letting your bratty little feelings show on your face. This one is for being a novice and not knowing your place. And this one –' here he hit me so hard I fell forward and gasped with pain '– this one is for being so fucking beautiful, whore girl.'

I scrambled back into position, my bottom burning and my ridiculous little pussy throbbing. That last remark threw me for a loop. Until that time, he hadn't seemed to be terribly pleased with my appearance. I stopped analysing the situation when he resumed the spanking, focused entirely on his task of turning my poor ass crimson red. I started to whimper, despite my best intentions to stay quiet.

'Yes,' he hissed in my ear. 'Yes, baby. Cry. Cry, little slut girl. Daddy will make you cry, because you are a bad little girl, and you deserve to suffer.'

My tears were flowing freely now, and I couldn't have stopped if I wanted to. My flesh was on fire and I wasn't sure how much more I could take.

Suddenly he stopped and appeared in front of me. I tried to hide my face, wet with tears. But he pulled it up by the chin and forced me to look at him. 'Look at you, slut. Crying but still flushed like a whore. Stand up. I want to feel your pussy.'

With tears still staining my reddened face, awkwardly I stood in the cramped space. I was keenly aware of my ridiculous outfit, of my breasts spilling out, and my crotch exposed by the split in the fabric.

Captain Rather leaned in close and brought one hand to my pussy. I felt his fingers, fat and sweaty, against my lips. Roughly, he spread them and pressed a finger up inside of me. It took all my control not to pull back and away from this repugnant little man.

He grinned and said, 'Oh my, aren't you the little slut girl? You are sopping wet!' He was right. Despite finding this 'master' repelling, my perverse little pussy was on fire. As he spread the juices from my own sex across my breast, I blushed in a confusion of anger and desire. Captain Rather's eyes were hooded with lust as he held the leather whip-handle between his fingers.

'Bend over, slut. I want to see that ass again. It would look so pretty with this whip-handle sticking out of it, just like a pony's tail. Bend over, I say.'

I was almost in a panic. I didn't want to disobey and yet I just didn't feel I could handle having a whip-handle shoved up my ass at that moment. It was too much, too fast. The panic began to rise as I realised I might end up decking the bastard and being thrown out of the Corps before I even made slave status. Trembling, I bent over as ordered.

Just then a little bell dinged from the office outside the bathroom. I was startled by the sound. For a moment he looked confused too. Then recognition, coupled with disappointment, lit his face.

'Time's up,' he said simply. 'Saved by the bell, eh, little missy? Well, don't you worry. I'll get you again. And when I do, be prepared for some fun! You will be my little filly and I will break you once and for all, wild thing.' There was a slight scuffling noise in the outer office. Captain Rather snapped his mouth shut and stepped away from me. As he backed away, his features seemed to melt and soften before my eyes. It was curious to watch him change in just a few seconds from stern taskmaster back to the doting, kindly professor. I found the effect chilling.

'Pull on your things. You're dismissed. I'll send my write-up through the appropriate channels.' Abruptly he turned and walked out of the little bathroom. Audibly sighing with relief, I pulled on my underclothing and uniform, and was lacing up my boots when Captain Rather stuck his head in the bathroom.

'Hurry it up, cadet. I have more important things to do this afternoon.' I jumped up, ass still hot from his spanking. I wasn't sure if I was supposed to say anything. I wanted to ask what the write-up he was going to send was all about. I decided to wait and ask Amelia.

'Uh, thank you, sir. For your time, sir.'

'You're welcome, Cadet Harris. I do hope we will meet again. Good luck on your project.' His voice was smooth now, and impersonal. His eyes were pleasant, but indifferent. It was hard to believe that this was the same man who had just been about to ram a whip-handle up my ass. My eyes followed his to his office door and I saw Ms Martin waiting politely, folders piled in her arms.

It wasn't until after I had scooted out past her that I realised the lingerie was still in a little pile on the bathroom floor.

Chapter Seven
The Colonel

My next assignment didn't come for several days, though I diligently checked my mailbox each night. I'd had a few days to process my experience with Captain Rather. I was confused by my own mixed responses. I had to admit that I had thrilled to what had happened to me. I thought about it a lot and decided that it really didn't matter if I didn't particularly like who was doing it. This wasn't a love affair, after all. It was slave training! I was looking forward to the next assignment. Hopefully the next master wouldn't be such a jerk.

As I opened the little envelope, I felt the thrill of anticipation. It said, 'Colonel Ronald Hewitt, 0900 hours, office.'

I stared at it a while longer, not believing the words. The colonel! Colonel Hewitt was famous on campus. Along with being a military tactics professor at Stewart Academy, he held some high position in the Pentagon and was known to receive phone calls from the President of the United States. He was highly respected and not a little feared on campus. I was instantly terrified at the prospect of having to present myself to him. Still, duty was duty, and there was nothing to do but put an army face on it and be a good soldier.

The next morning found me outside Colonel Hewitt's office at precisely 0900 hours. Eloise Hawkins, the colonel's secretary, smiled at me pleasantly. I was sitting on a wooden chair set across from her desk. The telephone on her desk buzzed and she picked it up. 'Sir? Yes, sir, she's here. Yes, sir.' The pretty young woman nodded toward the door. 'You are expected, Cadet Harris. You may go in.' She smiled at me and her eyes seemed to twinkle with some secret mirth. I felt a faint flush, sure from her attitude that she knew why I was there.

When I entered the room, the colonel didn't look up. He was busy writing on some important-looking document. I stood quietly at attention, staring just past his head, as a good cadet is taught to do, but I could see him peripherally. In his late forties, the colonel had a commanding presence, even sitting down. His nose was hooked between deep-set, dark eyes, shadowed by dark, straight eyebrows on a broad forehead. He had that ship-shape look of a career army man. His dark hair was cut regulation short, with a grace note of grey. His uniform was perfectly creased and starched so heavily I imagined it must stand by itself at attention by his bedside, waiting for him to step into it upon his awakening. His face was stern and impassive as he finally looked up. He looked at me for a moment, as if wondering how I happened to be there.

His eyes were dark and penetrating. I almost

flushed from his direct gaze. He looked at me slowly, first my face, then my throat, my breasts, my hips, my legs, his gaze lingering at each spot. I felt embarrassed but also oddly thrilled by his attentions. He exuded control as he stared at me; it was as if he were claiming each separate part of my body.

Though clad in the dress uniform of dark-green skirt, tailored just below the knee, and paler green blouse, tucked in at the waist, I felt naked in front of him. I stood still, erect, willing myself to remain calm.

The colonel spoke at last. 'Ms Harris, I understand that you are available for my use.'

I was surprised by the use of 'Ms'. It had been some time since anyone had called me anything other than Harris, or cadet, or slave. Before I could respond, he continued in a voice that sounded as if it had been oiled: smooth and deep.

'At ease, Ms Harris. Strip. Stark naked. Then present yourself to me over here by my desk.' He looked back down at his work, shuffling papers, seemingly unaware of me again. My heart had already jumped into my throat, but I hoped my agitation didn't show in my face or manner. I dared to speak; I had to.

'Excuse me, sir. The door?' It was open. His secretary was in full sight outside his office, bent over her own work at her desk.

'What about it, Ms Harris? Did I tell you to close it? Do you have a problem with an open door? Shy, are you?' He spoke in clipped tones, like someone not used to wasting his breath. I was taken aback, but realised his secretary must obviously be in on all this.

'Do you have trouble obeying an order, cadet?

Not good. Not good at all. We will have to work on that. Whip you into shape.' His mouth curved slightly, just the hint of a smile, the thin lips like the edge of a knife.

Nonplussed and a little unnerved, I started to disrobe. Ms Hawkins gave no indication that she was aware of what was happening but I felt fairly certain she was very aware. When I was completely naked, I walked over to his desk, my nipples already perversely hard. Something in me thrilled, as usual, to the commanding tone, the casual assuredness that I would obey him, that I was a slave to his dominance and to my own lust.

He looked up at me and his eyes seemed to smoulder as they travelled slowly over my naked flesh. I realised I felt proud at last, proud of my naked, firm body, my large, round breasts, my well-muscled legs. Maybe that was it – the pride in my face, in my carriage – that made him see me as a challenge. Whatever it was, he stood slowly and came very close to me. He was a tall man, and, leaning down, suddenly he slapped me, hard, across the face.

I cried out as the sting spread along my cheek. I had been unprepared for the assault, and had no idea why he had hit me. As usual, when someone slapped my face, I felt a rush of panic, offset by a heat in my blood that set me afire.

'Pride,' is all he said, as he sat calmly back down. 'It's all over your face. You are too proud. You think you're something special, Ms Harris. And that's OK. Maybe you are something special, for all I know. But –' he paused for effect '– but, if you have any chance at succeeding in the Corps, wipe that pride off your face. Stand at attention, but don't flaunt your body like that. Offer yourself, but don't be so brazen.' He looked away from me, toward the open door.

'Eloise. Come in. Bring the crop.'

I felt a moment's panic. There I was, stark naked as the colonel had put it. And he was calling the secretary to bring in the crop! I wanted to bolt out of there. Somehow I managed to maintain my composure. Eloise entered quickly, closing the door softly behind her, and I saw she was carrying a long, thin riding crop of black leather. I looked down, too embarrassed to meet her gaze.

'Ms Harris. Please bend over my desk, hands behind your head. Don't move.'

I bent, relieved to be able to hide my face. It's funny in retrospect to think that I was more embarrassed to be naked in front of another young woman than in front of a colonel in the United States Army. In the barracks we were often naked around each other and no one seemed to give it another thought. I suppose it was the context: I was the slave girl, ready and expecting to submit to a master, not to a fully clothed secretary.

'Eloise. Whip her. Fifty strokes. Hard. Then both of you get out of here. I'm busy. I'll send for you another time, Ms Harris. When you've learned a little more about humility.'

I couldn't see their faces. I could hear the colonel rustling papers. He was going about his work as if I weren't even in the room! Eloise hadn't said a word but I felt her move up close behind me. Then I felt the smacking of the little leather loop against my ass. It was tentative at first, but quickly became strong and hard. As always, the pain of the beating was juxtaposed with the arousal at my situation.

111

My breathing came ragged and fast as she continued the relentless torture. I could feel my pussy tightening with need as the leather heated my flesh. Methodically she covered my ass and upper thighs until I was whimpering and doing a little involuntary dance in place over the colonel's desk.

As suddenly as she had started, she was done. Still without a word, I felt her cool fingers on my shoulder. She was pulling me up, and I quickly followed her unspoken order and stood. She led me to my clothing, which I had left in a little heap near the door. As I slipped my T-shirt over my head, Eloise positioned herself behind me, holding my uniform blouse so I could slide my arms in easily. As I was buttoning my blouse, I looked at her. She had dark-brown hair that curled prettily around her heart-shaped face. Her eyes were large and dark, so dark I couldn't tell the pupil from the iris. Her large eyes looked even bigger compared to her small nose and little cupid's bow mouth. I wouldn't have called her beautiful, but somehow something from within seemed to light her features. Her face was flushed, whether from exertion or arousal I wasn't sure.

She looked over at the colonel and I saw the unmistakable look of adoration. This girl was clearly head-over-heels. The colonel did not return the love-struck stare. He hadn't even bothered to look up from his papers. The only sound in the room for a moment was the scratching of his pen across the page. Eloise looked over at me suddenly, and saw that I was observing her. She glanced down quickly which allowed me to continue to scrutinise her. There was a faint flush creeping across her cheeks. She was embarrassed! Eloise had just whipped me, naked across the colonel's desk, and was helping me pull on my uniform over my red ass, and she was embarrassed. I couldn't quite suppress a little grin at the absurdity of it.

As if suddenly remembering the colonel's orders, she hurried me to finish my dressing and led me quickly out of the room before closing the door noiselessly behind her. We stood together for a moment. Then I looked at the clock on the wall and remarked, 'Wow. He sure got rid of me in a hurry. I still have half an hour till I'm supposed to report back. I hope I'm not in trouble. I mean, I guess I really messed this one up.'

'You haven't. Not your fault. And no one has to know you got out early.' She stood a moment longer, as if weighing something in her mind, then said, 'Would you like to come to the break-room and have a cup of coffee or juice or something while you collect yourself? I mean with me. Have a cup of coffee with me.' She trailed off, as if she were embarrassed and unsure of herself. I realised that she couldn't have been much older than I was.

'Sure,' I said. 'I'd love to. I don't often have coffee with a woman who has just whipped me.'

Eloise grinned and said, 'Just following orders, cadet.'

I followed her down the hall to a small break-room. As we entered, I saw the sun was shining though the windows, dappling the room with light. It reminded me that this was just another weekday morning. I should have been out running an obstacle course or studying for my computer science exam. Instead I was a member of a secret society that had opened the door to my wildest fantasies.

Eloise was pouring coffee into a mug and asked me, 'What do you like? Cream, sugar?'

'Oh, I don't really like coffee. Water would be great though.' She got a glass from the cabinet and poured me some water from the cooler, then handed me the cold glass. Eloise gestured toward a chair as she sat at the little table in the centre of the small room, her own mug in hand.

We sat quietly for a moment, sipping our drinks. I shifted my weight on the hard seat, my ass still sore from her beating. Eloise watched me, grinning. 'Hurts, huh? Sorry I had to do that, but I always obey the colonel. He owns me.'

She said it so simply. He owns me. I drank from the glass, and then set the cup down carefully on the table. Curiosity got the better of me as I blurted out, 'He owns you?'

'Completely. Has for two years. I hope it will be forever.' She looked so happy sitting there, sipping her coffee. Again I sensed that serenity emanating from her.

'So are you in the Corps?'

'Oh, no. He would never let me do that. Corps slaves are Corps property. If I were in the Corps, he would have to share me. The colonel doesn't like to share.' She grinned, a satisfied look on her face. 'I used to be, though. That was how we met. And don't feel bad. He almost never uses anyone the first time. Usually just sends them packing, their heads hung in shame. You got a whipping, even though it was only me. So you must have some potential. And he'll call you back. When you're ready.'

'He will?' I wasn't sure if I was glad or not. 'And doesn't it bother you that he "uses" all these different people, with you right there watching?'

'Why would it bother me? If it pleases him, it

114

pleases me. I am here to serve him, not the other way around. And he doesn't see all that many, you know. Maybe only once a month. The rest of the time I am all he needs to torture and tease. I live for him. I would die for him.'

'Do you love him?'

Eloise stared into her glass, as if in the bottom was an answer she didn't quite have. Then I heard the catch in her voice as she answered, and realised I had asked a sensitive question. 'Yes. With all my heart.' She sounded so sad that I knew something was wrong.

'I'm sorry,' I started, 'I didn't mean to be so nosey. I –'

'No, no,' she interrupted me. 'It isn't your fault. You couldn't know. He's married, you see. She doesn't know about any of this. I have him during the day, but she will always have him at night.'

'Oh.' We were both silent. What a lousy situation for her, I thought. Never catch me falling for a married man, was my next thought.

'Well,' she said, her voice too loud, her smile falsely bright. 'So how did you get into the Corps? Do you like it so far?'

'I don't even know. Well, that isn't exactly true. I love it and I hate it. I have never been at once so humiliated and so exalted; so pissed off and so excited all at once. I don't really understand it yet. But it's getting in my blood, you know? Like, I go to the mailbox every day, sometimes several times a day, to check for my next assignment. And when there isn't one, I feel so let down. Though as soon as I see that envelope, my heart starts to pound and I wonder for the millionth time what the hell I've gotten myself into!'

Eloise laughed, throwing back her head. 'You've got the bug, all right. And that's exactly how to put it: in your blood. It's like an addiction. Once you taste the pleasure of submission, the intensity of it, you can't go back to vanilla, not ever.'

'But how did you get out? I mean, it didn't even occur to me to think about getting out. Is it easy to do? Do you just resign or what?'

'Sure, it's easy. This isn't real slavery, you know. It isn't even the Army, which is a lot harder to get out of, let me tell you. It's an agreement, and you can end the agreement anytime. As long as you keep your mouth shut about it. But it wasn't my idea to resign. It was the colonel's. He decided he didn't like my "assignments". He wanted me for his own. And he asked me what I thought and I said I would be honoured. I fell in love with him the first time he used me. He started calling for me more and more often. It was almost just a formality when I officially resigned from the Corps. But I still keep in touch with a few Corps members. The Colonel likes the occasional play-toy, you see.'

Eloise looked at her watch and stood up suddenly. 'Oh, shit. I didn't notice the time. I have to get back to my desk, fast. Listen, maybe sometime we could do something together. Or you could come over to my place or something. I don't live far from campus. But I do have to run now, Remy.'

'Oh. OK. Yeah. That would be really cool. Thanks, Eloise. Thanks for everything, I think.' I grinned at her, rubbing my sore butt with an exaggerated gesture. Eloise laughed and hurried back down the hall. The colonel was waiting.

Chapter Eight
A Truce

My third assignment came later that week. I was just pulling the envelope from my mailbox, eager to read what it might hold, when who but Jean Dillon should slip up behind me. With a sudden movement, the envelope was out of my hand and into hers.

'Hey! Give me that!' I reached toward her but she was too quick for me. She slipped it into the elastic of her pants at the small of her back.

Laughing a cruel, little laugh she said, 'What'll you give me for it, eh, Harris? Wouldn't be too cool not to show up for your assignment, eh, slave girl?' Luckily no one was around to hear what she was saying. But she was being very indiscreet and I was furious.

'Listen, Jean. You know I need that. If I don't show up, your ass will be in the sling, too, you know. You aren't a ranking mistress yet.' I tried to act tough, but I was feeling slightly desperate. Jean only laughed.

'Oh, I'm so scared,' she taunted, dancing away as I tried to grab at the envelope at her waist. This bitch was going to mess things up for me, one way or the other. I decided to switch tactics.

'OK, Jean. What do you want?'

'Ah! Now you're on the right track. I do want something. I want you to get on your knees, slave girl, and beg me for the envelope. Then I want you to kiss my ass. Then, if I feel like it, I'll give you the stupid assignment.'

This was too much. I didn't feel the slightest bit submissive as I reached for her. With a sudden movement, I had her arms pinned behind her back. Ratcheting one up until she gasped, I used my free hand to grab the envelope from her pants. I threw her forward as I retrieved it, and she fell to the ground. The envelope was torn, but not too badly. I would still be able to read whatever was inside.

'You're dead, Harris,' she hissed up at me as she slowly stood, rubbing her shoulder and arm. 'Dead.'

I didn't answer her, but went to my bunk to see what my next assignment was. When I got there, Amelia was waiting for me.

'How's it going, Remy? We haven't had a chance to talk lately. I've been so busy.' She blushed prettily as she said that, and I knew what she had been busy doing.

'Oh, pretty good, I guess. But that bitch Dillon is on my case again.' I told Amelia briefly what had happened. She looked worried.

'Remy, that isn't good. Don't forget, she is going to be in a position of power over you one day. You could get yourself in a lot of hot water.'

'Well, I'll have to take my chances. I couldn't have done what she demanded. I would die first.'

'Pride, Remy. You have too much. You are going to suffer because of that.' Well, she wasn't the first one to tell me that. I didn't understand why pride and submission should be mutually exclusive, but at the time I didn't have the understanding or experience to protest. I nodded glumly, wondering if I was cut out for all of this after all.

'Well, aren't you going to open it?' Amelia asked, changing the subject.

Eagerly I took the envelope, pulling it open. 'Dr Margaret Wellington, 0800 hours, Friday, office.' Underneath, in small, bold letters was the single word 'mentor'. Dr Wellington! All thoughts of my nemesis vanished as I thought about my next assignment! My mind was flooded with images of the lovely professor. She was so unlike me, with her small, slender figure and delicate features. To me she was the essence of femininity. The stunning overlay of dominance perfectly complimented that femininity. It gave her a power that I couldn't yet define.

Amelia leaned over my shoulder, reading what was there. 'Dr Wellington will be your mentor! Oh, you are so lucky! To get a woman. I got a man but I really wanted a woman. And she is so sympathetic, so sensitive! You are so lucky.' She sounded wistful. I wondered who her mentor was, but she hadn't volunteered that information, and I was learning that discretion was definitely the better part of valour as far as the Corps was concerned.

The next morning, I rushed through my shower, and then put on non-regulation panties and bra. I grinned at myself, realising I had a crush on another woman! This was a side of myself I had never explored. I had often found other women attractive,

119

or interesting, even sexy. But it never occurred to me that it might be a sexual interest on my part. I always thought I wanted to be like them, or be them. It never occurred to me that I might want to explore something more intimate.

Yet I couldn't deny the pull in my pussy when I thought of her leaning over me as I made myself come that fateful night of initiation. I hadn't seen her since, and really hadn't thought about her much. But I was thinking about her now as I walked briskly toward the chemistry building, looking purposeful, my mind whirling with the possibilities. The last few weeks of experience had opened something inside of me, and now it was as if I were hypersexual, and hyperaware of that sexuality. This new-found desire encompassed not only my usual male fantasy, but now included women as well. The petite and lovely Dr Wellington had asked for me. She wanted me! At least she wanted to train me. What if I let her down? So far my first two assignments had not gone very well, at least as far as I could see. I was afraid that, even though I loved it, I wasn't really cut out of a submissive cloth.

When I got to the little waiting room of her office, the secretary's desk was empty. Maybe non-military professors didn't rank a secretary. I wasn't sure if I should knock or just wait. I was a few minutes early, so I decided to sit tight.

When it was time, I stood to knock on the door. Just then, it opened, revealing Dr Wellington on the other side. She was wearing another closely cut dress that emphasised her pert, little breasts and tiny waist. Her eyes were dark and shaped like almonds; she had a decidedly Oriental quality. Waving me in, she said in that low voice of hers,

'Come in, come in. I've been looking forward to our little visit. We have plenty of time today. I have you cleared for two full hours.'

Two hours! I didn't say anything, since I remembered her admonition once about not speaking unless directly asked to do so. She closed the door quietly behind us.

'Before we start, come and sit down.' She gestured toward her desk, a large affair with stacks of papers and little blue exam books neatly piled to one side. Close to the edge of the desk where I sat stood a long, glass vase filled with a huge spray of yellow and purple irises.

She sat behind the desk and took a slim manila folder from one corner. She opened it and stared at the pages in front of her for a moment. I realised I had the same sick feeling that I used to get when I got sent to the office for some infraction or other in grade school. I sat on the edge of the seat, resisting the temptation to bite my nails.

She looked up at me, her face pleasant, but serious. 'Remy, I have to be frank with you. So far you have mixed reviews.' My heart sank as she started to speak. I was sure both Captain Rather and the colonel had found me to be a miserable excuse for a novice. I was a failure: I would be kicked out before I even had a chance to learn. Somehow, though I loved the excitement of submitting, I didn't seem to be the submissive type, apparently.

I was dying to ask what was in those reports, to grab them from her and read them myself, or at least to defend myself. But she hadn't asked me a direct question, and I wasn't going to blow it now, if I could help it. Dr Wellington stood and walked gracefully over to the couch on the side wall. As she sat down, she pointed to the floor at her feet. Hoping I was reading her cue correctly, I left my chair and kneeled beside her, hoping this was what she intended. I looked down, waiting for the bad news.

She was still holding one of the pages in her hand. She looked down it again, and said, 'Let's see. You have arrived on time and obeyed everything asked of you. You have submitted to their demands with relative grace. I say mixed reviews because both assignments to date report that you are too proud. I understand the colonel even sent you away, unused. But then, he often does that.

'I don't often warn slaves, but be careful of the colonel. Just between us, I don't think he has a place in the Corps. He likes to break people. He has sent more than one slave over the edge. He is too brutal in his approach. But then, they don't ask me about these things.' She laughed as she said that, but I was troubled by her remarks. She brought me back to the issue at hand as she continued to speak.

'Still, Remy, there seems to be something lacking in your make-up; lacking that is, if you really want to serve others. Call it humility, perhaps.'

I sighed, then realised with horror that the sigh had been audible. Still looking at the carpet, I waited for the recrimination. Instead I felt a soft finger caressing my cheek, smoothing back my hair.

'Do you want to know what I think? I think both those men lack understanding about novices. They forget what it is like when you are at the beginning. They forget that a person isn't born a perfect slave. You may have intensely submissive sexual feelings; you may long to serve and merge with another who has complete power over you. But that doesn't mean you automatically know how to act or how to submit with grace.

'Especially a girl like you, Remy. I'm familiar with your record to date: most impressive. But it's the record of a strong personality, one might even say a dominant one. One only needs to look at you to see you are athletic and capable. I personally don't think that has to count against you. To teach someone like you to really submit: now that would be an accomplishment.'

I felt a warmth suffuse me as she spoke. She seemed to not only understand me, but to accept me as I was. She had faith in me, I realised.

'Now, Remy. Here's the thing. I want to give you a final chance. I want to test you, really test you. I don't want you to "submit" to something that sexually arouses you. I already have some idea about that, don't forget.' I bit my lip, remembering that she knew all too well what aroused me. She of all those present at the initiation had seemed to understand the thrill I got from exposing myself to their cold stares as I came with abandon for them, after having been beaten and humiliated by those virtual strangers.

'I don't intend to satisfy your lust today, Remy.' As she said that her hand trailed down to my breast, her fingers grazing my nipple, causing it to instantly stiffen to attention. 'No,' she said, pulling her hand away. 'Today we will see what you are really made of, novice. Today we will see if you deserve the title of slave or if you are just masochistic. Are you prepared to submit for me, Remy? To truly submit, not for your pleasure, but at my command?' Her eyes rested on me so heavily I could almost feel the weight of her look.

'Oh, yes, ma'am. Yes, please.' I did want it. I wanted it so badly I knew I would do anything to please her.

'That is what I had hoped to hear. Get up, girl. Get up and strip. Then stand in the centre of the room, arms clasped behind your back at the elbow.'

I scrambled up, eager to do as she bid. I waited, trying to calm my breathing, which already was coming in short, shallow breaths of anticipation.

'You can come in now, Jean.' Oh, God. I couldn't have heard that. Maybe it was coincidence. But no. I felt something sharp catch in my chest as little Miss Jean Dillon came sauntering into the room from a door I hadn't noticed until that moment. She swaggered over to me, her little body smartly fitted in a black leather corset and skirt. Her heels were high, so high she almost stood eye-to-eye with me in my bare feet. I had to admit grudgingly to myself that she cut quite a sexy figure. Her honey-coloured skin looked creamy against the shiny, black leather of her corset. Her little breasts were raised and pressed together appealingly. She wore very little make-up, but her lips were painted a bright, cherry red. I was drawn back to the situation quickly by Dr Wellington.

'As you know, Remy, Jean is in training to be a mistress. It is unusual to allow novice dominants to interact with novice submissives, but General Dillon feels Jean is ready and, of course, I will be directing the activity.' So that explained it. Little niece Jean had used her formidable connections to get her way. She had promised she would get me, and boy was she going to. Dr Wellington reminded me of my promise.

'Remember, Remy. You aren't here to please her, you are here to submit. I know something of your situation. I know something of the, er, relationship between the two of you. It doesn't matter. It's irrelevant. What matters is that you are here to serve me. And it pleases me to see you here, naked, in front of Mistress Dillon.

'And you.' Now her attentions were mercifully turned from me to my enemy. 'You must remember who you are and what you represent. You are the Corps. When you assume the role of mistress, you also assume the responsibility. This isn't a chance to exact revenge for whatever perceived slight there is between you. This is your chance to persuade me that you have what it takes to make a true dominant, not a bully girl. Understand?'

'Yes, ma'am.' Jean spoke softly, her head ducking slightly in submission as she nodded her compliance to Dr Wellington. I had never seen Jean like that and was momentarily fascinated by her seeming humility.

'Good. Then we will begin. First, Jean, I want to see how you wield your whip. Thirty strokes should be sufficient. Novice, kneel on your knees, keep your body up so both sides are accessible, and put your hands behind your head.'

I did as ordered, now becoming truly afraid. I was certain Jean would find a way to really hurt me, or at least humiliate me. I was determined not to let her do so. I would show her, and Dr Wellington, that I could submit, even when the mistress was someone who I was certain had no place in the Corps.

Biting my lip to stay quiet, I waited, heart pounding, for the torture to begin. Dr Wellington handed Jean a long, slim riding crop. The loop at the end was very small. Jean came forward, until she was standing close in front of me. Slowly she moved the handle of the crop across my stomach, which caused me to flinch slightly. I wanted to pull back, but forced myself to remain still. Stepping back, she walked around behind me. I stayed still, holding my arms behind my head, willing myself to be calm.

'Count, slave.' Jean said, her voice no longer humble. Suddenly I felt the stinging slap of the leather against my back. I gasped.

'Is that how you count? Now. We'll start again, novice.' The disdain was obvious in her voice. Again she struck me with the whip, hard. This time the blow mercifully landed on my ass, which at least had some padding.

'One!' I called out. 'Two! Three!' She slapped me with the crop twenty more times on my back, ass and thighs. My body was on fire from the constant caress of the leather. I was breathing hard, trying to keep control of my voice as she whipped me harder and harder. Finally Jean stepped around in front of me. She was slightly out of breath from her exertions. Her eyes flashed as she raised the crop to my breast. I couldn't help but squeeze my eyes shut as the crop came down on the soft swell above the nipple.

'Twenty-four!' I managed. Down came the crop on my nipple. This time I couldn't keep it together. I screamed with pain and fell out of position, my hands flailing out to break my fall. I couldn't catch my breath as I hurried to scramble back into position, putting my now-tired arms back behind my head.

Dr Wellington remained implacable, watching us from her position on the couch to my left.

'Five extra strokes for losing position,' Jean announced, looking toward Dr Wellington, perhaps for confirmation. I was still looking ahead, but Jean must have got the go-ahead, so I steeled myself for eleven more strokes to my flesh.

Jean smacked me methodically, from breasts to belly to thighs and back up again. The final blow was delivered to my other nipple, just as hard as the first time. I sucked in my breath sharply, but somehow managed to stay in position, as I grunted, 'Thirty-five.'

'Nicely done,' Dr Wellington remarked.

I wasn't sure who the remark was meant for, but Jean replied, 'Thank you, mistress. She is nicely reddened, wouldn't you say?'

'Indeed, I would. But the praise wasn't for you.'

Jean actually had the grace to blush herself at that point. Dr Wellington wasn't focusing on her, though. She had gotten up and moved close to me, leaning down to stroke my face. 'You took that with real grace, slave.' Slave. She had said slave, not novice. I tried not to attach too much importance to her remark. 'You did fall out of position but the second time you took it with real courage.

'Now for the rest of your assignment. I want you to ask Mistress Dillon how you can please her today. And then do it.'

I froze for a moment, feeling a sickening finger of dread pull its way through me. Giving Jean *carte blanche* would certainly end up with us in a fistfight, or worse. God, this was hard. Much harder than submitting to the crude Captain Rather or the pompous colonel. They were abstracts. Jean Dillon was real, and she was now in a position to control me, while I was to remain defenceless and at her mercy.

I saw that Dr Wellington was staring at me, waiting to see how I would respond. She smiled slightly, perhaps encouragingly. I felt myself rising to the challenge despite any misgivings. I could do this. I would do this, for Dr Wellington, for myself. I would truly submit.

Jean meanwhile had walked over to the couch. She stood confidently, her hands on her hips, her corseted body beautifully outlined in leather. Her dark hair was loose and wild from the exertions of the cropping. 'Novice,' she said imperiously, 'crawl over here on your hands and knees. And let's see those big tits sway back and forth.' She sat down as she spoke, exuding confidence and arrogance. I felt anger rise and mingle with shame. I had started to feel proud of my well-shaped breasts, but somehow, around these two perky-breasted women, I again felt big and awkward. Somehow Jean had latched on to my insecurities. She had cut to the quick with her crude remark.

Still, I was determined to obey, to the letter. Face burning with shame, I crawled toward the young woman sitting on the couch, her legs crossed, long heels dangling. I reached her feet and waited for the next order.

'Now. Kiss my feet. Leave the shoes on, and make love to my feet. Use plenty of tongue. Convince me that you love it. This is just where you belong, and just where I want you.' She laughed cruelly, extending one pretty foot for my attentions.

My eyes narrowed with distaste but I had to admire her choice of torment. What better way to reduce your enemy to nothing than by forcing them to kiss your feet, no, your shoes, for God's sake. Again I became aware of Dr Wellington standing nearby, very intent on my actions. She gave me the courage to continue.

Slowly, tentatively, my tongue darted out to lick the tip of Jean's patent-leather-clad toe. I leaned forward, carefully taking one foot between my hands, as I started to kiss and lick the shoe in earnest.

'Don't forget the soles, novice.' There was actually a small clod of dirt on the bottom of one of the shoes. Jean was apparently aware of this as she barked, 'All of it. Every square inch. Clean it off with your tongue. You are my wash rag, novice. Do it like you mean it, like you love it. Worship me.' I swallowed, steeling myself to the duty at hand. I had eaten plenty of mud by accident, during basic training, especially in the pit. It wasn't so bad. I could do this.

I started to lap her shoe, carefully cleaning the blob of dirt from the sole with my tongue. I tried to swallow it quickly, as I continued my oral homage to this woman. I had to admit that, even though I hated her, she had a style about her. She had a commanding presence. If only she could get past the bully phase, she might someday be a worthy dominatrix.

My jaws were aching and my tongue felt like raw sandpaper when at last I felt a tug on my hair. I thought at first it was Dr Wellington, granting me a reprieve at last. But when I looked up, I saw it was

Jean herself. She actually patted my head and smiled at me.

'See,' Dr Wellington said, obviously pleased. 'That wasn't so bad. For either of you. You both have shown real potential to be a part of the life. And now girls, I get to have some fun. I like to watch. I want to watch you two sexy things kiss and make up. Oh, and to quote my little friend Jean here, do it like you mean it.'

I knew exactly what she wanted, though Jean seemed a little slow on the uptake. Dr Wellington prompted her a little bit more as I kneeled up and back on my heels. 'Let this slave girl help you off with your corset, Jean, dear. Don't forget you are still a novice, too, and as such, at my command. Let's even the field a bit. Get naked and then kiss this lovely blonde girl. Like you mean it.'

Jean stood, a little shakily, and for a moment I almost felt sorry for her. I was used to being naked and exposed at this point, but apparently it was something new to her. She blushed prettily as I stood behind her and untied the satin bows and released the little hooks that held her tightly in place. She leaned forward slightly, allowing the corset to fall. I took it and laid it carefully on the couch near Dr Wellington, who smiled sweetly at me. Then I unzipped Jean's little leather skirt and she stepped out of it, still in her stiletto heels. I placed the skirt with her corset and returned, waiting for direction.

'Don't forget the shoes, though you do look lovely like that, Jean, naked in your spike heels. But I want you both naked, and facing each other.' As the professor spoke, Jean stepped out of her shoes and kicked them toward me. I took them and set them neatly standing on the floor by the couch.

I had actually seen her naked before, in the showers, but somehow I had never noticed her petite figure, or at least I hadn't appreciated it. Her breasts were small and high, with dark-brown nipples standing out against her tan skin. Her hips flared slightly from her small waist. Her little pubic patch was lush with short, black curls.

Dr Wellington settled back, clearly having a good time. 'Now, the fun begins. Start with a kiss, my darlings.'

Jean seemed almost shy as she approached me. Gone was the tough-girl swagger, gone was the competitive cadet. In her place stood a naked young woman, though admittedly one who had just beaten me. My flesh still stung from her crop. And now we were supposed to 'kiss and make up'. I had never kissed a girl before. She leaned toward me, her hands clasped protectively around her own waist. I leaned down, as scared as she was, until our lips met. Her face was so soft against my own.

After a moment of chaste kisses, her lips parted slightly and her tongue licked across my lips. I parted my own, finding myself curiously eager for her kiss, for the invasion of her tongue. We were still only touching at the mouth, our naked bodies held away from each other by our uncertainty. A word from Dr Wellington changed that.

'Yes. That's right. All wrongs between you are righted now, my little girls. Now make love to each other. Girls can be so tender where men are so rough. Let your bodies come together. Taste that special sweetness of female flesh.' Her low voice was even lower than usual, husky with her own apparent lust. Still, she made no move to come to us, or to have us serve her directly. As she said, she liked to watch.

Perhaps it was the freedom of having been given a direct order. Neither of us had to wonder if we were gay or if we wanted this. We simply had to obey orders. Both of us certainly understood that concept. I wondered briefly how this girl, who had called me a 'dyke bitch' back at the beginning of the term, was going to handle being forced to interact sexually with another girl, to make love to her.

I forgot to wonder as she reached out and gently fondled my breasts. Her hands sent an electric current of pleasure through me. As if in a dance we'd practised many times before, we leaned forward into each other, falling slowly together to the soft carpet. Our arms wrapped around each other as we continued to kiss.

Jean's hand crept down my belly to my blonde, pubic curls that covered my dark-pink and now swollen labia. I felt her fingers reach out to touch and explore. I moaned with pleasure as she found my clit. I was soaked with desire by now.

Leaning my own head down, I found her dark nipples already stiff with need. Gingerly, I took one into my mouth. It felt wonderful, at once soft and erect. I rolled it with pleasure between my teeth, eliciting a little moan from Jean. She lay back flat on her back and I followed her, my mouth unwilling to let go of that perfect little marble of feminine flesh from between my teeth. After several moments Dr Wellington again intervened.

'Jean, you've done this before. You take the lead. Pleasure this young woman as if she were your mistress.'

The idea at once frightened and excited me. As I lay back, Jean dutifully crawled between my legs, which she spread far apart. The Oriental carpet felt rough against my still-tender skin. I forgot any discomfort as her tongue crept out and licked my outer lips. I stayed still, but I was very aroused. I wasn't sure how I was allowed to react. Should I stay still and quiet, as with the beating, or let myself go? After a second, her hot little tongue darted out again, and this time she didn't stop, but began to explore the folds and secret places of my sex.

As the pleasure washed over me, I was struck by Dr Wellington's remark that Jean had done this before. Perhaps a part of learning to dominate involved submission as well. An intriguing idea that was quickly forgotten as Jean's tongue and fingers shut down my conscious mind, turning me over to complete pleasure and lust. It didn't matter how I was 'supposed' to react: I could no longer control myself. I was in heaven.

Just as I was about to come, I heard Dr Wellington's commanding voice from the haze of my arousal. 'Stop now, Jean. We don't need to let the little slut come. She hasn't earned that right yet.' Oh, God. Shades of Jacob and his constant denials were brought back and I almost cried out in frustration. My pussy was on fire and so swollen I could barely close my legs as Dr Wellington commanded me to get up and stand at attention.

While I stood, forcing myself not to whimper with frustrated need, she said, 'Come over here, Jean. Let's let the slut girl service us both at once. Sit here on the couch with me.' As she spoke, Dr Wellington lifted her shapely little ass from the cushions and slid off her underwear. With a kick, the little, red-satin panties landed at my feet. Jean eagerly sat next to Dr Wellington, who at once took her in her arms. They were so well suited to one another, both petite and yet curvaceous, though Jean's body was strong and angular, where Dr Wellington's was softer and more feminine.

I would have again felt too big and awkward, except that I was too busy drinking in the sight of those two lovely women caught in each other's arms. They both spread their legs wide. I trembled slightly as I kneeled before them. Dr Wellington's pussy was shaved bare, something I had never seen before. Her labia were a lovely dark pink, and already swollen with lust, spreading prettily so that her entrance was exposed. The contrast was striking: the pale, white skin and naked pussy of the professor, and the darker, honey-brown flesh of Jean's thighs, with the dark, silken pubic curls partially obscuring her pussy. They were both beautiful.

For the moment, they ignored me completely. Jean unbuttoned Dr Wellington's blouse, pulling it open to reveal two perfect, little round breasts tipped with rosy, pert nipples. The two women seemed comfortable together; I got the distinct impression that not only had Jean done this before, but with Dr Wellington.

She disentangled herself from Jean's embrace long enough to say to me, 'Get to it, slave. You may worship my pussy with your mouth while you use your hand for Mistress Dillon.' She pulled my head forward, grabbing a handful of my hair, mashing my face into her hot, open crotch. For a moment I was paralysed. It was one thing to allow another woman to kiss me there, but to do it myself? To lick

134

someone's spread pussy? To suckle and kiss the hot little folds of flesh? I didn't think I wanted to. I was scared; I was shy. What if it tasted funny?

A sudden thwack to my back startled me enough to cause me to yelp. Dr Wellington had used the crop on me and at the same time she said, her voice less patient, 'Slave, obey orders. Now.'

That was that. I had no choice. Licking my lips nervously, I opened my mouth, and allowed my tongue to cautiously taste the musky scent of her pussy. In truth, she didn't have much of a taste at all. But there was a heady, spicy scent, mingled with her perfume. I liked the feel of her silky lips against my mouth. As I started to lick and suckle her the way Jean had just done to me, she let out a soft moan, which was muffled by Jean's mouth on hers.

I remembered that I was expected to pleasure Jean, too. Reaching out my right hand, I found her delicate little pussy and pressed my finger into her opening. It was so hot and tight as the muscles clamped down on my finger. I continued to kiss Dr Wellington, exploring the folds of her hot pussy with my mouth.

Dr Wellington fell back, opening her legs further for my access. She took my head in both her hands and held me in position as she gyrated on my face. Jean leaned over her, suckling her nipples. Faster and faster Dr Wellington moved, mashing my open mouth against her very hot, swollen pussy. I could feel the little nub of her clit against my tongue. But I wasn't kissing her; she was using my face and mouth, fucking herself on me. After a few more moments she tensed and shuddered, crying out with passion as she came. She let go of my head and let her own fall back against the back of the couch.

I leaned back on my heels, watching as her spasms subsided. Her face and neck were flushed. Slowly she opened her eyes and looked down at me, giving me a lovely smile. Then she said, 'Not done with your duties yet, slave girl.' She pointed toward Jean, who smiled like a cat as she lay back, spreading her legs wide.

I moved over toward her. My jaws were aching and my face was smeared with my own saliva and Dr Wellington's juices. But I didn't even have a chance to wipe my mouth against my shoulder when Jean grabbed my head and forced me down on her lap. At once I started to lick and tease her pussy. She tasted different from Dr Wellington: slightly salty but not at all unpleasant. I concentrated on the task at hand, hoping she would come soon so I could rest.

I wasn't disappointed. After only a few moments, Jean's breathing quickened. She started to shudder and moan and I continued to lick her hard little clit. Suddenly she pushed my head back and rubbed her own pussy with her hand. With the other hand she slapped my cheek, hard.

Tears leaped to my eyes and a hand flew to the spot where she had struck me. Jean ignored me, coming hard and long, with Dr Wellington cooing over her and kissing her breasts as she did so. As her orgasm ebbed, Dr Wellington held her in her arms. I felt very alone and naked at their feet, confused and frustrated.

At length, Dr Wellington noticed me there. 'Oh, look at our poor little lamb. Are you worried that you somehow offended Mistress Dillon here? Don't worry, it's just a little quirk of hers. She likes to slap someone when she is coming. Such a pervert!' They both laughed, Dr Wellington with a low, throaty chuckle, while Jean's laughter was higher-pitched and girlish.

I wasn't particularly amused, but I was relieved to know I hadn't done anything wrong. My own pussy was still throbbing with denied release. I wondered if Dr Wellington would allow me to repeat the performance of the initiation night.

But no. She was sated and no longer interested in me or my desires. She stood slowly, stretching like a cat. Then she beckoned toward me. 'Help me out of this, slave. You'll find my "day" clothes in that wardrobe over there. Jean's army-issue monstrosity is in there too. Get them.' I did as I was told, my head still fogged with unrequited lust.

The professor allowed me to help her dress, turning gracefully to allow me to zip her up, and lifting a dainty foot for me to slide on her conservative pump of fine leather. I started to stand after putting on her shoes, but a touch of her cool hand on my bare shoulder kept me at her feet.

Jean dressed quickly, looking again like the familiar clone cadet in the uniform of the day. It was almost hard to remember the hot little girl in her leather corset and stiletto heels.

Dr Wellington spoke to me for the last time that day. 'Remy. Once again I congratulate you. You are a slave. You've made it. I am taking Mistress Dillon out to celebrate now: she's made it too. You stay here, on your knees, until we are gone. Then you may play with yourself if you like, dress, and get back to classes.' She consulted her watch. 'You have about fifteen minutes.' With that, they were gone.

Part of me was angry. Angry to have been left alone, naked, on my knees, while they went off to celebrate. But then, wasn't this just right? Wasn't this just where I belonged? All my life I had striven to be the best and the toughest. Right now I was just a slave girl. One who had made two beautiful women come. And my mistress had given me permission to come as well.

Need overcame any false pride and I lay back to rub my hot little pussy. In a very short time I came hard, images of Jean and Dr Wellington filling my head. What a lucky little slave girl, indeed.

Chapter Nine

Said the Spider to the Fly

Well, it's one thing to watch other slaves up on the little stage, going through their carefully choreographed routines. It's quite another to be up there yourself! But Dr Wellington had decided it was time for me to get up like the rest and give a little demonstration of my supposedly acquired grace and discipline. I was assigned to perform with two males, one submissive and one dominant. We were to coordinate our own programme.

The only requirement for our particular show was that we use 'The Web'. The Web was a cleverly designed sort of restraining device that someone had built. It consisted of a black frame of aluminium metal pipes, built in the shape of something like a soccer goal net. The netting consisted of soft nylon ropes crisscrossed in every direction and attached up and down the frame so that it really did resemble a spider's web. At various intervals along the rope were little leather cuffs with velcro closures that could quickly but securely bind someone in place. It was kept in the bell tower and used in the various torture chambers. I had seen it, but had never seen it 'in action'.

Bill and Mark met with me one afternoon to choreograph our performance. We had already talked over the basic premise for our show. Even though Bill was dominant, he didn't try to control things, which I appreciated. He encouraged us to participate as equals, with the basic goal to create a sexy and exciting show.

We decided to do a kind of dance, with a theme of Bill as a kind of spider who would capture each of us and use us for his pleasure. Mark was a gymnast and very flexible, while Bill was athletic and very strong. The performance was to be twenty minutes long. That may not sound like very long, but when you are trying to make it interesting and sexy, it can seem like forever.

The night came all too soon when we were scheduled to perform. How odd to peek from backstage and see the little tables filled in the dim, little room. I saw Dr Wellington, of course, and Sergeant Sinclair. Even Ellen Roster was there, sitting with several men at a table to the side of the stage. I saw Sam Brady, looking attentively from his place on the wall where he waited with other slaves to respond to a beckon or nod from anyone at the tables who needed a fresh drink or anything else. I remembered how, only a few months before, I had had the honour of sitting at one of those tables, watching Sam on this very stage.

Now it was my turn. My stomach clenched and it felt like I was in an elevator whose bottom had just dropped out. Even though I was barely dressed, I felt hot: my palms and underarms were wet with nervousness, my mouth was dry. My outfit was a red satin G-string and large, red satin ribbons that crisscrossed over my body, only barely covering my breasts. I looked like a present for someone to unwrap. Mark was similarly clad, his cock and balls secured in a bright-red pouch. Bill and the slave assigned to help us backstage secured Mark and me into the web.

We had decided to show off Mark's gymnastic abilities, as well as his capacity to suffer. He was positioned with his hands and feet on the ground, his body arched up so that his cock and balls were raised appealingly in their red covering. He was secured against the web by one wrist and one ankle, his head thrown back, Adam's apple bobbing. I was completely suspended against the web, secured by my wrists, waist, thighs, and ankles. My arms were raised high around my head and my legs were spread far apart. My feet were resting lightly against Mark's upraised torso. Because of the angle of the web, which tilted back slightly, I was actually rather comfortable, with my back leaning into the give of the mesh created by the rope. As a final touch, we were both blindfolded in the same crimson satin.

Bill was dressed in a black shirt and pants, to represent the spider who would capture his prey. Bill was African-American, and his dark skin gleamed attractively against his black collarless shirt which was unbuttoned to the waist, revealing his hard-muscled chest. At a signal from him, the music started, a slow, instrumental piece of African origin with drums and pipes. I could hear the slow, ratcheting sound of the curtain rising, my sense of hearing heightened by the blindness. Actually, I was

141

grateful that I couldn't see the faces out there, watching, waiting expectantly to see our little show. I only hope the nervousness I felt didn't show in my face or body. I could actually feel Mark's heart pounding against the soles of my feet.

The first part was easy, for me at least. Though I couldn't see it, I knew what was happening, as Bill approached Mark, a single lash in his hand. He moved slowly, edging toward Mark like a spider languidly secure that he had captured his prey in his sticky webbing. He lay the lash vertically along Mark's taut body so that the handle end touched his cock. Mark had to stay very still to balance the whip. Bill slid his hands over Mark's body, and under it, sensually cupping his ass cheeks, his balls, tweaking his nipples, placing his large hand around Mark's bared throat. I didn't hear a clatter, so I had to assume the whip had stayed in place, thank God, during this mood-setting scene.

Then I heard it, just a fraction of a second before Mark must have felt it: the whoosh and whistle of the lash as it flew through the air to land on his naked flesh. Again and again I heard the whistle, and then the slapping sound as the lash met with skin. Mark moaned softly with each strike, but stayed in position under my feet. Luckily for me, Bill was quite talented with the whip, and he managed not to strike me by accident while whipping the poor slave below me.

The audience was silent as the whipping continued. I felt Mark's body grow wet with sweat from the exertion of maintaining his position while being so cruelly treated. When it was over, Bill released the simple bonds that held his charge and helped Mark to stand. We had chosen the single lash because of the lovely, long lines of fire it leaves on the skin, especially fair skin like Mark and I have. I knew that Mark was now displaying his marked and sweat-glistened body to the audience, for their review and approval.

Then the sound of Bill leading Mark, still blind-folded, to a spot behind the web, where he stood, head bowed, symbolically 'claimed' by the spider, who now moved on to new prey: me. I could smell Bill as he moved in close to me – his sweat mingled with a spicy cologne as he leaned in to touch me – to prepare me, as he liked to say, for my whipping. Though I knew it was coming, I shuddered slightly when his hands began to touch my body. I only hoped no one had noticed from the audience, as that could be interpreted as non-compliance, and punished.

His strong fingers caressed my cheek, the movement soft and sensual. They trailed down my throat. Then I felt the sudden tug as he gripped the flimsy bands of satin that barely concealed my breasts and belly and pulled until they ripped away, leaving me naked save for the small piece of fabric covering my mons.

I felt his hand on my right breast, which he cupped and then let fall. Then I felt the lovely sensation of his fingers tugging and twisting at my nipple, first gently, then less so, until I was breath-ing hard, pressing my lips together to keep a cry from escaping. The second breast was similarly teased, the nipple twisted and flicked until it stood as hard and eager as the first.

Bill then did something which wasn't choreo-graphed into the scene. It took me a moment to register what was happening, and, as he clamped

143

first one and then the second clip on to my poor nipples, I cried out softly. The little teeth were covered with a soft rubber, but still the press of nipples gripped tightly in the little vices took some getting used to. This was not part of the programme and, even as I became accustomed to the sharp pull against my tender flesh, I felt a rush of anger that he had dared to change the scene without clueing me in. But I was hardly in a position to protest at that point. I had never had clamps applied to my nipples before but, of course, I knew that was what it had to be.

Ironically, I was so intent on my own resentment at the clamps that I forgot to mentally prepare for the single lash, the little stinger that was about to mark my body from head to toe. When the first stroke came, I cried out in earnest in a voice certainly audible all over the little theatre. Now my heart was pounding, and I was terrified because of my indiscretion. These shows were silent, a test of the slaves' endurance and grace, to be borne without an undue display of emotion. What would happen to me?

The lash continued to fall, striking randomly, leaving little burning trails of fire across my naked body. I struggled to regain control, to remain silent, to breathe deeply and flow with the pain. As Bill's skilful lash continued to rain against my flesh, I fell into the rhythm of the whipping, my skin adjusting to the heat, becoming numb.

I could feel the sway of the metal chain that held the clamps together. I became aware of my wet pussy as the whipping continued. Had my sopping vagina stained the red satin, revealing my obvious lust to the audience? I squirmed slightly, aware that they had an excellent view of my spread and barely concealed pussy. I was now so aroused by the situation, the whipping, my bonds, Bill's sensual, heady scent in my nostrils, the awareness that all eyes in the room were on me, that I could have come from a touch to my aching pussy.

I became aware after a moment or two that the whipping had stopped. Every part of the front of my body was burning from the lash. Then Bill did another thing that was not choreographed into our show. He leaned forward and kissed me gently on the cheek, while slipping a hand into the satin of my wet G-string. As his fingers brushed roughly past my clit and pressed into my wet and open entrance, I again sighed aloud, my body arching toward that lovely, hard hand. I shuddered, one stroke away from coming right there on the stage. The audience seemed to sigh with me. I had disobeyed protocol, but what could I do? As usual with me, lust had won out over discipline.

His lovely hand was withdrawn, leaving me aching and frustrated. I felt the bonds being released, and then the blindfold was also removed from my face. Mark had joined us centre stage, and we bowed, heads low, until the lights dimmed and, mercifully, the curtain fell.

We rushed backstage to clean up and dress. Dr Wellington liked to see her performers when they were done. I was scared to see her. I had been so overtly aroused and sexual on the stage. In the few shows I had seen, the slaves were very controlled and rarely let any emotion escape, even during a strenuous whipping.

I pulled on the pale-yellow silk dress I had chosen for the occasion. Dr Wellington had asked me to dress because after the show she wanted me to sit at her table. She asked that I please wear something other than khaki, something feminine for a change.

Her head was thrown back, her throaty laugh filling the air as I came out on to the floor to sit at her table. The talking stopped as I arrived at the table and I felt all their eyes boring into me as I kneeled next to her, waiting for that cool touch on my shoulder that would indicate that I could rise. It came after a moment.

'Remy, love. You did splendidly!' I was speechless with surprise. She went on. 'Sometimes these shows can be so dull. I mean, they are beautifully executed, minutely choreographed little whipping scenes or whatever, but they lack heart! No emotion, no real indication that the slaves are even alive, much less moved by what is happening to them. But you, Remy – when Bill clamped your nipples, and at the end when he finger-fucked you – God, I could feel it with you! You became sex, raw sex, raw desire, raw need. It was terrific.'

I felt myself blushing hotly at her praise. I was at once intensely relieved and delighted at her effusive comments, as well as embarrassed by the attention. A man at the table, who I recognised as one of the two that had been at my 'audition' said, 'If she were mine, I'd whip her to shreds for that blatant display. She's nothing more than a slut.'

'Well, she isn't yours, Maynard, so you'll have to content yourself with your own fantasies. She's mine, and I like my slaves full of lust and life. She's real, for God's sake, not some automaton. Who wants a blow-up doll that can take a beating, for God's sake?'

Maynard was quiet, looking malevolently at me.

146

I looked down quickly, not wanting to be accused of being forward by looking directly at a master. But inside I was glorying in her defence of me and my behaviour.

'I thought it was a most impressive show,' said a woman who I hadn't met. She smiled at me and said, 'I liked the colours – the red little insects trapped by the black spider, or the blood red of the welts and the black of the evil master having his way – very theatrical, very poetic. I liked it.'

'Thank you, ma'am,' I whispered. Inside I was thinking, thank God it's over!

Chapter Ten
The Life

*O*nce I had been admitted into the Corps on a permanent basis, things became almost routine. If you can call being regularly whipped, bound, and forced to sexually serve a variety of masters and mistresses 'routine'.

As Amelia had promised, I was subjected to hours of training classes, sometimes with other slaves, sometimes alone, where I learned how to kneel gracefully, how to maintain uncomfortable positions for long periods of time, how to take a whipping without so much as a whimper. We also did aerobic and isometric exercises to slim and hone our bodies. All of this was done in the nude.

Even when not in slave classes or on assignment, we were reminded of our positions. One day Sergeant Sinclair split the group that was scheduled for that day's physical training into two sections. One section he sent off to run several courses with his assistant drill sergeant. I recognised several members of the Slave Corps around me, but of course gave no indication of this. Nor, appropriately, did any of them. The sergeant opened a large duffel-bag full of small packages. He called us up to take one each.

We were dressed in shorts and T-shirts that day. Unwrapping our packages, we each found a medium-sized butt plug. It seems everyone in our little section was a slave! And Sergeant Sinclair, of course, knew who we were. Laughing at our embarrassed confusion, he instructed, 'Slick it up as best you can and stick it up your collective butts. Keep it in till lights-out. Then you can dispose of it as best you can. Don't let anyone find it though. You'll all be severely punished if any of these plugs turn up anywhere.'

He watched with amusement as we licked and spit on our anal plugs. Sam Brady was next to me, and his blush, as usual, was vivid on his pale, freckled skin. But we all did it; by this time we were well trained, I suppose, both to follow orders by a sergeant and by a master. Going through the day, the erotically uncomfortable anal plug making me squirm in my seat during classes made me so horny that my panties were soaked by the end of it. I would look around my class, seeing a person here and there who I knew was in the same situation as I. The kindredness and connection I felt toward them is hard to describe.

To tell the truth, I don't know if I'm describing any of this right. It wasn't just about being humiliated and tortured. I felt something somehow sublime in my condition, my situation. It seemed to affect others as well. Sam had tried to describe it to me before I had joined the Corps, and I was clueless. But now I understood. Something about being controlled, used and abused by a whole cadre of people

149

who could snap their fingers and make you do things you would never have dreamed you were capable of, with the constant thick overlay of sexuality. It was an intense experience.

Amelia especially seemed changed by the life. Those not in the Corps probably assumed it was just the rigorous military training that had changed her. It wasn't that she had lost a lot of weight, though she did seem somehow firmer, stronger. She stood straight, with her head up now, instead of shyly eyeing the ground when others spoke to her. She seemed proud, not only of her ability to serve with grace, but of her own natural beauty. She confided in me that for the first time she didn't always turn to food for comfort. She had found herself in her calling to serve others as a slave.

Interestingly, I had found peace within myself as well. I was no longer driven to be the best at PT or in my classes. Yet ironically, perhaps because I let go, I was doing very well in all my courses and in my training. The Slave Corps seemed to suit me.

I loved the excitement and perverse pleasure I derived from submitting to strangers who could demand whatever they wished of me. I loved the stage shows where I got to perform with other exhibitionistic slaves for the little gatherings of dominants down in the bell tower basement. Occasionally I had twinges of longing for something more romantic, but usually I was too involved in the scene, in serving and pleasing and testing the limits of my sexual endurance, to ponder anything deeper.

I was just completing my freshman year, having been a full-fledged slave for some months now, when the colonel called me back. I had found an envelope, as usual, in my box. Opening it, my heart gave a little involuntary lurch as I saw the words 'Colonel Ronald Hewitt, 1900 hours, Thursday.' At 1900 hours! That was 7.00 at night! I had never had a night assignment before. I wondered about the logistics of it, and then remembered that Thursday was a special night-time training programme. We would all be out all over the place running drills. I would never be missed.

Thursday found me waiting outside the colonel's office at the appointed time. I was disappointed not to see Eloise there, though it made sense, since it was so late. We had never gotten together, as she had suggested. It wasn't that I didn't want to: it had just never seemed to materialise. I realised the fact that she wasn't there that evening made me a little nervous. Colonel Hewitt was not a man I felt very comfortable being alone with. But at the same time, I was pleased that he had called me back. I felt I had come so far since that day when I was still a novice, the day he had his secretary crop me while he signed papers and looked bored. Hopefully today's session would be more successful!

Timidly I knocked on the office door. I noticed this time the small, gold plate with the words, COLONEL RONALD HEWITT etched into it. I heard his voice say, 'Come in.'

Opening the door, I pushed and entered. As before, he seemed engrossed in his work. Papers were spread everywhere as he bowed his head over his work. I had come a long way in the patience department. I stood calmly, at attention, waiting to be acknowledged. At length he looked up and said, 'Slave. Strip. Then lock the door.'

That was it. No preamble. No welcome back. Just strip. I did, as quickly and quietly as possible. Then

I walked to the door and turned the deadbolt until it clicked into place. For some reason the action didn't make me feel particularly safe. Rather than taking comfort from the fact that no one could walk in, a part of me now felt locked in myself.

'Come closer.'

I approached him, wondering what was next. Pulling open a drawer, the colonel withdrew a small chain with two clips attached to it, one at either end. It was a pair of nipple clamps. Other than that time on stage, I had had little experience with clamps. I hadn't forgotten their sharp little bite, though, and my nipples tingled in dreaded antici-pation of what was to come. These clamps were different from the ones Bill had used. Those had been tipped with rubber, while these were little alligator clips, with nothing to protect delicate flesh from the sharp, metal teeth.

Without speaking to me, the colonel reached out and took hold of both my nipples. He roughly pulled and twisted them until they were erect. I couldn't suppress a soft moan of pain as the clips closed around each nipple like a vice. Oh God, it was much worse than the other ones! It took all my willpower not to pull them off. But after a while the pain subsided and was replaced by a dull tension that wasn't entirely unpleasant. The colonel tugged at the chain. He seemed satisfied that it was secure, and let it drop. I dared to look at his face while he was busy in a drawer. His expression was blank, neutral, but his eyes were bright, piercingly intense. I shivered slightly, resisting the urge to wrap my arms protectively around myself.

Next he drew out another chain. This one, I saw, had only one clip on the end. On the other end was a clasp of some sort. I watched, more curious than afraid, as he attached the chain by the clasp to the centre of the chain dangling between my breasts. With a sudden, blinding realisation, I knew what the third clamp was for.

'Spread your legs. Expose your clit.' He spoke in almost a monotone. He seemed bored. Just a few months before I couldn't have done it. The thought of those sharp, metal teeth biting into my delicate pussy flesh would have been more than I could have borne. But months of training in submission and endurance made me know I could take it.

Hoping he didn't see that my fingers were trembling, I spread my own labia, offering up my little hooded clit for his pleasure and torment. Deftly, he attached the clamp to the hood of my clit so quickly it was over before I knew it began. He had obviously done this many times before. The instant he was done, my body registered the pain. It was excruciating. I began to breathe deeply, willing myself to handle the pain, as we had been taught in our slave classes. I stood still, naked and chained in front of the colonel.

He wasn't even looking at me. He was looking down at his papers again. Without looking up he said, 'Bend across my desk on your back. Here.' He cleared a wide path through the papers with a sweep of his arm. With a strong hand he pressed back against my hip, forcing me back on to the desk. My legs spread as I struggled to maintain some kind of balance. I finally settled on tiptoe, my knees splayed outward. The effect was that I was bent back with my naked pussy clamped and in full view. The chain felt cold against my belly.

The colonel ignored me, it seemed, as he continued

to read his papers, occasionally scribbling something in red in the margin of his work. The wood of the desk was cool and hard under my bare back and buttocks. My clit had numbed somewhat, and the pressure was bearable. It was very disconcerting to just lie there, without having anything done to me.

I wanted to do something, to force some kind of reaction from him. But of course I lay as still as I could. I knew the drill. After some interminable period, the colonel put down his pen and stood up. He moved directly in front of me. Leaning down over me, he took the chain in his hand and pulled up. The tug sent spirals of pain coursing through my nipples and pussy.

He released the tension, still not speaking. Then I felt his finger, hard and probing, at the entrance of my vagina. To my embarrassment, I was wet as usual. Naked and in pain on this strange man's desk, I was totally and inexplicably aroused.

'Slut,' he hissed into my ear. I closed my eyes. His face was very close to mine. Again I felt the tug of the chain as he reached down and grabbed it. Suddenly pain flooded into my cunt. I realised as he held it up that the colonel had released the clamp. The resultant blood flow brought all my delicate nerve endings back to life. I gasped from the intensity of it, pressing my thighs together, desperate for relief.

The colonel barely seemed to notice. He was intent on removing the now-unneeded chain from the one between my breasts. Once it was off, he laid it next to me and lifted up, hard, on the remaining chain. This forced my breasts up as my nipples were elongated by the tension of his pull. I cried out and he slapped me.

Jerking my head away, I realised even as it was happening that I was losing control. He realised it too, as he slapped the other cheek just as hard and barked, 'Get control of yourself, slave! Where is your grace? Take it! You know you need this. You know you crave to suffer and I can give that to you. Take it!'

He slapped my face again and again, still pulling up on the chain all the while. I began to cry. I was still aroused, but becoming too overwhelmed to handle what was happening. It was amazing that he had found the one area that I was especially sensitive to. I still had never managed to get over my fear of having my face slapped. And this sadist had honed right in on that fact.

Dropping the chain, his face contorted with disgust, he quickly released the clamps and my hands flew to my aching nipples. I was crying quietly as he began to speak. 'None of you Corps slaves can take real torture. You're just a bunch of pussy sluts looking for an easy master to jerk you off. You make me sick.' He walked around behind my head so I couldn't see him. I heard him unzip his pants.

'What do I expect from a bunch of army brats. Oh, well. At least you can be of some use. I presume they taught you how to suck cock?'

The question must have been rhetorical, because he didn't wait for an answer. Instead he pulled me up further across the desk, until my head was hanging off the other side. After positioning himself in front of me, his cock even with my face, he pressed the round, fat head against my lips, forcing them apart. As the cock slid back past my teeth, along my tongue to the back of my throat, I started to gag. But there was no getting away. The colonel was silent as he used my mouth. He didn't touch me in any other way, just slid his rigid member in and out of my mouth. Tears pricked my eyes and threatened to spill over again.

His pace picked up and I tried to position my mouth to create the most friction. Presumably the faster he came, the faster I could get out of there. He may have been Eloise's romantic ideal, but he certainly wasn't mine. After what seemed like forever he finally started to move in a rhythm that signalled impending release. His eyes fluttered shut. Other than that I wouldn't have known he was about to come; he didn't make a sound.

Pulling out suddenly, he shot his load across my face and chest. A glob landed in my hair. I lay still and quiet, like an animal that has been trapped and hopes to avoid notice by its predator. The colonel zipped up his stiffly starched pants and returned, face again placid and indifferent, to his desk. 'Get up. Don't clean yourself. Just get dressed.'

He sat in his chair, and he leaned back and actually smiled, his thin lips again reminding me of a knife blade. The smile didn't register in his eyes though, which remained cold. As I pulled on my fatigues he remarked, 'Not so proud now, eh, cadet?'

'No, sir,' I whispered, hoping I sounded humble.

He was wrong though. I was very proud. I had endured him without giving in. I had submitted more truly than I ever had before. I was more than proud; I was exultant. I had made it past the colonel without breaking. I was intact, at least in spirit, despite the gooey come dripping from my hair and staining my uniform.

'Now get out. I'm busy.'

Chapter Eleven
Jacob's Dungeon

*I*had completed my freshman year, spent a summer at home in Atlanta and was back for the autumn semester as a sophomore. I could barely get through that interminable summer. I didn't know anyone 'in the life' back home. I felt so different now. So apart. I didn't care about shopping at the mall. I didn't give a damn about rock concerts or boyfriends. I just wanted to get back to the Corps.

My very first assignment of the year caught me completely unprepared. 'Jacob Stewart, 1200 hours, Friday, bell tower, room 5B.' Jacob had graduated the prior year, and was completing officer training begun during his senior year at the Academy. Somehow I had managed to avoid him most of last year. But now, not only was I going to see him, I was expected to submit to him.

On my way to the tower, I remembered how it had felt when Jacob had broken up with me. I remembered how the light had seemed flat when he had left. What would happen when I came face-to-face again with the first man to claim my innocence? Would love rekindle? Would the magic still be there?

I entered the tower from the side door, using my key that I still kept on a gold chain around my neck. I went down the now-familiar basement stairs and followed the numbers to room 5B. I had never actually been in room 5B before, but I knew about it. It was soundproofed and rigged out like some medieval torture chamber, complete with a St Andrew's Cross, a whipping chair, and a rack.

I stood before the door a moment, gathering my courage. Tentatively I knocked. The door opened, though for a moment I couldn't see anything in the darkened room. I realised as Jacob closed the door behind me that the only light came from candles set here and there throughout the room. As my eyes adjusted, I saw him standing there, as tall and handsome as ever, dressed all in black, his shirt open at the throat. Just behind him I noticed a rich tapestry of medieval knights on plump horses.

Jacob smiled at me. 'Remy,' he said. 'How beautiful you've become. Submission suits you, as I knew it would.'

I looked into his face, seeking out the man I had once thought I loved. But I couldn't find him. This man was handsome, make no mistake. But I felt no thrill of desire, no secret recognition in either my body or soul. The feelings of passion and romance that had so consumed me the year before had shifted to mild interest, if that.

'I requested you especially, Remy. I think you're ready at last. Ready to submit to me as you were meant to from the beginning.'

I didn't answer. Luckily, he hadn't asked me a

direct question, so no response was expected or required. I must say I was feeling rather unsubmissive at the moment. Indifference was shifting somewhat to anger as I remembered how I had suffered when he let me go. I looked down, hoping my feelings didn't show in my face.

Taking my action for compliance and perhaps agreement, Jacob pressed gently on my shoulders. I understood the signal and sank to my knees. 'I want to test you today, my love,' he said.

I inhaled rather sharply at his usage of the endearment, but reminded myself silently to maintain control. My personal feelings should have nothing to do with submitting with grace to a master of the Slave Corps.

'We have an hour and a half. During that time I will take you to new limits. Are you ready, slave girl?'

Direct question. 'Yes, sir, Master Stewart.'

He seemed slightly offended. 'Don't call me Master Stewart. Sir or Jacob will be fine. We are old friends, after all.'

Oh, is that what we were. Very well, then, sir. Of course, aloud, I only said, 'Yes, sir.'

'Take off those nasty army things and put on this.' He handed me a very pretty white dress. It had little pearl buttons all the way down the front. I unbuttoned it enough to slip it over my head. It was slightly too snug at the breasts, which forced them up and together, showing a lot of cleavage. Jacob seemed to like the look, as he stood in front of me, unbuttoning one and then one more of the buttons at my chest.

'There,' he said. 'Perfect. French peasant girl. Long blonde hair, bare feet and all.' Taking my hand, he led me over to a small table. 'Bend over. I want to redden those cheeks a bit before we begin.'

I have to admit, standing there in the candlelight of Jacob's medieval dungeon, in my pretty white dress, naked underneath, I was getting pretty turned on.

As I bent, he pressed one large hand against the small of my back, forcing me far over the table. I rested my cheek against the smooth wood as he flipped up my dress. I felt a faint draft on my bare flesh, and then Jacob's hand smoothing my asscheeks, then pinching the flesh ever so slightly between his fingers. Then the hands were gone and I knew, the split second before I felt it, that he was starting the spanking. His hand was slightly cupped as it came down hard on my ass.

People think a whipping is the worst, but sometimes a spanking can be much harder to take. Perhaps it is because of the large area that a man's hand can cover at once. So many more nerve endings are awakened by a hard palm than by a few strips of soft leather. And if you hold your hand just so, a spanking can be brutal.

I felt the heat spread under his hands as he smacked me over and over, warming my entire bottom and upper thighs. After just a few minutes I was panting and clutching at the table top, tears seeping from under my tightly closed eyelids. I was determined to remain quiet. I was sure he hadn't forgotten my outraged protests when he first tried to dominate me. I wanted to show him how far I had come, without any help from him.

Finally the spanking stopped and Jacob pulled me by my hair. 'Learning to take it at last, eh, girl?

I wasn't sure you had it in you. Maybe I should have given you more time.' Maybe.

He looked at me critically while I tried to catch my breath. I was dying to touch and soothe the burning skin of my ass, but I didn't dare. I had to bite my tongue not to say aloud that yes, maybe I had needed more time, more understanding. But we were past all that now. No going back.

'Well, so much for the warm-up.' His voice was brisk, businesslike, as he led me to the centre of the room. 'Raise your hands high over your head. Yes, like that.' As he spoke, he was adjusting some kind of pulley apparatus that was hanging from the ceiling. He lowered it until a short, thick wooden board with wrist cuffs nailed into it was at the height of my raised wrists. Without speaking, he pressed each of my wrists into a cuff and snapped it shut. The cuffs were lined with sheepskin and felt warm and soft, though decidedly snug.

Stepping back to the pulley, Jacob cranked it, raising the wooden board, which forced me to stretch up until I was on tiptoe. I couldn't quite keep my balance, but the cuffs held me in place. He stepped forward and kissed me, hard, on the mouth. I remembered those lips and, despite myself, I felt some of the old passion flaming into being as he crushed my lips with his, his tongue probing deep and insistent in my yielding mouth.

He pulled away, a little smile playing on his lips. 'Still a slut, I see,' he grinned.

I bristled and bit my lips to keep from responding with some smartass retort. Before I realised what was happening, he reached out for my dress and, grabbing firmly on each side just above my breast, he ripped the fabric. Little buttons sprayed as he rent the pretty fabric, leaving the dress hanging open.

'Oh, God, I remember these tits,' he murmured, as he squeezed and held them in his large hands. I was so unprepared for his action, and so stunned that he had ruined my beautiful dress, that I barely noticed what he was doing.

Looking at me, his eyes glittering with lust, Jacob said, 'Peasant girl. I am a knight here to claim my prize.' He was inspired by the room we were in, no doubt. But I had to admit to myself that the image was exciting, if contrived. 'You are powerless to resist me. I have you bound and now I am going to beat you, and then fuck you.'

I gasped slightly. He couldn't take me by force. It wasn't 'allowed'. Surely he wouldn't dare go against the rules of the Corps. I didn't have time to worry about this, though, as again he pulled me against him and kissed me. His mouth trailed down my throat to one breast, where it found a stiff nipple eager for attention. He bit it, just a little too hard, causing me to pull away slightly. Jacob stood back and slapped me, hard, on my cheek. I was breathing deeply now, trying not to panic.

'Let's get one thing straight, slut. You will not pull away. For the next hour you belong to me. Completely. No matter what I do to you, you take it. Understand, slave?' His voice was low and insistent. I had no choice but to nod. Yes, I understood.

More gently he said, 'Remy. Don't fight me. I am your knight, come to rescue you. I just want to taste the fruits of victory. I want to whip the flesh that is my prize. I want to deflower the little peasant girl at my mercy.'

OK, so he was back to the fantasy. He had actually taken my virginity once. Why not pretend to a second time. As long as it was pretend. Even if there hadn't been rules protecting me, I didn't want Jacob to fuck me. Not like this. Not as part of his little game. I had no choice but to trust that he would abide by the rules as he played out his role as my captor knight.

'I assume we understand each other, peasant girl. If you behave, I will spare your life. But first you must suffer for me, just a little.' Jacob took a long, heavy braided whip from the wall. He snapped it several times in the air near me so I could hear the whistle of the leather against the air. Slowly, almost languidly, he began to stroke my flesh with the whip. Long, slow lashes that caressed more than stung. I felt the heat creeping back into my pussy as my skin warmed to the gentle whipping. I was suspended, my toes barely touching the ground, my clothing torn, in the candlelight of this man's torture chamber. Just pondering my delicious situation made me hot and ready for more.

With perfect timing, Jacob increased the tempo and intensity of the whipping. It was starting to sting now and, despite myself, I began to writhe in my bonds, trying to avoid the lash. But of course I could not. Again and again the whip struck my flesh, the pain mounting until I was screaming. But I never screamed 'stop'. It wouldn't have occurred to me; I was only sensation, only responding to the lash. I was beyond the conscious thought-process that would have allowed me to make a request.

I felt my head falling back and my mouth falling open, as if I had no control over my own body. The heavy, stinging pain of the lash seemed to abate until all I felt was the caress, the kiss, of leather on my skin. But I knew he was still beating me as hard as before. He hadn't changed: I had. I felt languorous and a deep feeling of peace settled over me like a mantle.

As he continued to whip me, he must have sensed the change. 'Yes,' he whispered, his voice husky with emotion. 'Oh, yes. You are there. You have succumbed. You have risen above the pain. You are worthy at last of my cock.'

I couldn't have answered if I wanted to, though I was aware of what he was saying. I was in some perfect, submissive place and I never wanted to come down. I realised after a moment that Jacob was no longer beating me. He was pulling off his own clothes, revealing that hard, long body I remembered so well.

Moving to the pulley, he quickly released the chain so that I was let down. I slumped to my knees, my arms still raised and locked into the cuffs. Then Jacob was there, unlocking the cuffs. As he did, I fell forward, my body like rubber. Jacob took me in his arms. Sensation was coming back; I was coming out of the submissive trance he had put me in. I wanted to go back; I wanted to taste that piece of heaven again. But it was not to be.

Jacob's cock was pressing hard against my leg. He lifted me up and lay me back on the carpet. 'I would have you again, Remy. I don't care about the Corps. I want you. I want to claim you, finally and completely. Now. I want to fuck you. You must belong to me.'

Only a few months before, if someone had told me that Jacob would want me back, I would have died from happiness. But between then and now, something had changed. I was no longer the eager girl infatuated with the first boy to make love to her. I had come to my own place of strength and serenity and Jacob, to my own surprise, had no part in my new life.

I realised with startling clarity that I didn't want to belong to him. I didn't want to break the Corps rules and I didn't want to fuck him. I was still for a moment, unsure of what to do. He had said he was going to fuck me and, if he persisted, he would get his way. I had to set him straight.

'Excuse me, sir.' My voice was husky and I cleared my throat and tried again. I wanted my tone to be deferential but firm. 'That is against Corps regulations. I am a member in good standing of the Slave Corps. What you are asking could result in my expulsion from the Corps.'

'Who would have to know? Why are you always so damn fixated on rules for God's sake? I was hoping you had grown up a little from the "regular army" brat you were back then. Come on, baby. Give. You're just a slave; you have to.'

'Please, sir.' I was struggling against him now, as he tried to push me down and force my legs apart. This was no longer a game. I had never been compromised before with any master or mistress of the Corps. I was tested, certainly, and brought past limits I had thought I could handle. But I had never been asked to do something I wasn't ultimately and willingly prepared to do. Until now.

Jacob tried to kiss me again. I could feel his knee forcing my legs apart. I felt a rising panic as he manoeuvred himself to enter me. Pushing hard against him, I managed to pull away just a little. 'Jacob! If you do this, it will be rape. And not some fantasy of yours about knights in shining armour.

165

You won't get away with it, I can promise you that. I'm not your girlfriend anymore, in case you hadn't noticed.'

My words seemed to deflate him. With disgust, he pushed against me, knocking my head back to the floor. Standing, he said, his voice cold as a razor blade, 'Get up and get dressed, slave. Do you think I wanted to fuck you because you were my girlfriend? Do you think you'd have been the first slave girl to break the stupid Corps rules? I've fucked any number of you stupid sluts. You'd just be another in a series of whores masquerading as "members in good standing in the Corps".' He spat the words out with disgust.

'I'm done with you. Nothing has changed. My original assessment was right.' There was a bitterness that tinged his words like the bite of an under-ripe orange. 'You're a hopeless, regulation-filled automaton who couldn't think for herself if a gun were up against her head. Get out. Dismissed, soldier. Beat it.'

I didn't waste a second pulling on my uniform, hurling the torn dress from me as if it were contaminated. I couldn't believe that the man who had taken me to the edge of such ecstasy was capable of such cruel and insensitive behaviour. He wasn't a master at all; I knew that now. He was just some self-absorbed, hypocritical control freak looking for an easy target. I ran out of that room, slamming the door behind me. Jacob had gone too far. He'd confided in the wrong person about his abuse of the Corps' slaves. If I had anything to do with it, he would be out of the Corps for good.

* * *

166

It turned out that I didn't have to do anything. Several months later, I heard from none other than Jean Dillon that he had been thrown out of the Corps and was away on 'indefinite leave' from Officer Training. Seems he picked the wrong girl to mess with. He tried to make her to break the rules and when she resisted he tried to force her.

She not only fought back; she broke his wrist in the process. He tried to get her thrown out of the Corps for assault and for disobedience as a Corps slave, pressing formal charges through the Corps' tribunal process. He swore under oath that she had broken his wrist out of malice and disobedience. He further swore that she had begged him to break the rules and have intercourse with him, but that he had refused, resulting in her assault on him. It would have been his word against hers, and his probably would have carried more weight, but he hadn't counted on the fact that the whole thing had been videotaped.

Apparently she liked to hide a camera when she was able to, to capture her erotic experiences on tape for later viewing. She was able to produce the evidence that made a liar out of Jacob Stewart.

I was stunned by the whole thing. And to think that I had thought I was in love with the guy! I was also surprised but pleased that Jean had confided in me. I guess that things were never the same between us after that fateful day at Dr Wellington's. Jean no longer harassed me; there even seemed to be a grudging respect and friendship developing between us. Sometimes I would look at her and think about what her pussy had tasted like, or how she had forced me to lick dirt off her high heels. I wondered what it might be like for her, as a mistress-in-training. What did their assignments consist of? What was it like to whip and humiliate the submissive men and women at her mercy? One day I got a chance to ask her, and what an interesting tale!

Jean and I were on KP (kitchen patrol) duty. Each of us was sitting on a stool in front of a huge mound of raw potatoes that we were peeling for that night's dinner. We were making small talk about campus life. Out of the blue, she said, 'Hey, remember Ellen Roster, the Freshman Corps Commander?'

'How could I forget!' I answered. 'She seemed hell-bent on making my life miserable that first semester. Until I got into the Corps, that is. Then she pretty much left me alone.'

'I'll bet she did. You should have seen her face when she showed up for an assignment and I was the mistress-in-training!' Jean laughed at the recollection. 'She stopped calling me slime-bucket after that, let me tell you!'

'Oh, God! Tell me everything! That must have been quite a scene!'

'Oh, it was, all right. I showed up with Mr Kowolski. Do you know him?'

I shook my head.

'Well, he's an accountant in the administrative office. He comes across like this typical egghead nerd kind of guy. He's kind of short, with a little moustache and no chin. He's always very polite and deferential with "beg your pardons" and "oh, excuse mes!" But wait till he puts on his "Master Costume" and turns into Master K.! Then you better hide your little slave butts, girls, because that man is wicked! And what a foul mouth! He even gets to me!' She was grinning as she said this, but I made a mental note just the same. I might be assigned to Mr Kowolski one day.

'So anyway,' she went on. 'We show up and there I see none other than Sergeant Ellen Roster, kneeling on the carpet in his office, where she'd been instructed to wait. He apparently has a thing for her, and he uses her a lot. It was really a trip seeing old bitch Roster there in a little white negligée kind of thing that he likes her to wear. No perfect starched uniform to hide behind. Just Ellen in her undies, forehead to the ground. She had no idea it was me there with him, though he had warned her that a novice mistress would be coming today to train with her.

'She didn't look up when we came in. Mr Kowolski said in a loud voice, "Hey! Your master's here. I've brought a friend. Crawl over here and lick her boots. But keep your head down. You aren't worthy to look at us, bitch." Roster did as commanded, inching her way over to me, feeling with her hands along the carpet since she wasn't allowed to look. She found my boots and kissed them, completely subservient. It turned me on right away to have her down there like that. She has a pretty good body, you know. She's got a big butt, which is great for whipping.'

As I nodded, recalling Sergeant Roster's ample but attractive figure, Jean went on.

'So, as she was sucking my boot toes, Kowolski leans down and slips a blindfold over her face. He puts a finger to his lips indicating that I should be quiet. I grin, realising she isn't supposed to know that it's me, her slime-bucket cadet, at whose feet she's kneeling.

'"Get up, slime bitch," Kowolski barks at her. He's always barking when he gets to be master. "Lift your arms above your head. This mistress here wants to see how you handle a cane." Roster actually gasped out loud, a kind of yelp almost. Mr Kowolski turned to me, an evil leer on his face. "My Ellen is scared of caning. She can take a good whipping with a flogger or crop, but bring out the cane and poor Ellen just falls apart, don't you, girl?"

'As he said that, he grabbed her by the hair and pulled her head back so her blindfold-covered face was pointed to the ceiling. Her lips were trembling and I was afraid she was going to cry. Man, it was way cool to see Miss High and Mighty Corps Commander, who had gotten me up once at four to clean the fucking latrines, with her head bent back, all scared of the caning that I was going to give her.

'Well, Mr Kowolski brought out this long bamboo rod and started whooshing it through the air. Roster actually fell down and huddled, begging him not to cane her. "Don't worry," he said to me. "She's such a goddamned wimp. I'll just tie her up so you can cane her properly." Kowolski pulled Roster to her feet and dragged her to a chair. Forcing her across it, so she was straddling it, half her body hanging over one side and half the other, he quickly tied her wrists and ankles to the chair legs. Roster was whimpering the whole time but she didn't try to get away or anything.

'Then Kowolski said, "Want to see how wet this slut is? She acts so scared, but she's creaming in her panties, right now, aren't you, slut whore?" He reached down and stuck his hand in her little panties. Pulling out a finger, he wiped her pussy-juice on my arm. That kind of grossed me out. I mean, she was my unit commander, you know?'

I nodded again. That would have grossed me out for sure. But I wanted to hear the rest before anyone came around to interrupt us. 'Go on, Jean! I can't believe this. What happened then?'

'Well, he pulled her panties down and she was kind of moaning and saying stuff like, "Please, sir, not the cane. Anything but the cane." Mr Kowolski ignored her, but said to me, "Don't worry about marking her; she isn't a student, so she's exempt from that particular rule. You really can't help but mark with the cane, isn't that right, whore?" As he spoke, he slapped Roster's big ass hard. She started to beg again and Mr Kowolski seemed to get irritated.

'"Damn bitch can dish it out to her cadets but she sure can't take it, can she?" As he was talking, he was getting out something from his desk. I saw it was a ball gag, a big, shiny red one. "Open wide," he said, as he shoved the gag into her mouth, quickly securing it around her head. Her whimpers were muffled after that.

'"OK, hurry up. Let's see some nice fiery lines on that fat ass," he said to me. So, I was kind of nervous. I mean, I hadn't ever caned anyone before that, and I didn't want to hurt her permanently or anything. Mr Kowolski saw my hesitation, I think, because he took the rod from me and said, "Here, let me demonstrate." He took the supple cane and brought it down on Roster's butt. She jerked and moaned but she was tied pretty good to that chair.

'Like I always do when I see someone being whipped, I instantly got soaking wet and full of this power lust. It's hard to describe, but I get this kind of blood lust. Like I could lift up the world or something. There is nothing sexier to me than a slave, writhing and screaming as I beat them until they beg for mercy. Then I want to use them, make them fuck me or eat me or whatever I feel like at the moment. It is so hot! I just love the life!'

Jean sat there for a minute, her face flushed, staring into a middle distance, no doubt fantasising about whipping some slave. I was getting turned on by her excitement, too. But I wanted to hear the rest of the story. 'So you caned her?' I prodded.

'Yeah. I sure did. I left marks all over that lovely white ass. When I was done, Kowolski had her suck him off, and then suck me off! We took turns, standing in front of her, still tied to the chair. She had to lift her head and hold it up so she could reach us with her tongue. It was so hot. I came in like twenty seconds.

'Then Mr Kowolski let her jerk herself off. He untied her hands but left her legs tied to the chair. She got her hands under there and fucked herself good, moaning and sighing with pleasure. When she was done, he took off her blindfold and said, "Now thank the pretty little mistress who caned your sorry ass, slut girl. And don't forget to tell her how delicious her pussy tasted." That Kowolski is a sadist, all right.

'Well, for a second after she took off the blindfold, Roster couldn't see who I was. But when her eyes focused, you should have seen her! She turned totally pale, and then blushed beet red. It was really kind of cute.

'"Well?" Mr Kowolski reminded her. Looking like she was eating nails, Roster managed to say, "You have a delicious pussy, mistress. Thank you for caning me." Mr Kowolski laughed and actually bent down and kissed her face. Then he untied her and told her to go clean herself up and wait for him in the bathroom. They're actually lovers too, him and Roster. Can you imagine? That dyke bitch and that wimpy accountant are slave and master?'

'That's some amazing story!' I had totally forgotten to peel potatoes as I listened to her. 'It must be hell to be a slave and in a position of authority like she is.'

'Oh, she gets off on it!' Jean laughed derisively. 'Mr Kowolski told me: she loves to be humiliated like that. It's her biggest turn-on. And she loves to be caned, too, though it really does terrify her. One of those weird paradoxes, I guess.'

We were both quiet for a while, peeling our endless piles of potatoes. Finally I said, 'My life is something of a paradox, I guess. Always on top in schoolwork and sports, but on my knees, naked at the mercy of whoever commands it. I can change at the drop of a hat from tough woman to submissive slut girl.'

Jean grinned at me, her eyes narrowing as she studied me. 'I think I like the submissive slut girl the best,' she said, almost shyly.

'And Ellen Roster is a tough woman/submissive slut girl too!' I laughed. 'So maybe Ellen Roster and I are more alike than I like to admit!'

Jean laughed. 'Scary thought!'

Chapter Twelve

E.'s Lot

*A*fter that first time I met Eloise – the colonel's exclusive slave girl – I had never gotten around to taking her up on her invitation to come to her place sometime. We really just didn't cross each other's path after that. But one day, in the spring of my sophomore year, we were both attending a picnic held in honour of some benefactor to the Academy. I happened to settle near Eloise on a blanket with my flimsy paper plate loaded down with barbecued beef and potato salad.

I recognised her at once but wasn't sure she recognised me. She was staring down at her plate, looking pretty miserable actually, and I thought I should say something nice. 'Hi there, Eloise. I don't know if you remember me –'

She looked up suddenly, as if startled out of some reverie. It took her a second to focus, but then her dark-brown eyes seemed to light up.

'Remy Harris! Of course I remember you. How could I possibly forget?' She grinned wickedly and

I was sure she was recalling her role in beating my poor little butt in her master's office that winter day last year.

'Well, it's been a long time,' I remarked casually. Of course, neither of us would mention the circumstance of our acquaintance. We were surrounded by innocents with no clue of our secret lives.

'It sure has! What do you say we get out of here and you come back to my place? I never did get to show you where I live. Might be a nice change from campus life.'

It was Sunday, which was a "free" day as far as PT and classes. Still, I had to be back by 1800 hours for a barracks inspection. But that was four hours away.

'Don't you want to stay and enjoy the picnic?' I asked, as I bit into a delicious piece of spare rib.

'Not really. I only came because he insisted. But she's here, so what's the point?'

I followed her gaze to another blanket some fifty feet away. Seated there were the colonel and a middle-aged woman I could only presume was his wife. She looked tall and statuesque, sitting straight, platinum-blonde hair pulled back in a ponytail from her angular, tennis-court tanned face. She was smiling at something Colonel Hewitt was saying. At once I understood Eloise's desire to get away.

'Well, I don't mind leaving, I guess. I've made my appearance. But just let me finish this stuff here. It's too good to leave.'

She nodded, smiling, and sat back, folding her hands placidly in her lap. After stuffing my face a little more, I stood up, drinking deeply from my cold bottle of Coke.

'OK, I'm ready. Let's go!'

175

Eloise jumped up, grinning. Together we walked off the field toward the east side of campus.

'I live just off campus in the Village Apartments. We can have a glass of wine or something and catch up on each other's lives since we last met. I bet you have a lot of stories!'

I nodded, grinning. I did indeed.

Her place was cute – if a little dull. One small bedroom with a tiny kitchen and living room which opened out on to a modest patio. Because it was such a lovely day, we decided to sit out on the patio. It was enclosed by high walls that made it quite private.

Eloise brought the bottle of white wine out with us and set it on the little garden table. We sat in the wrought-iron chairs on each side.

'So, tell me everything. I want to hear all about your assignments,' she said.

I filled her in on the more interesting assignments, in a general sort of way. The sun was shining brightly overhead and I unbuttoned my sleeveless blouse one more button at the neck. As I did so, Eloise slipped off the outer blouse that she had been wearing over a dark-blue tank top. As she leaned forward, elbows on the table, I noticed that her back, where it was exposed around her tank-top straps, was a crisscross of purplish marks.

'What's that on your back?' Even as I blurted it out, I knew. Those were whip marks. Corps masters and mistresses were very careful not to mark Corps slaves, for obvious reasons. But Eloise wasn't in the Corps. She flushed slightly but stuck her chin out in a little gesture of pride, or perhaps defiance.

'Like you don't know? Those are my marks of courage. My badges of courage. That's what the colonel calls them. He beats me until I pass out sometimes. He says I can take it, not like those wimpy Corps wannabes. Oh!' She realised as she spoke that she was addressing just such a wimpy Corps wannabe. 'Not you! I mean, no offence –'

'It's all right, really Eloise.' I couldn't think of what else to say. I was at once horrified and fascinated by the marks on her back. What did this man do to her? The voyeur in me was out in full force: I had to know. If I showed my horror at her treatment she might withdraw and that would be that. If I focused instead on my fascination with her ability to submit, which was a legitimate fascination, perhaps she would open up.

'Wow, Eloise. That's so intense. Your badges of courage. Do you think I could see them? I mean, without the shirt?'

'Well, gosh.' She hesitated. 'I don't know. I mean, I don't usually get naked without the colonel here to oversee.'

'Oh! You don't have to get naked. Just lift the back of your shirt.'

'Well, it isn't just my back, Remy. It's everywhere. He beats me every day to keep the marks fresh. His constant reminder of my position, he says.' She went on, talking faster now. 'I don't usually get careless like that. I don't want just anyone to see, of course. They wouldn't understand. Even you Corps slaves –' Again she faltered, but then she pressed on. I could see that really she was dying to share it. It must be lonely to suffer like that for one man, and have no one to share with, not even him, except when he could spare the time from his wife and family.

'Show me, Eloise. I won't betray your trust. Show

me what you have suffered for your master.' My words, and her own evident desire to show someone got the better of her. Rising, she went inside, beckoning me to follow. I came after her, curious and a little nervous. She opened her bedroom door and went in. It took my eyes a moment to adjust to the darkened room. All the shades were drawn.

'Jesus,' I couldn't help but utter, as I saw the incredible array of whips and chains hung on every wall in the room. There were small leather whips, rubber whips, cat-o'-nine-tails, chains of every thickness, coils of hemp and nylon rope. Crops with small loops and long rectangular loops, manacles, cuffs, collars. And from the ceiling hung pulleys, hooks and chains to rival anything at the bell tower. I kind of fell into the little armchair near her bed as I took in the amazing torture chamber.

'Well,' she said, smiling a little nervously. 'It's something, huh? The colonel hung every whip and chain himself. One by one, after they had been used on me.' As she spoke, Eloise slowly peeled her tank top from her slender body. Her torso was revealed, braless and slim, with round, heavy breasts and large, pink nipples. Her breasts, like the rest of her, were crisscrossed with whip marks, some purple, some red, some faded to pale pink. But she didn't stop there. Unzipping her short skirt, she stepped out of it, now standing completely naked before me.

'I never wear underwear,' she explained. 'He doesn't allow it. He wants my body sensitive to its surroundings. Just like O, I never sit on furniture without lifting my skirt first. In fact, he calls me E. I love it. Just like the novel.' She looked at me, and again that little defiant tilt of the chin dared me to say anything negative. I was too busy staring. Her pubis was shaved bare. I had seen a few naked women completely shaved, since entering the Corps, but somehow I could never get used to that plucked, little-girl look. Seeing my glance linger at her sex, Eloise spread her legs and gestured toward the labia. I looked and saw an oblong gold ring hanging heavy from one side. She was pierced.

'Are you happy?' I asked, seething inside with confusion, arousal, and my own judgmental attitude toward her evident 'perversion'. Even as I asked, I knew the answer. It radiated from her.

'Gloriously happy.' She smiled like an angel. 'I know my situation would freak most people out, even people initiated into SM like you are in the Corps. But you can trust me when I say that I am never happier, never more at peace, never more fulfilled, than when the colonel is here, and I am suspended from the ceiling, covered in welts, dildos shoved up my ass and cunt, a penis gag silencing my cries.'

Who was I, who only dallied in this business, to judge what moved her or anyone else? She had more to say, though. It seemed, once the veil of silence was lifted, she couldn't wait to tell her tale. I reproduce it here, in her own words as best as I can remember.

'When I first joined the Slave Corps I was so excited. I've been a "pervert" since the minute I could think clearly. All my fantasies revolved around being taken prisoner, being ravaged, beaten, and sold into sexual slavery. Even when I was a little kid, I would do my best to manoeuvre the boys into some game involving kidnapping and some kind of bondage. I used to get my two older brothers to play this

179

pirates game, where they would capture me and tie me up and pretend to flog me. I didn't recognise it as a little kid, but these were very sexual games for me. I would beg them to play until they got bored and told me to get lost.

'In high school I discovered *The Story of O* and the Victorian anonymous works and you couldn't pry me out of the bathroom, where I masturbated so much I got blisters on my fingers. I was constantly in a daydream about being whipped till I bled, like in the Victorian novels, and being chained and used by the guards and drivers like in *O*. I would never wear panties, even then, and I secretly shaved my pussy from like age sixteen.

'I tried desperately to get the few boys I dated to treat me rough or something, but they just didn't get it. I would hint that I "liked a strong man" or something, but they would just end up flexing their muscles or something. When I dared to be more specific, or show them some bondage magazine that turned me on, they would run for the hills. I was so lonely and confused, but always horny, and always dreaming of submission.

'I stumbled on the Slave Corps totally by accident. When I was in secretary school, several openings came up at the Academy. I applied for one and got the job, as a secretary in the central office. The work was fine, and the pay decent. I started to notice that one other secretary in the office was always being called away 'on assignment'. Something to do with army training: it was all rather vague. I became friends with Jane – that was her name – and one night we went out for drinks after work.

'I asked her where she was really going all the time. I was only joking when I said, "Come on, I know you're out servicing all the officers, satisfying their sexual needs. Don't deny it." I expected her to laugh it off, but she blushed suddenly and looked away from me.

'I knew I was on to something. Call it pervert radar. Anyway, I pressed her, pretending I knew more than I did. Finally she admitted that where she went wasn't exactly "protocol". "It's like this," she explained, the margaritas we'd been drinking all night no doubt causing her to let down her guard. "I like to play the slave girl. I like to submit." Well, as you can imagine, my hair just stood on end at the very words. I was riveted to her, willing her to say more. She did. "There's this kind of club see, but it's secret. I could get in big trouble just for saying anything about it. So don't you ever breathe a word, you hear me, Eloise?"

'"Never," I whispered, almost dying with excitement. "Tell me, Jane. Tell me. I have to know. I want to be in the club. Please. How do I get in?"

'"Wait a minute, you nut!" She laughed at me; I was probably being way too intense for her. I couldn't help it. These were my deepest secrets, my most constant longings she was hinting at. "You don't even know anything about it!"

'"So tell me, Jane. Please." I guess something in my tone finally convinced her I meant it. She started telling me about the Corps, whispering, and looking over her shoulder all the time to make sure she wasn't being overheard. I was enraptured. I wanted to enlist right away. She explained that it wasn't so easy, that I would have to apply, with her recommendation, and that I would have to pass certain tests.

'The very next day I got Jane to take me after

work to a stage show. I was floored by what I saw. I was so excited I almost came right in my chair without even touching myself. I was allowed to try out, or whatever you wanna call it. I actually fainted when they were whipping me, but it wasn't from fear or pain or anything. I think I just swooned from sheer pleasure.

'Well, needless to say, I got in. I loved it from the second I was in. I could barely focus on my job. I started getting more and more assignments. I would do any and everything asked of me. I kept waiting for someone to really take me to the edge. It sometimes just seemed like a game. A fun game, but not the real-life suffering and submission I craved.

'I think I got a reputation or something, because I started getting the really hard-core masters. Like the colonel. I didn't know anything about him back then. I didn't know much about the academic side of things, you know, or who was who. I just got my next assignment, and I went.

'He used me the very first time. Which I found out later is very unusual. The second time he took me down to the chambers in the tower. He suspended me upside down and fucked my mouth with his cock. Then, after he came, he whipped me really hard. I remember swinging and twisting, hanging there upside-down, the blood in my head making me dizzy and disoriented. I was blindfolded and gagged.

'After the whipping, he left me hanging there, and spread my legs far apart, fingering me until I came. Which was in about ten seconds. I have never been so turned on in my life. Thank God I pleased him, because I was obsessed by him. Totally absorbed. I was actually bored now by my other "assignments". They couldn't give me what I needed. They were too tentative, too careful. They didn't want to mark me, for God's sake. Bunch of wimps. I only wanted to serve him.

'Well, by some glorious chance, he had found his soul mate at last in me. He wanted me for his own. When he asked me if I would resign from the Corps and become his personal property, there was no hesitation. I instantly agreed. That was two years ago. I couldn't imagine life without him.'

She looked at me expectantly. I didn't know what to say. It wasn't the extremity of her lifestyle that bothered me. I mean, it was too intense for me, but that didn't mean it wasn't right for her. What I was thinking of was the sadness. Her obvious loneliness and the fact that he was still married, whether or not happily, to someone else. I didn't feel I had the right to pry, though.

'Well,' she pressed. 'What do you think? Bet I had you fooled the first time you saw me in the office, right? Sweet little goodie-two-shoes type, right? People always think that.'

I nodded and smiled, glad that she had shifted the direction away from requiring a response from me. But just as quickly it shifted back. 'You think I'm a jerk, don't you?'

'What?' I was genuinely surprised.

'Sure. I know you do. You think I'm an idiot for staying with a guy who won't leave his wife.'

'I never said that. Anyway, maybe he will.'

'No. He won't. He made a commitment to her, he says. Duty, all that shit. I'm just a slave; a possession. I don't rank. No status. Just a toy.'

'You don't believe that.'

'I have to. I don't know what to believe. I can't

183

believe he loves her, but I don't dare believe he loves me. So I just console myself with the fact that he is the best thing that ever happened to me. I'll take what I can get. I do get to see him every day. I work for the guy, for God's sake. And he takes me here, every day at lunch time, and beats me and uses me until I taste the stars in heaven. What more could a person ask for?'

What more, indeed?

Just then there was a knock at the door. Eloise, who was still curled up naked on her bed, jumped up, alarmed. 'Oh, my God! Get the door! Oh, shit! What if it's him. I'm not ready! Hurry!' She was racing around the room, pulling on her clothing, smoothing her hair, all in a frenzy. The knock sounded again, more insistently. Eloise fairly shoved me out of her room saying, 'Tell him I'm in the bathroom. Hurry, don't keep him waiting!'

I walked quickly over to the front door and looked through the little peephole in the centre. It was the colonel, just as she had said. He must have ditched the wife and kids somehow and popped over for a quickie. I wasn't sure if I should open it, when the colonel saved me the trouble by taking out his key and inserting it in the lock.

Quickly I pulled the door open. He looked up, angrily, and then looked confused, when he saw it was me, and not his slave girl. 'Hello, sir. Nice to see you again, sir.' A lie. Just seeing him reminded me of his humiliating treatment of me at our last meeting.

'What the hell are you doing here? Where the hell is Eloise?' If he even recognised me, he gave no indication.

'She's in her room, sir. Um, in the bathroom.

184

She'll be right out.' Thank God, Eloise burst out of her room at that moment, smoothing her hair, smiling nervously at the colonel.

'You kept me waiting, E.'

Eloise blanched visibly. I know it was what she said she wanted, but it was just a little too close to abuse for me to stomach. I didn't want to stick around for the 'angry master exacting retribution show'.

'Well, wow. Look at the time,' I said, aware that my voice was falsely bright. 'I have to get ready for inspection. It was fun, Eloise. Goodbye, sir.' I practically ran out of there. Neither one of them said a word. I don't even think they had heard me. I guess true love will do that to you.

Chapter Thirteen
The Stars in Heaven

After I left Eloise's I was in a kind of a funk. Here I was, twenty years old and I had never experienced the kind of intensity of feeling that she seemed to experience on a daily basis. I don't know, though, that I would call what she had with the colonel love exactly. I was clueless myself. What was love, anyway? I had to laugh at myself just a little. I mean, isn't that the age-old question?

I had thought I was in love with Jacob last year, but I came to realise it was just infatuation. He was older, handsome and sure of himself. He was the first one to finally sneak a little way into my heart. But not very far. And I eventually realised that I had never loved him. I mourned the loss, not of him as a human being, but the loss of the situation. It had been nice to have a boyfriend, to have someone to look forward to seeing every day.

Not to mention the sex, which was great. But really, he was still my one and only. I had had lots of sexual adventures in the 'Hard Corps', but I had never made love again. Not only was it against the rules, but the Corps wasn't about that. The Corps satisfied a deep longing in me to submit, to surrender to another, but it sure wasn't about love.

Spring break was right around the corner. I drifted through my classes and army training and before I knew it, the break was here. I wasn't going home this spring. My parents were travelling to Italy for a vacation. Instead I was to go see my aunt in Columbia, South Carolina. She was a widow, who had lost her true love, my Uncle John, about five years back, to cancer. She had told me she would never remarry; a love like that just doesn't happen twice, she told me. But she was so full of life and vigour that nothing would keep her down. She had as many beaux, as she called them, as she could handle. Her life was always exciting, it seemed to me. Always spur of the moment.

When I arrived, she was there at the bus station, all out of breath, waving and smiling at me from the platform. She was about twelve years younger than my mother, and more like a girlfriend than an aunt. Her dark-blonde hair was barely contained in two tortoiseshell combs, framing her round, cheerful face and setting off her large, blue eyes. 'How are you, Remy sugar?' She kissed me and then held me at arm's length. 'My God, girl. You must be six feet tall! You look like some gorgeous Amazon with your shock of blonde hair and that coppery tan. The Army life is good for you, I guess!'

I laughed and agreed that it was. If she only knew.

'Listen, sugar. I have a proposal to make. And if you don't like it, I'll just change my plans. But you are a grown woman now, after all.'

'What is it, Aunt Salome?' I was beginning to worry a little. Aunt Salome's 'proposals' were something to watch out for.

'Well, darling! Something wonderful's just popped up. I have a chance to use someone else's ticket and hotel reservation for Atlantic City! You know how I love to gamble! But I only have the one ticket and it's only good this week! Of all weeks, when you are coming to see me! But I thought, well, Remy is a woman now. Maybe she can stay here alone and kind of enjoy the solitude. You always were a loner, girl, ever since I knew you, off on your bike God knew where, with a book and a Coke.'

'Wow, Aunt Salome. Alone? Mom and Dad –'

'I called them. I made sure it was OK before I even asked you. Because I didn't want to offer something they wouldn't approve of. They said you are old enough to make your own decisions. I told them I wouldn't go if you want me to stay. I won't, sugar, if you don't want.'

What could I say? She looked so eager, even though she was trying to play the proper aunt, willing to stay with little niecey if little niecey couldn't handle being alone for a few days. In fact, as I thought it over, the idea did rather appeal to me. My very own place for a whole week! After the crowded barracks, a little time alone would be fabulous.

'Sure, Aunt Salome. You go ahead and have a grand time! I think it would be fun to stay alone! I've never done it before. It's about time I tried it out, right?'

'Oh, you wonderful girl! You really are grown up now! I'll be back Saturday morning. So we'll still have all day Saturday and Sunday to catch up on things. And here: here's some money so you can buy food and just enjoy yourself. Go to the movies or something. Buy yourself a dress. Do you ever wear a dress? Always the tomboy.'

I interrupted the lecture I knew was about to begin about being a tomboy and not catching a man. 'Yeah, sure. That would be great. When do you have to go?'

'Well, my flight's not till ten tonight, so we even have time for some dinner.'

Tonight! I had thought we would at least have a day or two to visit. But I kept that thought to myself. I didn't want to make her feel bad.

'Oh. Well, OK then. I'm pretty hungry, actually. Should we stop off at your place so I can leave my stuff?' My stuff consisted of my duffel-bag and a backpack full of books I had to read for next term.

'Let's go!' Linking arms, she led me to her bright yellow Porsche, illegally parked in a fire lane. As usual, there was no ticket on the window shield. Aunt Salome got away with everything. After a dinner at her favourite diner in downtown Columbia, I drove her to the airbus stand and we bid our farewells.

Driving slowly back to her apartment, I savoured the unusual freedom of my own car and my own place. Imagine! My own bed with no bunk overhead and no nine other girls tossing and turning around me. I got back to her place, a comfortable, spacious two-bedroom apartment done in pinks and greys. I watched TV for a while and then curled up with a one of my English Lit. books.

I awoke to a beautiful dawn slipping through the slats of Aunt Salome's bedroom window. So used to rising early from my military life, I jumped out of bed and hopped into the shower. I pulled on my favourite faded dark-blue T-shirt and some cutoffs.

Going into the kitchen, I laughed with pleasure when I opened the refrigerator to a whole shelf of Coca Cola, in the six-ounce glass bottles, just the way I like it. Good old Aunt Salome.

The morning would have been perfect if only I'd had my bike. Still, it was a lovely spring morning and I looked forward to getting out. Armed with a backpack full of Cokes and some good books, I set out for a walk. Leaving Aunt Salome's apartment building, I made my way down a little hill to a nearby park. The park was empty at this hour; the sun just hitting the trees, promising a warm day ahead. It must have been pretty early still, maybe 7.30. I found a nice little spot on a bench near the fountain to get on with my reading.

I was deep into Walker Percy's *Love Among the Ruins* when I noticed someone sitting down next to me. Looking up, I saw a young man, maybe twenty-four or twenty-five. He was sitting so that the sun hit his hair, lighting it to a coppery red, shot with gold. He looked over at me and smiled. His eyes were what struck me first. They were a lovely blue-green colour that was identical to the T-shirt he wore over blue jeans.

'Beautiful morning.' He had that unusual South Carolina accent. It is a rolling sound on the tongue that I've never been able to imitate, at once deep South and some kind of European twist that never quite got lost in the melting pot. On him it sounded delightful.

'It sure is. Perfect spring day.'

'No work today?'

190

'I'm on break. Spring break. I'm a college student.'

'Oh, that's neat. Here in Columbia?'

'No, at Stewart Military Academy.' I felt vaguely defensive as I said it. Lots of people didn't understand anyone wanting a military career. But he seemed politely interested.

'No kidding. What year are you?'

'Sophomore.'

'Huh. I never went to college. Just didn't find the time.'

'Oh. What do you do?'

'I'm a writer. I write for various magazines. And I've written a few novels.'

'That sounds so cool! What do you write about?'

'Oh, stuff.' He got vague suddenly and looked away uncomfortably.

'Well. It's nice to meet you. I'm Remy Harris.'

'Remy.' It seemed to roll off his tongue like a round, perfect grape. I was enchanted. 'Eric Darby, at your service.' He bowed from the waist as he spoke, in an exaggerated gesture of formal greeting. Suddenly his expression changed from gracious good humour to a scowl. He glared at his watch, as if it were at fault.

'Oh, shit! I was just going to try and charm you into breakfast with me. Your enchanting beauty must have driven all thought of my dreaded visit with the dentist from my head.'

I laughed, disappointed that he was apparently leaving me so soon, but pleased at his gallant excuse. 'Well, what reminded you?'

'My dentist. He's waving at me.' Looking around, I saw a tall, thin man in his mid-fifties waving heartily in our direction. Sure enough, above his

191

head, over a bright-red painted door, the word DENTIST was neatly etched in black letters on a white sign. Looking apologetic, Eric said, 'Perhaps tomorrow? Anyway, it was a pleasure. I hope I'll see you around.' He loped off, turning back to smile as he disappeared into the dentist's office.

I watched that red door for a while, wondering if I should stick around and wait. But that would seem too obvious. Anyway, what if he was there for a root canal? He would hardly be in the mood for clever banter with a stranger after that. I sighed, packing up my book. I was even vaguely resentful that I had to move from my cosy spot on the bench, just to prove to him and myself that I wasn't sitting there waiting for him to come out.

That evening my aunt called. She reported having a fabulous time in Atlantic City. I told her I was having a terrific time as well. I would have been, too, if only I hadn't met Eric like that. I would have been savouring the Chinese take-out and the video I had rented to watch that evening. I would have been perfectly happy with my quiet evening alone, ending with a hot bath and an early bed.

Instead I found myself inexplicably musing on the stranger I had only met for a few minutes. I could see his handsome face, the blue-green eyes, the glossy, reddish-blond hair. His lips were full and sensual, his jawline firm. I liked the way he held his body, as if he were comfortable with it, with himself. Sitting with my head in my hands, dreaming of this stranger, I realised my problem: I was horny.

As I turned on the hot water and dropped some of Aunt Salome's bath oil into it, I thought about my situation. Here I was, in a sexual club where I wasn't even allowed to have sex. Well, that wasn't strictly true; I was allowed to have orgasms. I was certainly allowed to give orgasms, and to receive the sting of a lash or the burn of a rope. All of which I loved. But I wasn't, indeed expressly wasn't, allowed to make love. To lie in the tender embrace of another human being.

It wasn't that the club precluded me having a boyfriend. But with school and army training and my 'assignments', who had the time? Not only that, I didn't think I could settle for a 'vanilla' boyfriend at this point. A timid, cautious, uncertain college boy who barely knew how to kiss a girl, much less leave her weak with passion and desire.

I eased into the tub, soaking in the hot, fragrant water as I ruminated on my plight. Without quite realising it, my hands had found their way to my pussy. Slipping a finger inside, I rubbed the palm of my hand against my clit, enjoying the heat of the water and the pressure of my hand.

The hot water was still on, at low pressure, to keep my bath warm. Suddenly I had an idea that hadn't occurred to me since high school. When I lived at home, I would often masturbate by positioning myself under the water faucet in the bathtub. It was a safe and easy way to come, without worrying about anyone finding out what I was doing.

Inching forward now, feeling a little silly, but determined nonetheless, I scooched up under the faucet and adjusted the water until it was a warm, forceful spray on my spread pussy. Sighing as the spray hit just right, I held myself open, imagining that it was Eric holding me that way. Eric had taken me home and forced me into the tub. He had held my legs open and wouldn't let me up until I passed out from coming over and over again under the hot jet of water.

Then he would pull me out, wrap me in a big, warm towel, carry me to the bed, and fuck me silly. Not very imaginative, I admit, but, in my needy state, it didn't take much. Soon I was coming hard under the water's intense and direct pressure to my clit. Moaning aloud, I shifted slightly, but stayed under the stream until my shudders subsided into stillness.

At last I felt that maybe I could get to sleep, and I climbed out of the now-tepid water. After wrapping myself in a big, warm towel, I brushed my teeth and went to bed, hoping for sweet and spicy dreams.

The next morning I took more care with my appearance than usual, putting on my only dress, a pretty, soft cotton floral print that was cut close to the body and then flared at the hips, swirling down past my knees. I even put on a hint of make-up, and brushed my hair until it shone in the sunlight streaming through the window. My old, brown leather sandals completed that outfit. It was either them or sneakers.

I found the same bench, again empty, and sat down to wait, hoping it wasn't obvious that I was doing so. After several minutes, I had actually gotten rather involved in my novel and was startled by the sound of a male voice close behind me.

Turning, I saw that it was Eric! He had come back. I couldn't suppress the smile that burst through my self-promised attempt to be nonchalant. He looked even more handsome than the day before in a black T-shirt that showed off his muscular arms and chest. His jeans were faded, with large holes at the knees. His feet were bare. Quite the opposite of military-perfect Jacob, in starched uniform and spit-shined boots. I decided I liked the contrast and definitely preferred the former.

'Remy! I was hoping I would find you here! For some crazy reason, I can't get you out of my head. What am I talking about? Nothing crazy about it! A gorgeous blonde with the body of a model and the face of an angel was sitting on a park bench being pleasant to me and I left her to get a cavity filled! I spent all of yesterday cursing myself for being so stupid and not cancelling my appointment.

'I spent the night alone in my house, miserable that I'd let such a lovely person disappear, maybe forever. I set my clock for five so I would get here at sunrise, just in case you were a very early riser, and just in case you would come back to this bench to read again. Then I fell into troubled sleep and when I woke up the sun was already up in the sky and I was sure I had lost you! The damn clock didn't go off!

'But you're here! You're here. And you weren't a dream after all.' He ran out of breath and fell heavily on to the bench next to me. I was completely dumbfounded by his long and breathless speech. How could this handsome, funny man possibly be so smitten with me?

I suspended disbelief and just sat back, enjoying his show.

'So, now that I've made a complete and total ass out of myself, how about a belated invitation to breakfast? I know a great little dive near here that makes the most incredible corn muffins.'

Laughing, I said I was starving and would love to get some breakfast. We walked toward the little block of stores and restaurants, our arms occasionally touching as we strode along. Each time I felt his skin against mine I felt an uncontrollable little shiver of pleasure. The place we entered was called Pete's Grill. Eric told me the owner was Greek and they catered to the working man who got up at 4.30 for the early shift. They were closed by 2.00 in the afternoon.

We ordered a breakfast of hot coffee and corn muffins from the counter and then went to sit in a booth near the window. Our food came: long, flat muffins sliced in half and grilled in butter, and big mugs of steamy coffee with plenty of fresh cream and sugar to ladle in the way I like it. For some reason the food tasted incredibly delicious, better than food has a right to taste.

We ate in happy silence for a while. Then, as usual, my curiosity started getting the better of me and I came back to the conversation at the bench. 'So, I really want to know. What do you write about? What is your area of expertise, or whatever they call it?'

'Well.' He seemed to be appraising me, giving me some kind of secret test in his head. At last he said, 'I don't usually talk about it. I mean, I usually tell people I'm a carpenter, because I do that too. I make furniture for a local store here when I'm not writing. I don't even know why I told you that yesterday morning about being a writer. Maybe I wanted to impress you.'

I smiled, pleased at the idea that he had wanted to impress me. I waited.

'OK. I can see you aren't going to let this drop.

196

I'll just tell you flat out. I write erotica. I have a very active imagination and an active libido to match.' He smiled, his eyes crinkling with mirth. 'Figured I might as well make some bucks at it.'

'No kidding! How did you get into that? I mean, how do you even think of doing something like that in the first place? Who do you write for? How did you get the idea?'

'Well, I was a very horny and very lonely teenager with acne and a stutter.' No trace of either now, that was for sure. 'And,' he continued, 'I bought a lot of soft-porn magazines and got on-line a lot too, downloading endless series of pictures and stories I found on the web. I was almost always disappointed. The stuff in the magazines was usually so poorly written you couldn't even masturbate to it without getting distracted and disgusted by the bad writing.' He blushed a little as he said this, which I found absolutely endearing.

'I thought guys were into pictures. Girls like to read about it, boys like to look at it.'

'Well, that's a bit stereotypical, don't you think, Remy?'

Now it was my turn to blush a little. He was right. I was being sexist in reverse. 'Yeah, I guess you're right. Sorry.'

'No, it's OK. You're right for the most part, I guess. Anyway, I started writing out stuff I would like to read about. Written in proper English with some sense of a storyline. But still full of sexy stuff. You know, to be read with one hand while the other is, uh, busy.' Again the faint blush, but I could see he was enjoying himself, and trying to gauge my reaction.

'And what do you like to write about?' I asked, teasing him, hoping to catch the blush again.

'Oh, the usual. Whips and chains and naked slave girls begging for mercy.' Silence. I felt a little catch in my chest as I looked down at my plate. Probably he was just kidding, throwing out something 'perverted' to see what I'd do.

'Well you sure got silent all of a sudden. Cat got your tongue? Or was it something I said?'

'You're kidding, right? About the whips and chains?'

'Why would I be kidding? Don't be a prude. It's a free country. If two consenting adults want to play a few little SM games, why not?'

'Oh,' was all I said. I nibbled at my muffin, not really tasting it anymore.

'Remy.' He seemed concerned now. 'Hey, I'm sorry. Sometimes I get out of line. I forget, because I'm in the business, that not everyone is open to that sort of thing. I'm sorry if I offended you.' He looked so worried and contrite at the thought of having upset me that I burst out laughing.

'What? What's so funny? You really have me confused, Remy!'

I was laughing now so hard the tears were rolling down my cheeks. To think that this man was worried about offending a girl who had just spent most of the last two years involved in a club where she was regularly stripped, bound, and beaten for fun. Whips and chains indeed.

Laughter is contagious and finally Eric started laughing too. At last I ran out of breath and slowed to a halting, hiccuping stop.

'OK, Remy. You can let me in on the joke now.'

'You sure you're ready, Mr Porno Writer, sir?'

198

'Oh, come on, I'm not –'

'I'm just giving you a hard time. The joke is this. I'm a slave. I mean, a real sex slave! I'm so into your whips and chains I can tell you stories that would send you screaming to your mamma. Or running to your publisher, maybe.'

He stared at me, those big, blue-green eyes wide with disbelief. Then his mouth twitched up into a little grin. 'Well, you don't say. Miss All American girl, miss girl-next-door beauty, is a perverted, depraved slut!' He started laughing and again we burst into uncontrollable hysterics. I hadn't had so much fun since, well, ever, I guess.

'Let's get out of here, Remy. You have some talking to do! Here I am, just imagining the stuff and writing fantasies, and I have before me a real live girl whose maybe done all the nasty stuff I contrive in my sick, twisted mind!'

We left the diner arm in arm. He invited me back to his place but I opted for the park bench again. I wasn't quite ready to go home with a guy I'd just met. Once we were settled comfortably, I got out two Cokes from my backpack, offering him one, which he took.

'OK, Remy. Now tell me what you really mean when you say you are a slave girl? Does your boyfriend tie you up and spank you?'

'I don't have a boyfriend.' That seemed to distract him for a moment. I liked the fact that it did. But he wasn't to be dissuaded.

'Well, so what do you mean, then? You can't just throw out something like that and then not follow up!'

'Well, I want to tell you. I think I do, anyway. I've never told anyone. I've never even talked about it with fellow Corps –' I broke off, having already revealed more than I meant to.

'Fellow core? What are you talking about? What are cores?'

I had been about to say Corps members, of course. I laughed at his misunderstanding. I felt so comfortable and happy being around him. It was really weird for me. A first, you might say. Even around Jacob I had never felt exactly comfortable. In some way I was always on my guard. With Eric, things felt so relaxed.

'Not core, silly. Corps. As in a military corps. Only this corps has a twist. I'm afraid to tell you, though, because of my promise. I am sworn to secrecy, you see. If I tell you, I might be betraying the trust of the other members. If it ever got back, I'd be thrown out for sure. I might even be thrown out of the Academy!' It was strange but, as I said it, I had the shocking realisation that I didn't particularly care.

Everything that had seemed so vitally important to me – the Academy, my military career, the Slave Corps – suddenly just didn't seem to matter so terribly much. It seemed pale, almost an imitation of real life. Sitting here with Eric felt like real life times ten. I was a little shaken by this. I didn't even know this handsome, strange guy next to me, and yet on some level I felt more comfortable with him than I did with anyone I had ever met. I decided to tell him, there and then. What the hell? Who would he tell, anyway? He didn't even live in the same state.

Eric was probably gearing up to swear to secrecy, leaning forward, looking sincere, but I cut him off.

'You know what, Eric? I'll tell you. I feel like telling you. Isn't that crazy?'

'No, that's terrific! Because I intend to hound you until you give in, anyway. So might as well be now as later, right Remy, darlin'?'

I sat back, feeling happy, but nervous that I was going to say out loud the deep, dark secrets of my life. Secrecy had become such second nature to me that I wasn't sure I could be very articulate about it.

'Well,' I started. 'It's like this. Underlying the basic military and college life at Stewart, there is a secret society, a club, kind of. You have to get invited to join, and even then you have to pass some pretty rigorous tests to qualify. It's called the Slave Corps, which is kind of a misnomer, since there are masters and mistresses in the club too. It's got the nickname "the Hard Corps", which might be more apt, really.'

He smiled and nodded toward me, indicating that I should go on. He was leaning further forward, listening intently. I took a deep breath and continued.

'Slaves get assignments. That's what they call it. Every week or so, or a few times a week, for an hour or two, you meet with an assigned master and they get to abuse you for a while. Whippings, bondage, sex, but no intercourse. Just about anything goes but they can't mark you. Wouldn't look good in the public showers.' I looked sideways at him to see how he was taking all this. He was staring at me, his eyes bright, his mouth slightly open. I plunged ahead. 'I guess you could say it's a place where people with like interests – in this case sadomasochism and dominance and submission –

come together in a formalised process to express their needs and desires.'

'Huh?'

Laughing, I expounded, 'It's a sex club. Either you are submissive, and get beaten and sexually used and tortured, or you are dominant, and get to do the abusing. Get it now?'

'No way.' He was shaking his head in disbelief. 'No way. How could the students ever get away with that? They'd be caught in a New York min –'

'Who said it's only students? The most powerful and active members of the group are professors and military staff on the campus. And it doesn't stop there. I've heard we have members all the way up through the Pentagon. We students are just little cogs in the big perverted wheel that is the Hard Corps.'

'That is absolutely incredible!' Eric leaned close to me, looking at me intently. 'And you are submissive? You look so, I don't know, so tough. No, that isn't the right word. You look so confident, so strong and sure of yourself.'

'Well, thank you, I think. But why do being submissive and being strong have to be at odds? I think to truly submit takes way more courage and confidence than just whipping someone's ass with a paddle. You know?'

'Yeah, I guess I hadn't thought of it like that.'

'I know. I was like you at first. I confused submission with passivity. I had no idea of the grace and courage it takes to submit with honesty and passion.'

'Wow, listen to you! You should be the writer! You have a very poetic way with words.' I looked down, embarrassed but pleased. 'Remy.' Again my name rolled on his tongue like honey and melted butter. 'Remy, you are the most exciting woman I've ever met. Beautiful, intelligent, honest. Listen, I want to confide something in you. But I'm a little nervous about it.'

'Oh, Eric! Come on. I just told you the biggest secret of my life. You can tell me a secret too now. After all, it'd only be fair.' I was grinning as I said it, but very much in earnest.

'I know you did. And I believe you. It sounds impossible, but something in your face, in your voice, makes me know you are telling the truth. And I want to hear all about it! I will hold you my prisoner until you confess every word!' We laughed again, though my perverted mind instantly seized on the phrase, 'hold you my prisoner'. Sounded yummy.

'So back to you, then. What did you want to tell me?'

He sat back, looking toward the fountain, as if the answer might be in the clear water splashing over a triad of stone fish perched up on their tails. 'Well, you know we share the same passion of dominance and submission. But your passion is tested. Mine is academic. I've written about it, fantasised about it, dreamed about it. But I've never had the courage to do a thing about it in real life. I think I've secretly believed that there is something wrong with me. That's why I don't usually tell people what I do for a living. They would scream "pervert" and run away. And I have never dared even hint about it to my girlfriends.'

I must have made a face at that point, because he hastened to explain. 'Past girlfriends. I don't have a girlfriend now.'

I smiled at him, embarrassed that I was so obvious.

'Anyway,' he continued, 'I can't tell you how often, when I've been with a girl, that I've wanted to try something, pin her down, or smack her bottom. But I never dared.

'See, here's the weird thing. I regard myself as a feminist, or humanist might be a more accurate term. And I've never been able to reconcile those feelings that we should all be equal with forcing a girl to do things, and tying her up and whipping her, you know?'

I smiled. I had wrestled with precisely the same demons. 'I used to think that way, too. Before I understood the true nature of dominance and submission. It isn't about you forcing her, or taking something that you have no right to. In a real D/s relationship, there is an open, acknowledged exchange of power. She gives you the right to do the things you do. She gives herself to you. And, really, in a way, you give yourself back. Because when you take control of her, you also take the responsibility for her, to keep her safe and loved. I think it's the most romantic exchange possible.'

'Wow. And you found all that in the Slave Corps?'

'No.' I felt sad for a moment. 'No, I have just come to imagine that this is how it should be, really. The Slave Corps is just a game, when you get down to it. It's a very intense, exciting game. But there is no love exchanged. At least there hasn't been for me. It's more like mutual masturbation, I guess you could say. It's very exciting and very demanding, but it isn't romantic. Not to me. So far I guess it's just the best I could hope for.'

We both fell silent. I suddenly felt very shy around Eric. As if sensing, or sharing, the change in feeling, Eric stood up. 'We talk too much. Let's take a walk. I'll show you my furniture shop.'

I jumped up, glad for the suggestion. Things were getting a little too intense for both of us. Eric walked me down the block and around the corner to a quaint little shop with a bell by the door. A sign hung over the bell: FRANK'S FINE FURNITURE. Eric rang the bell as he walked in. 'Hi, Frank, come meet my new friend, Miss Remy Harris.'

A short, heavy-set man with a merry face came out of a little room off the side of the showroom. He was wiping his hands on a cloth. Then he held one out to me. 'Pleased to meet you, Miss Harris. A friend of Eric's is a friend of mine.' I took the offered hand.

'Show her around, Eric. I got to finish oiling up this armoire for Mrs Cluney. Nice to meet you!' Frank was gone before I could respond in kind.

'He's a great guy,' Eric said. 'Lets me make stuff in his workshop, and then sell it on consignment here. I do real well with it, actually. It's sort of my therapy.' Eric showed me some furniture he had made. The pieces he showed me were of a light, pretty wood. There was a low, deep rocking chair that made you want to curl up in it with a good book. There was a futon frame, minus the cushion. It was curved on the sides, giving the hint of motion somehow. In front of it sat a low coffee table shaped like an S that was all curves and beautiful wood grain. I was enchanted.

'Eric! This stuff is gorgeous! I want it!'

He laughed, and I caught that slight flush to his cheeks that was so appealing.

'I'm glad you like it. I don't produce much, though. I spend too damn long on each piece. Then I end up attached to it somehow and don't want to sell it. Isn't that dumb?'

'Not at all. Such pretty stuff; I would want to keep it too. Especially if I'd made it with my own hands.'

'Wanna see more?' He suddenly looked like a devilish four-year-old with something up his sleeve.

'Sure. Is there another showroom somewhere?'

'Yep. One just chock full of the stuff. About two blocks from here.'

'Oh! What's it called?'

'My house.' He laughed and I couldn't help but laugh with him. Why not, I figured, and off we went, calling our farewells to Frank as we headed toward Eric's place.

Eric's house was on a pretty little lot with carefully tended flowerbeds on each side of the walkway. The house had a big, open front porch where two of his beautiful rocking chairs sat, looking empty and inviting.

'Do you live here alone?'

'Sure do. I like my solitude. I'm too old for a roommate, anyway.' I turned toward him. 'Twenty-four,' he said, anticipating my question. 'Anyway, here it is. My humble abode. Come on in.'

We entered and I liked it right away. Eric's signature furniture was nicely spaced around the room. On a futon frame rested a bright, overstuffed futon cushion with splashes of yellow and gold against a teal green. The room was open and had a spacious feel to it, with blond, hardwood floors and little throw rugs here and there.

Giving me a tour, he showed me the study, where

206

his computer rested in a corner on a computer table of his own design. It was built to nestle into the corner of the room, with several tiers of shelves, laden with books and papers, rising to the ceiling. A long, low couch occupied the other wall.

There was a little kitchen and then finally, the bedroom. His bed filled most of the room. It was a king-sized bed with tall posts at each corner. There was a gauzy netting draped over the posts, creating a canopy effect. The window was open, and breeze blew through at just that moment, causing the netting to sway.

'This is so great. It is like a dream room.'

'That's my dream canopy!' he said, surprised. 'I sort of imagine it catches my dreams. I know it's corny, but I like the idea.'

'No, it's neat. I like it too.'

We were standing close to the bed. Suddenly his arms were around me. His mouth found mine and we kissed for a long moment. It wasn't like Jacob's crushing, probing kisses, all force and teeth and tongue. It was gentle, but deep. It was almost like we were drinking each other in.

After a long moment, he let me go, and we both sort of fell together on the bed. Slowly, sensually, Eric started to unbutton the row of tiny buttons that held my dress closed. He pulled them open one by one, until my breasts were exposed, though still covered in the lace of my pink bra. Eric's mouth found the swell of my breasts. His tongue slid over the lace fabric till it reached my nipples, where he playfully bit and tugged until I was rigid with desire.

Not willing to wait for him, I reached behind my back and unclasped the hooks of my bra. Eric at once took over, pushing up the delicate fabric with his hands. My eyes shut in pleasure as I felt his kiss again, this time on bare flesh. Eric focused on the tender, stiffening tips, drawing a moan from me.

He kissed and suckled me like a starving man, his mouth devouring me while his hands moved up and down my sides. I wanted him. I wanted him to take me, there and then. My arms circled up around his neck and I pulled his body on to mine. We rolled so that I was on top of him. Straddling him at the hips, I leaned down and kissed his perfect mouth again and again.

I could feel his impossibly hard erection pressing against my inner thigh. After a few more kisses, he sat up. 'Remy.' His voice was hoarse with desire, with need. I rolled over as he stood, pulling his shirt over his head and quickly unbuttoning his jeans. His cock was perfectly outlined in his pale blue cotton underwear, long and thick and painfully erect. There was already a drop of pre-come at the tip, making a little wet spot on his underwear.

As he stood there, strong and beautiful, with dark, reddish-blond chest hair tapering off in a thin line down his belly, I inhaled his beauty. He was gorgeous. I was almost transfixed by his muscular, lean body, as I stripped unselfconsciously in front of him. I slipped out of my dress and let the useless bra drop to the floor. I could feel my nipples straining as the blood engorged them. They were literally aching to be kissed again. I wriggled out of my panties and stood for a moment naked before him.

Being exposed so often and with so many different people had given me a certain confidence – or at least ease – about my body. I stood still and straight as he stared at my naked form. I wanted to give him a chance to examine me. I felt somehow that he had that right. Eric didn't speak, but his eyes were bright with desire.

Without planning it, without deciding to be submissive or otherwise, I kneeled on the floor at his feet. It felt like the natural place to be. Using my hands and my mouth, I carefully pulled his underwear down past his engorged cock. It popped out, jutting toward me.

I put my hands behind my back, kneeled carefully up, and took that gorgeous cock into my mouth. First I swirled my tongue around the hooded head of his penis, feeling the groove with my tongue. Then I let him slip into my mouth, relaxing my throat as Jacob had taught me, until his cock was all the way back. I couldn't breathe. His cock was actually blocking the air passages of my throat.

I eased forward slightly, breathed deeply, and then took him back again into my throat, my tongue and mouth muscles working to massage his cock from tip to base. Eric moaned and pulled my head into his hands. He grasped handfuls of my hair and held them as if they were reins. Moaning, he arched into me. I took him in, revelling in the sexy, musky scent of his pubic hair. Still I kept my hands behind my back. I wanted to please him using just my mouth.

After just a minute more, he pulled away, his cock sliding out as he let go of my hair. I looked up at him. Had I failed to please him in some way? His penis was still rock hard, and now shiny with my kisses. He held out his hands to me and pulled me up, then lifted me into his arms. I wrapped my legs around his hips, feeling his cock press up against my pubic bone.

Leaning over the bed, Eric dropped me gently on to the covers. Then he fell on top of me, pinning me with his perfect weight. My arms fell over my head, and his hands found my wrists. Taking each one tightly, he held me, pinned under him. His cock found its way with little trouble to my sopping wet, eager pussy. With one thrust he was in to the hilt. He lay still for a moment, perhaps savouring the feeling of being enveloped by my hot, velvet walls.

I couldn't stay still. My hips started to rotate, trying to take him further into my body. Still he didn't move, but lay heavily on top of me. I groaned, trying to pull my hands free, but his grip only tightened. Suddenly he pulled out a little and thrust back in, hard. This forced a gasp from me. Again and again he pulled back and then thrust, creating a perfect, intense rhythm as his pubic bone struck my clit while his cock impaled my pussy.

I was moaning and writhing under him. His mouth found mine and he kissed me, more forcefully this time, as his cock pounded my pussy until I thought I would faint from pleasure. Finally, with his own long, low moan, Eric arched up and thrust his seed into me. I kept moving, desperate to come now, but he pulled back and away suddenly.

'What is it?' I asked, half crazed with the need to come.

'You didn't come, did you?'

'God, I'm so close. Come back. You're still hard.'

'No. I want to watch you. Make yourself come with your hand. Keep your eyes open. I want to see your eyes as you come.'

Just his commanding voice was enough. I felt myself becoming his. I felt that subtle transition from lover to submissive. Staring at him, my body

210

on fire, I put my fingers to my swollen pussy. First
slowly pressed two fingers into my vagina. Leaning over, he pressed his own hand over mine,
forcing my fingers in as deep as they would go. The
intensity of the movement made my body convulse
with desire. He let go, and sat back again, watching
me intensely.

I slowly withdrew my fingers, and began to rub
and swirl around the hot, wet surface of my pussy.
I was so aroused, I knew I could come instantly. As
if it were the most natural question in the world, I
said, 'Please, sir. May I come now?'

And as if it were the most natural answer in the
world, Eric answered, 'Yes. Do it for me. Now.' On
the word now, my body began to convulse with
spasms of pleasure. I was wracked with waves of
intense release. I struggled to keep my eyes open
and fixed on his. But they kept fluttering shut. My
hand dropped away from my sex, and I fell back,
my breathing still loud and ragged. Suddenly I felt
his fingers where mine had just been. He began
kneading the hard, little nub of my clit with rough
fingers.

'No,' I said weakly. 'No, I can't come anymore.
Stop. I've had enough.'

'Ah, but I haven't.' He smiled slightly but his eyes
were hard. 'I want to see you come again. For me.
Come for me, Remy.' His fingers were relentless. As
they swirled and tugged and pressed against me,
his mouth came down on one nipple, kissing and
biting it. I fell back, completely giving myself over
to the sensations. I was treading on the edge of
consciousness. I felt dizzy and hot. The intensity of
feeling radiated up from my pussy. I became

211

nothing more than a pussy. Just feeling, just sensation, just raw sex.

I heard a high-pitched squealing sound that seemed to go on and on. I realised as my body convulsed, wracked with the most intense orgasm I had ever experienced, that the wailing came from me. My body took complete control, then, and I heard no more. I came and came until I fell back, completely spent, tears streaming down my face.

I felt his arms around me then, enfolding me against his warm, supple body. He was kissing away the tears that had trickled down my cheeks of their own accord. I sighed and snuggled into his chest, deeply happy, completely exhausted.

We must have fallen asleep, because when I awoke, still crushed in Eric's tender embrace, the sun was slanting through the window at a much lower angle. I kissed Eric's stratchy cheek, and slowly his lovely, blue-green eyes opened. For a moment he looked confused, and then desperately, touchingly happy. Again I felt that slight catch in my chest. Remembering Eloise's description of how the colonel made her feel, I wondered, was this going to be my taste of the stars in heaven?

Chapter Fourteen
Submission

*T*hat night Eric and I ate at a little seafood place that had the best fresh oysters I ever tasted. It was weird, but somehow food just tasted better when I was with him. A squeeze of lemon, a dash of Tabasco, and down went the slippery little morsel. We'd follow it up with a healthy swig of ice-cold beer. After neither of us could eat another bite, we decided to go for a little walk.

It was a new moon, so you could really see the stars, pricking the sky in all directions. We held hands and walked quietly for a while. Eric led me down a winding path behind the park. It was secluded and quiet, with a little grove of trees obscuring the path just ahead. Eric turned to me and stopped. I stopped too, about to ask what was up, when he silenced me with a long, deep kiss.

I felt my nipples harden and my pussy grow moist with desire. My body was already softening in anticipation of whatever might follow. Without a word, Eric drew back, looking at me with an expression at once tender and fierce.

'Remy,' he whispered. 'I want to taste you. No one can see us.' As he spoke, he pressed me up against a tree. Pinning me there with his body, he kissed me again. While his mouth was busy on mine, his hands reached up under my dress. With one quick pull, my panties were down to my ankles. I struggled against him, trying to get away.

'Eric! What are you doing! Someone will see!'

'No one will see. No one comes around here at night. And if they do see, so what? Don't you want to take risks for me? Don't you want to please me in this way? Because it would please me, Remy. To know that you are submitting, yes, submitting to me.' He seemed to savour the words, to get excited just from the sound of them. I was getting excited too.

I stopped struggling, and felt that wonderful sense of peace dropping over me like a cloak. I have never been able to adequately describe the feeling I get when I let go, when I give myself up to someone else's control. It is sublime.

Eric kneeled down before me. Placing a hand on either thigh, he gently spread my legs. 'Put your hands over your head, Remy. High. Grab hold of each wrist. Don't move or speak until I give you permission. Do you understand?'

'Yes, sir.' The 'sir' just slipped out. It seemed like the most natural thing in the world. I raised my arms high above my head, locking my wrists together as instructed. I leaned back against a tree, feeling its rough bark pressing through the light fabric of my dress. Then I felt his mouth close to my bared pussy. His breath was hot against me as I

214

felt his tongue, wet and tentative, on my delicate folds.

Remembering his admonishment to be quiet and still, I bit my lower lip, trying to keep silent as he picked up his pace, licking and tasting every part of my pussy that he could reach. Using his hands, he spread the lips wide, leaving my clit bared and defenceless to his onslaught.

I couldn't help but moan as he licked and bit my tender little bud. Soon I had forgotten all warnings to be still and was writhing against him, so close to coming I could feel the pull deep in my pussy as my body prepared for its sweet release.

On and on he kissed me, holding me still with his hands on my hips. I did manage to keep my arms up and raised as he had told me, but my cry pierced the still night as I came on his face. Bucking and arching into him, I came again and again.

Eric stayed kneeling for a while, his arms wrapped around my thighs, till my heart slowed and my breathing calmed. Then he stood and took my face in his hands. In a very quiet voice he said, 'Remy, darling. You failed to obey such a simple request. Tell me this. What did I ask you to do?'

'Oh, Eric. I tried. Anyway, you can't be serious. I –'

'Remy.' His voice was insistent, almost cold. 'Answer the question. What did I ask you to do?'

'To not move or speak until given permission.'

'That's right. And what did you in fact do?'

'Well, Eric, you would move too, if someone was doing that to you. It's impossible to –'

'Stop. Now.' His voice was quiet, but commanding. I lapsed into flustered silence. I was only making excuses, and he knew it.

'Remy.' His voice was gentle now. 'I know we are brand new, and that you are only here for a few days. I know I might never see you again after this. But tell me, honestly. While you are with me, do you want to submit to me? To belong to me, even if only for a little while?'

I realised as he asked that the answer was yes, oh emphatically yes! I did want to belong to him, for however long we had together. I nodded, hoping he would understand my longing without being scared off by it.

'Then listen, Remy. When I ask something of you, I expect it to be done. Do you understand? I don't expect excuses, or lapses. I know this isn't always easy. And I know that there is trust involved, and that we are still new together. So all I can do is ask you to trust me. And to let go. For now you belong to me. Do you understand, darling girl?'

I flung my arms around him, not trusting myself to speak. This was what I had craved, without even knowing it. First with Jacob I had sought something romantic, without being in tune to my own submissive nature. He hadn't been able to reach me: his way was for him, not for us. He tried to take me where I wasn't ready to go.

And then the Slave Corps, while wonderful in its way, was limited by definition. One didn't seek love there, though sometimes one found it, I supposed. I certainly hadn't. But here was this wonderful man, who seemed to understand me and want me. And he was offering me the chance to submit. To truly submit, without games, without false control.

It's only now, in retrospect, that I can explain this all so clearly. Then I just held him tight, never wanting to let go.

'Remy! Are you OK, honey?' Eric sounded worried as he pried my arms from his neck and held me at arm's length. 'Why, Remy, there are tears in your eyes.'

I buried my face in his chest, still not trusting myself to speak.

'Are you happy, Remy?'

Mutely, I nodded, wrapping my arms around him again.

'Good. Because I want you freely, without coercion of any kind. First, will you stay with me tonight? All night?'

'I would love to.' The thought of curling up in his bed, wrapped in his strong arms, the dream canopy gently swaying overhead, was wonderful.

'I'm so glad, Remy. And now that that is settled, there is the matter of your punishment.'

I looked up at his face, wondering if I had heard him right. 'Punishment?' I asked in a small voice.

'Of course. For disobeying. You could think of it as a reminder if you like. A reminder that you belong to me, and when you disobey my rules, you get punished. It's really very simple.'

I didn't respond. I was at once frightened and excited by his words. I had never been punished. Not by someone who cared about me at all. I had been used, certainly. Humiliated, discarded, teased, and controlled. But no one had ever cared enough to teach me.

We were both quiet as we walked back to his place, my hand resting lightly in his. He unlocked the door and opened it, gesturing me inside. Once safely in, he shut and locked the door, the cylinders falling into place with a certain finality. There was no going back now.

Eric went over to the couch. 'Come here, Remy. I want you to lie over my knee, just like the naughty little girl you are. I am going to spank that lovely ass of yours until my hand gets too tired, or I need to fuck you. Come on. Right here.' He patted his blue-jean-clad thighs, grinning devilishly.

I came over to him, suddenly feeling oddly shy. Slowly, almost hesitantly, I pulled my dress over my head. Reaching back, I unhooked my bra and let my breasts fall forward. 'Leave the panties on,' he instructed. 'I'll take care of them.'

I lay across his knees, feeling big and awkward as I did so. With one hand he yanked down my panties, baring my ass to his hand. There is something about having your panties pulled down, and lying across someone's knee, that is very humiliating. I felt a hot blush of shame as I felt his fingers probing between my asscheeks. Finding the little puckered entrance, he pressed against it slightly, causing me to flinch.

'Ah,' he said, musing. 'You don't like your asshole touched, is that it? Shy, are we? We'll have to do something about that, Remy dear. Won't we, my love?'

I didn't answer right away, wondering what to say. I hated anyone to touch my asshole. A sharp smack elicited a response.

'Yes, sir.'

'That's better.' As he spoke, he continued to finger my asshole, though he didn't try to penetrate it. After a moment, his hands glided over my exposed bottom. I liked the feel of his rough hands massaging and stroking my skin. With a little push, he spread my legs a little more, so that my pussy was peaking through. Using two fingers, he grabbed the outer lips, squeezing together. Then he let go, and slid a finger in my – as usual – sopping wet pussy. I sighed and tried to stay still, hoping he would continue his exploration.

The sigh seemed to bring him back, though, and abruptly the hand was gone. 'Now Remy. I want you to remind us both why you are draped across my lap, your panties at your knees. What got you here, hmm?'

I felt acutely embarrassed at having to answer this. I knew he was teasing me, but I also knew he expected a response. 'I disobeyed you, sir. I moved and, um, made some noise when you were . . .' I trailed off, embarrassed, remembering his ravishment of me at the tree.

'When I was . . .?'

'Kissing me, sir.'

He laughed. 'Kissing you! What a delightful expression. OK, then. I'll accept that. So you understand that this is a punishment. This is not for your sexual gratification, or indeed, for mine. Though I must admit the sight of you draped over me like this does have me a bit, uh, aroused.' He pressed down on the back of my thighs as he said this, so I could feel his rock-hard erection against my leg.

'But seriously. This is a lesson. To help you remember to obey me, to the letter, at all times. Understand, Remy?'

'Yes, sir.'

'Then we begin.' His hand smacked down on one cheek, then the other, over and over. I felt a warm glow suffuse my ass as he spanked me. It really didn't hurt, and the end result was that I was getting incredibly horny. I subtly tried to shift my legs so my clit would rub against his thigh with each smack. But I think he was on to me.

'Remy,' he said, punctuating each word with a smack. 'You are a hussy!' I smiled to myself at the Southern word, but of course said nothing. 'You are nothing but a hussy slut girl who is only after her own little satisfaction. Where is the submission in that? If you get just exactly what you want, it isn't submission at all. It's hedonism.'

I secretly agreed with what he was saying, but I wasn't focusing too well as he rained down a shower of slaps on my now very tender ass. I was hoping he was almost done and we could get on to the delightful business of making love. But he wasn't done. Not by a long shot.

Suddenly he let go of me. 'My arm's getting tired. And you don't seem to have any trouble taking this little spanking. God, what was I thinking anyway? You've probably been subjected to much more rigorous corporal punishment.' He was right; I certainly had.

'So I have a better idea. Pull on that dress. Go out into my backyard. You can pull up your panties but don't button your dress. Go out there and cut me a switch, hussy girl. There's a nice big tree out back with low, hanging branches. Here, I'll get you a clipper.' I just stared at him as he went to a drawer and pulled out a little pair of pruning shears.

As he handed them to me, he said, 'Go on, girl. And make sure it's a big one. If I don't like it, I'll get one you're sure not to like!' I hurried out his back door, hoping desperately that no neighbour was out that evening, enjoying the fresh spring air. I stood on tiptoes and cut a long, thin branch from the tree. I clipped off the excess twigs and leaves and hurried back inside, carrying the branch.

I handed it to him without saying anything. My tender ass flesh was already twitching in dreaded anticipation of the switch.

'Bend over this coffee table here,' Eric said, pointing to one of his beautiful pieces. 'You get too horny over my knee. We'll just take the sex right out of this punishment.'

Almost trembling, I kneeled and lay across the table. Eric walked up behind me and pulled the panties down unceremoniously to my knees. Then he lifted my dress way up over my head and left it that way, covering my head like a shawl. He pressed me down until my breasts were mashed against the smooth wood. A hand on my head caused me to lay it, turning to one side so I rested on my cheek.

'OK, Remy. Time for a good old-fashioned switching.'

The first blow caused me to jump and grab my ass where it had landed. 'Jesus, that hurt!' I yelled.

'It's supposed to. That's why it's a punishment, silly girl.' Again the switch landed, just below the first spot. And again I yelled and clutched at myself.

'Remy. I thought you were a trained slave girl. What is all this about?'

'Oh, Eric! Please! They weren't allowed to mark us. I've never been caned or – or switched or whatever you call this. I'm not used to it.'

'Well, get used to it. Because I like it. You have two lovely welts on that creamy ass of yours, and before I'm done, you'll have plenty more. Oh, and one more thing, Remy darlin'. Grab yourself again and I'll tie you to this table. Got it?'

'Yes, sir,' I managed, gripping the table sides with trembling fingers. I was scared of the switch, but incredibly, fiercely aroused. I squeezed my eyes shut as the hard, stinging switch found its mark again and again. But somehow I didn't move out of position again, though I was making a lot of noise, yelping and crying.

Eventually I couldn't help myself and I cried out, 'Oh, please, please, please, please, no more, no more, no more.' It was like a litany that I couldn't control or stop. He finally took pity and dropped the switch, bending down to touch the welts he had raised with his own hand.

'I'll be right back,' he said. I barely noticed he was gone. It was such a blessed relief not to feel the sting of the switch on my tender flesh. In a moment he was back and I felt something deliciously cold on my skin. I realised after a moment it was ice. Eric smoothed the cold, hard ice across my sore bottom and thighs, easing the sting as my flesh slowly became numb with cold. Then I felt a soothing balm being massaged gently into my skin. It felt lovely as his hands caressed and smoothed my body.

'Can you get up now?' The stern master was gone, it seemed, and Eric was all concern.

I struggled to my feet, feeling a little dizzy and stiff after having crouched down for so long. Eric put his arm around my shoulders, and gently guided me to the bedroom. 'Go get yourself ready for bed, Remy. Tonight you will sleep at my feet, totally naked. You haven't yet earned your way back into my bed. But I'm feeling lenient, so you can stay at the bottom.'

I was startled by this statement. I had expected

some tender, passionate love-making at this point. But he expected me to sleep at his feet! I washed up in his bathroom, and came out, gingerly feeling the welts raised across my ass.

Eric sat in the centre of his bed, cross-legged, in pyjama bottoms. Despite the discomfort of my sore bottom, I wasn't impervious to his obvious, male charm. He looked so handsome sitting there, smiling at me from his perch. I walked toward him and started to lean into his arms. With a slow shake of his head, he gently pushed me away, guiding me down to the end of the bed.

I sighed, but curled up at his feet, suddenly feeling deliciously exhausted. Eric leaned down, kissing me tenderly on the top of my head. Then he got up and went into the bathroom, turning off the light in the bedroom as he went. The last thing I remember was a cool breeze gently blowing the netting overhead, before a deep, dreamless sleep overtook me.

I woke up some time later and found myself wrapped tight in Eric's arms. I didn't know if I'd crawled up or he had pulled me up, but his body felt wonderful and warm against mine. It was the first time in my life I slept all night with a man. I felt so safe and delicious.

We were nestled like spoons, with my back and ass pressed into his stomach and thighs. His hands were cupped, one on each of my breasts. Suddenly it occurred to me, as I came fully awake, that it was possible that I wasn't supposed to be up in this part of the bed. I didn't want to risk another punishment. As carefully as I could, I started to lift Eric's heavy arms from my body. He stirred and mumbled something. I froze, as still as a mouse on a moonlit night.

After a moment, his breathing became deep and regular again, and I tried, once more, to lift his hands from my body. I succeeded in moving them and was just sliding down when he said, 'And just where are you going, Remy, my love?'

'Oh! Eric, you startled me. I don't know how I got up here, but I promise it wasn't on purpose –'

He interrupted me with a laugh. 'Don't worry, sweetheart. I brought you up here. I just couldn't leave such a beautiful, soft, loving woman down at my feet any longer. I needed you in my arms.'

I lay back happily, feeling deliciously languid and peaceful. Eric began to kiss me, starting at my eyelids, moving to my lips, my neck. His mouth trailed down to my breasts and then further, to my stomach. I felt his lips caress my hips and then nuzzle into my pubic hair. 'Hmmm,' he murmured, as he spread my legs, quickly finding my already aching pussy with his mouth.

'Oh God, Remy. You taste so good. Like fresh rainwater and mushrooms and apricots. I can't get enough of you.' He stopped talking to concentrate on driving me wild.

Soon I was moaning and arching up into his mouth. I wanted him to consume me, to use me up. Just before I reached a point where I couldn't stop, Eric pulled away and propped himself on his elbow, wiping his wet face against his shoulder. I was sighing and shuddering with unfulfilled lust.

'Remy. Listen to me. I don't ever want you to come again without first asking my permission. You understand, dear? I want to possess your body. Think of it as my body. It belongs to me. You can't touch it, sexually, or experience release without my express permission. This will help you feel more owned. You need to be owned, don't you, Remy?'

I nodded, feeling that my body would burn up from the craving to belong to this man. I wanted him to finish what he'd started, but I didn't dare demand it. It was his body.

'Remy, when you go away, because of course you must in just a few days, I want to continue to own your body. I want to possess you as completely as I can. Do you want that too?'

'Yes, Eric. More than anything. But I don't want to go away. I want to stay always.'

'Oh, Remy. My darling girl. We'll find a way to be together. But until then, you must never use your body for pleasure when you are alone. And if you remain in the Corps, and you are forced to come for someone else, you must silently beg my permission. Remember, even when you are lending it to others, that your body belongs to me.'

I fell silent. I hadn't even thought ahead to that, for some reason. I was still a slave girl in the secret Slave Corps. I would undoubtedly find an assignment in my mailbox when I returned. And Eric wasn't asking me to give that up. How could he? We had only just met, after all.

Did I want to give it up? I didn't know; I would think about it tomorrow. Right now there was only one thing on my mind. 'Please, Eric,' I whispered in his ear. 'May I come?'

Chapter Fifteen
Pony Girl

*O*ur last few days seemed to tumble and race to
a close. On Saturday morning, as the sun was
just climbing up over the horizon, Eric and I went
out for a final walk together before I went to pick
up Aunt Salome. The sky was as blue as cornflow-
ers. Everything seemed to stand out in such bright
relief. I realised as we walked quietly together that
I had never really noticed the incredible splendour
of nature around me, the way a hummingbird hov-
ers over a flower, the way that flower opens. The
way the bud splits so gradually, and always the
same way, with the petals curling up and open
toward the sun's kiss.

I felt such a sweet ache as we kissed and parted.
I felt a little silly as I clung to him, not wanting to
let go. It wasn't as if I wouldn't see him again! I had
invited him to meet my Aunt over lunch at her
place that very afternoon.

As I climbed into Aunt Salome's little yellow
Porsche, I realised that my life had changed, maybe

forever. I had started down a new path, though I wasn't yet sure where it would lead me. As I pulled into the Airbus terminal, there was Aunt Salome, in a bright yellow-and-orange silk dress, waving wildly in my direction. 'Aunt Salome!' I called as I pulled up. 'I thought I was early!'

'Oh you are, sugar love. I took an earlier flight back. There was a space open in first class and this darling young man I met just insisted on paying my upgrade for the pleasure of my company. We met at the casino and became inseparable gambling partners. Lady Luck was right there with us! This trip more than paid for itself.' She beamed at me as if this sort of thing happened to her all the time. I had a feeling it probably did.

As she climbed into the car, Aunt Salome turned to me. 'So how was it this week, Remy? Were you lonely? Did you miss the hustle and bustle of school life?'

'Not for second. I don't want to go back. I love it here, Aunt Salome. I've been doing a lot of thinking about this whole army career thing. I don't know anymore.'

She stared at me and then tilted her head quizzically. 'You love it here? I admit it's a nice place, but that doesn't sound like my driven, dedicated niece, who is going to be one of the first lady generals in this country's army. What's come over you, girl? Wait a minute.' She grinned slyly at me, understanding registering in her eyes. 'Don't tell me. The impervious Remy Harris has succumbed to romance! You've met someone, haven't you?'

Aunt Salome could always figure me out. I loved her for it. I didn't answer, concentrating on my driving, but that in itself was answer enough, I suppose. She threw her head back, laughing with delight. 'Well done, my girl! I was wondering when you would ever find yourself a beau! The tomboy is growing up at last!'

'Oh, stop it, Aunt Salome. I just met a guy, that's all.'

'And when do I get to meet this guy? Where did you meet him? What does he do? What do his parents do? How old is he? Is it serious?'

'Hold on. Before you give me the third degree about Eric, you can meet him yourself. I've invited him for lunch today. I knew you'd want to meet him.'

'Eric, huh? Nice name. Sure, I'd love to meet him. From the glow on your face when you just say his name, I'm sure he's terrific.'

Not surprisingly, Aunt Salome and Eric got along famously. He was enchanted, as men invariably are, by her vivacious manner and interesting stories. Then she skilfully teased out his life story with a gentle interview about his intentions. Eric was forthcoming and friendly, though he did forget to mention that he supplemented his carpentry career with the occasional erotic novel. I just sat back, enjoying the show, munching my sandwich. Eric sat next to me, his hand resting casually over mine on the table. I felt his closeness and would have been happy to sit there forever.

After Eric had left, Aunt Salome threw her arm around me. 'Remy. He is it. I can feel it in my bones. Somehow you've managed to stumble on "Mr Right" your first time out! I get these feelings, you know. I knew it about your mamma and daddy and I've got the same feeling now. Be careful, Remy. Don't let this one go too soon.'

I was surprised but pleased by her words. It confirmed my own feeling that there was something beyond just fabulous sex between us. If only I didn't have to leave just when I was starting to find out. But Sunday arrived before I knew it. Eric and I had shared a last few hours the night before, but there was no getting around it: I had to get back to school. As I kissed Eric a final time before Aunt Salome drove me back to Stewart, he whispered in my ear, 'I'll see you soon, angel girl.'

It was hard to readjust to the stark regimen of classes and training after that lazy, carefree week in Columbia. As I donned the olive drab once again, I realised I would rather be in my soft, summer dress or shorts, walking barefoot with Eric by the creek. Somehow that energising feeling of efficiency and strength I used to get just from putting on the uniform was gone.

I felt a nagging sense of dread, rather than the usual anticipation, as I opened my little mailbox, sure that an envelope would be waiting for me. It was. I realised as I held it close to my body until I could get to my bunk and relative privacy, that I didn't even want to open it.

Inside were the words, 'Captain Rather, 0700 hours, Tuesday, stables.' Captain Rather, the pony girl fellow. And the fact that we were to meet at the stables made things pretty clear. His promise, or threat, to make me into a pony girl, as he called it, was about to come to fruition. As I stared at the assignment, I knew that I just couldn't do it. My heart wasn't in it. I had to talk to someone.

Amelia was waiting at the bench near the bell tower that afternoon, as we had arranged. Wordlessly, we walked together to the SCU, where we could talk privately in one of the little rooms. Once we were seated in the little chairs at the small table in a corner room, Amelia spoke at last. 'So tell me, Remy. What has happened? You aren't yourself since you came back from break.'

'That's the funny thing, Amelia. I am more myself than I have ever been. I just didn't know it yet before.'

'What? You're talking in riddles. What's going on?'

'I met someone, Amelia, over spring break. And he's wonderful! I can't do this Corps thing anymore. I belong to Eric.'

Amelia was quiet for a moment. Then she said, 'I think I understand what you are saying, Remy. You've met someone who you think you are in love with and –'

'Not think, I know I am,' I said emphatically.

'OK, you know you are. And you can't imagine subjecting yourself to submitting to some master in the Corps, when your heart belongs to Mr Right.'

'Something like that,' I mumbled, irritated that she made it sound so trite.

'OK, well just hear me out for a second, Remy. I don't think you should quit the Corps just like that. I think you should take a few days to decide about something like this. You still have two more years here and you've devoted an awful lot of time to becoming a Corps slave. To throw it all away over something that could just be an infatuation –'

'It's not,' I insisted again, feeling like a petulant child.

'Please, Remy, I don't mean to sound patronising. I'm just thinking about what your best options are. Why not try one more assignment and see what happens? If it still doesn't feel right, let's meet again and decide what the best path for you is then. Like I told you before, nothing is written in stone. You can get out whenever you want.'

She smiled at me, a very winning smile, and I decided she must be right. Against my own instincts, I agreed to give it one more try. To the stables with me, then. Let's see what the hell this pony business is all about.

Early Tuesday morning I went to the stables and into the stall where I had been instructed to go. A young man who I assumed was the groom was there waiting for me. He nodded curtly. 'Morning, I'm Joe. I'm to prepare you for the captain. He likes his ponies a certain way. Take off everything but your underwear. I have your gear here. I'll help you put it on.' Apparently Joe did this all the time. He didn't ask me my name, or make any attempt at small talk. I took his cue and remained silent. He seemed rather bored as he watched me strip down to my underwear. I did catch him eyeing my breasts, though. His eyes slid away when he saw me looking at him.

'OK, raise your arms.'

I did and he slipped a leather harness over my shoulders. It buckled in back, and he struggled for a moment with the clasps, pulling it snugly around my body. The net effect was that my back was covered in thick leather, with straps that came around in front just under my breasts. They were lifted and left exposed.

Opening a leather pouch, he took out what looked like two long, golden tassels. I saw that they were attached to little clamps. Joe matter-of-factly flicked at my nipples until they were stiff and then

231

attached a tassel to each nipple. I felt ridiculous to be adorned like this, but then, no one had asked me.

'Get on your knees. I have to put this on your head.' He was holding a sort of bridle: a soft, leather cap with reins and a metal sort of necklace dangling from it. I was confused and not a little wary of letting him put it on me, but I kneeled obediently. He fitted the cap over my head, letting the reins fall down my back. The metal necklace turned out to be a bit. 'Open wide,' he said, and slid the steel bar into my mouth. I clamped down on it, feeling the cold metal against my tongue. The bit curved to fit the curve of my face, and wasn't particularly uncomfortable, just very odd to get used to.

'OK, it fits. Make sure it doesn't fall out. The captain likes that bit in there. Makes you look more authentic, he says. Also keeps you from talking. If you take my advice, you'll keep the damn thing in. He gets really furious if one of his "ponies" talks. Ponies aren't supposed to talk, got that?'

I nodded mutely, only half believing this was really happening to me.

'Now,' he went on, 'you need your knee pads and gloves.' He had me lift each leg so he could buckle on heavy, thick leather pads that covered my knees. Then he slipped thick, workman-type gloves on to my hands. Was I going skating? I still hadn't figured out all the aspects of this getup, but I was sure I would know soon enough.

This was so bizarre! I was dressed up like a horse, with a bridle and reins and a bit in my mouth! What next? I quickly found out that the worst was yet to come. 'OK, now for the fun part. Pull off your panties and get on all fours. I'm going to put your tail in now. Don't worry. We sterilise these after each use.'

He opened a final pouch and showed me a long, full tail made of the same gold tassels that adorned my nipples. The tassels were attached at the base to a thick, rubber rod the size of a large penis. I kneeled in position as ordered, belted and buckled into leather cap and harness. My ass felt especially naked and vulnerable, lifted and exposed to this man. I tensed nervously as he walked around behind me.

'Don't be skittish. There, there,' crooned the groom, as if I was a real horse that needed calming. He stroked my back for a moment, and then my ass. His fingers brushed against my asshole and I shivered. This was going to be really hard. How could I let him slide that thing up my ass?

Do it for Eric, a voice whispered inside of me. Do it for your true love. Pretend you are submitting to him. No, don't pretend, do it for him. Make this a test of your love for your true master. That was it. That was how I could get through this. I would do it for Eric.

I felt something warm and gooey against my asshole. Some kind of lubricant, which Joe smeared liberally on me and on the phallus. Then I felt it press against the sphincter muscles. I willed myself to relax, to open to the rod being forced into my rectum. He eased it in very slowly, telling me what a good girl I was and how master would be pleased. It didn't hurt until the end, when the flared base popped into place, anchoring it firmly up my ass. I moaned into the bit, biting down and jerking forward, but it was done. I had a tail inserted into my ass.

'Good,' he said at last. 'You've taken it all. Make sure it doesn't fall out, or you'll be whipped within an inch of your life. I've seen it happen. Good luck, slave. He should be here in a few minutes. Just stay on your hands and knees and look at the ground. You'll know when he gets here. Good luck.' With that he patted my ass like it was a horse's flank and shuffled away behind me.

I waited, my padded knees and gloved palms resting comfortably on the hay that covered the stall floor. This was the strangest assignment yet. After what seemed like a long time when you're on your hands and knees, but probably wasn't more than ten minutes or so, I heard the sound of boots stomping and shuffling through the stall. I felt Captain Rather's presence as I looked at the ground, bit in my mouth, my body harnessed and bridled.

'Ah, lovely,' he murmured. I could see his boots from the corner of my eye; tall, rich, brown leather riding boots. I also saw the long, thin riding crop dangling carelessly from one hand, the looped tip touching the toe of his boot.

I felt his hand on the harness and bridle, pulling, feeling the fit. Then I felt the reins being lifted and the bit in my mouth was suddenly pulling back against the corners of my mouth. Without thinking about it, I raised my head to relieve the pressure against my lips.

'Good little filly,' he laughed delightedly. 'You respond well to the bit. Ah, and such nice, well-formed flanks.' He stroked my lower back, moving down the curve of my ass to my thighs.

'Your tail looks so pretty against your legs. I can't wait to ride you.' Ride me! Of course, I should have realised instantly, when Joe put on the pads and

234

gloves. Well, the captain was not a big man, though he did sport a lot of extra fat. But I was strong, and surely I could handle it if he didn't make me go too fast.

He mounted me, for lack of a better term, and leaned over, kissing my neck with wet lips. 'Let's see what you're made of, pony girl. Yah!' With that last yell, I felt the sharp sting of his crop on my ass. He grabbed the reins and pulled, forcing my head up high. 'Let's go, pony girl, and step high!'

He continued to smack my ass as I started to crawl around the stall with this little man on my back. 'Faster!' he yelled, pulling the reins and hitting at my thighs. I tried to speed up. It was hot in the leather bridle and harness and the sweat was already beginning to trickle from my forehead and underarms.

Around and around we went, until he directed me to go out into the open air. I was nervous, but knew I had no choice but to obey. No one was in sight, luckily, as I entered the bright sunlight of that warm spring day. With the sun now beating down and the weight of the harness and the captain, I began to sweat in earnest, and to breathe heavily as I tried to 'step high'. Would this ever end?

'Yes, yes, yes,' he kept muttering, as he leaned forward, the crop stinging my ass and thighs. I was slowing my pace; I couldn't help it. He relented at last as we reached the stall entrance and jerked at the reins. 'Whoa. Halt.' I stopped, grateful, sweat dripping into my eyes. I tossed my head in an effort to get the sweat off and the gesture seemed to please him.

'Oh, my poor, hot, little darling,' he crooned. 'Let's get you cleaned up.' He slipped off me and carefully lifted the leather cap and reins. I opened my mouth to let the saliva-covered bit slip out as he took the whole apparatus and tossed it on the ground near us. Then he began unbuckling the heavy harness, lifting it from my sweat-soaked body. When he removed the long tassels from my breasts I sucked in my breath as the bloodflow returned to my tender nipples. He didn't remove the tail, pads or gloves, but instead said, 'Stay on your knees, pony girl, and follow me.'

Exhausted, I trailed behind him, my muscles like jelly as I forced my body to cooperate. Once in the stall, he helped me off with the pads and gloves, and told me to kneel just on my bare knees. Then he took a large bucket of water, dipped a soft rag into it, and began to wash me down. The cold water felt heavenly on my heated flanks. He dunked the rag and lifted it, raining water on to my head and face. I lifted my face to the refreshing water, eyes closed. Then he held a cup to my mouth and allowed me to drink until I was satisfied. Roughly he towelled me dry and then he said, 'Lie on your back and spread your legs, pony girl. I want to see that pussy.'

I lay back, relieved to be able to lie down. I closed my eyes as he kneeled next to me, leaning his body over mine so that his face was close to my pussy. 'You look so good like that, with that beautiful tail stuck up your pretty little ass. Oh, and you are so soft.' As he spoke, I felt his fingers lightly touching my pussy lips. Slowly, delicately, he began to massage the flesh. He was skilful and, though this whole charade had left me exhausted and not at all turned on, his fingers began to awaken desire in me.

236

He inserted one, and then two fingers deep into my pussy, sending a shiver of sensation through me that made me shudder visibly. He laughed his pleasure at my reaction. He continued to rub and finger-fuck my pussy until I was moaning and arching up into his hand. Just as I was about to come, he stopped and stood up in front of me. I opened my eyes to see him pulling his small but very erect penis out. He began furiously pumping his cock, positioned over my prostrate body and spread pussy.

After a few moments, he moaned loudly and then began to spurt over my belly and sex. I was still aroused and unsatisfied, and wasn't really expecting to get to come. I started to close my legs but he said, 'Keep them open, bitch. I'm not done with you yet.' Then he held his now flaccid penis over me and did something I will never forget. He pissed on my spread pussy, the hot urine splashing in a steady, hard stream against my clit. And here's the really perverse part of the whole thing: I came.

Chapter Sixteen
The Freedom Club

*I*t was two weeks before I could get away from the requirements of the Academy for a leave with my sweetheart. He sent me the plane ticket and said he would meet me at the airport. I was more than a little nervous to see him after these two weeks. What if it had only been an infatuation, as Amelia suspected? What if the magic was gone, an illusion born of need and wishful thinking?

Any fears evaporated when I saw him waiting at the gate. He stood back a little from the crowd, smiling, his arms crossed on his chest. When I came to him he wrapped me silently in a strong embrace, his face buried in my hair.

'Remy,' he whispered. 'You came back.' As if I wouldn't! I pulled back a little, and offered my lips up for a kiss. He kissed me, that sweet, warm kiss that had melted all resistance the first time we had touched. He took my small duffel-bag and said as we walked out of the terminal, 'Good that you packed light; you won't be needing much.'

Back at his place we ate a nice lunch of chicken salad sandwiches and fruit that he had prepared and then he turned to me, his eyes warm but his expression serious. 'Remy, we've had time to think things through, you and I. We've been apart these last two weeks and had time to decide if what we had together is something we want to continue. I want to tell you now that I have decided I want you whatever way I can have you. And if that doesn't include D/s, that's OK too. It's your call, Remy. That's what I'm trying to say. But understand this.' He paused, making sure I was focused on what he was saying. I was.

'Understand that, if you enter this relationship with me as my slave, there is no going back. I know it was a kind of game for you back at school, but with me it will be different. You will be my possession. I will own every part of you, from your toes, to your pussy to your breasts to your heart to your soul. Do you understand that? I would demand that nothing be held back from me, not now or ever. You would pledge your devotion, your servitude and your love for as long as we are together. I in turn will pledge my devotion, my guidance and my love for as long as we are together. Is that something you want, darling?' The similarity to wedding vows was not lost on me.

'Oh, yes, Eric. I want it. I have always wanted it, and I never even knew it was possible until we met. But this isn't even about want for me. I have no choice. I already belong to you. I just thank God that you want to claim what is already yours.' He held out his hand, smiling broadly, but there were tears in his eyes.

I came to him, rising from the chair. He pulled

me on to his lap and kissed me long and hard. 'We only have a weekend for now to cram in everything we can. I don't want to waste a second! Let me tell you how it will be for this weekend. You won't sit on any furniture, unless expressly invited to do so. I want to help you feel your new status as quickly as possible. You won't wear any clothing except what I give you and when I tell you. You will always kneel in my presence, and keep your eyes on my cock unless I am speaking to you, then you can look me in the face.

'I'm familiar with "safe words", as I presume you are, but we won't be using anything like that. You are safe with me by definition. You are safe because you can trust me to explore your limits carefully and to stop when I, as your master, think it is time to stop. Understand that you no longer call the shots. Everything is up to me. For this weekend, again to help you to more quickly appreciate your position, you will take no action without my express permission and approval. You won't eat food, or drink water, or pee on the toilet, without asking me first. You certainly won't come without permission, and you must always thank me for whatever I choose to do to you. Do you understand, Remy?'

His words were having a hypnotic effect on me. Just the words alone, uttered in his lovely baritone, were enough to soak my panties. I felt that delicious languor of submission fall over me, slowing my heart rate, parting my lips, engorging my pussy and nipples with desire. I nodded, sliding from his lap to the floor as I did so. I kneeled there, head bowed, my heart so full of love it actually hurt.

I felt his hand on my head. 'Go wash up, Remy,

and leave your clothes in the bathroom. Come to me in the bedroom when you're ready. I want to use you.'

I hurried to the bathroom, unable to control the huge smile that spread across my face. I was in heaven. This was what I had not been able to articulate, but had known somehow was there. This was what it was really about for me. This was what I had yearned for with Jacob, but hadn't had the words or understanding to seek.

I stripped and used a warm, soapy washcloth to freshen myself. Then I brushed my teeth and splashed on some perfume. I undid my French braid and shook my hair free over my shoulders. I hoped he would approve; I desperately wanted to please my new master.

Eric was on the bed, his shirt off, only in his faded jeans. I wanted to come and cover his hard, well-muscled chest with kisses, but of course I didn't. I kneeled at the foot of the bed, head bowed, arms behind my back, to await his bidding.

'I've gotten some toys since you were last here.' Eric was up now, getting something from his bureau. 'I can't wait to try them out on my little slave girl. I've been practising my technique, but have yet to try it out on a real person, so you'll have to let me know if I'm doing it right, Ms Expert Slave Girl.' He laughed and I smiled.

'See what I have for you, slave?' I looked up and saw that he had a large, heavy flogger, a riding crop, leather wrist and ankle cuffs, several dildos and gags, a blindfold, and lots of rope. I was impressed, and said so. Just seeing all that lovely equipment laid out got me even hornier than I already was.

'Get on the bed,' he said quietly, 'on your back. Spread your legs and put your arms over your head.'

I did as I was told, feeling my heart already beginning to thud in my chest. He attached the soft, leather cuffs to my wrists and ankles, looking at me tenderly as he did so. Taking my left leg, he raised it and attached it to a tie already secured high up on the post. He did the same thing with my right leg, so that my ass was lifted off the bed. Then he took each wrist and secured them to the top posts. I was completely immobilised now, but not at all afraid. I would have trusted him with my life.

'Oh, God, are you beautiful,' he sighed, and I felt myself colouring slightly. I loved his attentions, but I still wasn't used to them. He went over and picked up the crop. 'I think I'll start with this,' he informed me. 'It's the easiest one to handle. Just lie back and relax –' like I had a choice '– I want to warm that lovely flesh all over to get you in the mood.'

He began to smack my ass with the little square of hard leather. The smack of leather on skin always aroused me, as did the sting of the little crop. It didn't hurt at all, at first, as he warmed my skin, moving from my ass to my thighs, and then up to my stomach, my breasts, and back down again. I was breathing harder, but controlled and deeply. He put down the crop for a moment and I felt his lovely fingers invade my spread and very wet pussy. He slid in several fingers and I felt my muscles contracting on them. I tried to move into his hand, to position myself to fuck myself on his hand, but I couldn't move.

'Naughty little slut.' He laughed. 'Did I tell you you could move? Time for lesson number one.

242

Don't move until invited to do so.' He picked up the crop and smacked my delicate pussy folds, causing me to yelp and twist in my bonds. 'You forgot already! There you are, moving again! Let's try it once more.' Again he smacked my pussy, and again I yelled and twisted, not having been prepared for the quick blow. I was longing to press my thighs together, to escape the hard, leather stinging my pussy, but of course I couldn't.

'Remy, this isn't a game. Behave, or I will really punish you. I will tie you under the bed and leave you there for hours. Don't make me do that, honey. We don't have the time for this silliness. Now, get ready. I'm warning you this time. Stay still when I spank that naughty little pussy, or we'll be at this all night.'

Smack! Down came the crop, but this time I managed it. I sighed deeply but I did manage to keep from twisting away from the crop. Then it came down on my nipple, and I screamed, but again did not try to squirm away.

'Much better. I knew you could do it, Remy. You can do so much more than you think you can. I am going to help you discover just how far you can go.'

I wanted him so bad just then. If I had been free I think I would have fucked him! But I was bound and helpless, and forced to endure the delicious torment. He continued the cropping, covering every part of my body he could reach with the wicked sting. Then his large, cool hands were on me, soothing away the fire, lighting a new one in my belly. 'Thank me,' he murmured, his face in the hollow of my neck.

'Thank you, sir,' I breathed, meaning it.

He kissed my mouth, my neck, trailing down my

body to my wide-spread pussy. When his tongue flicked against the little bud of my clit I moaned, longing to thrust up into him, but mindful of his warning about moving without permission.

Eric kissed his way back up my body, leaving me almost desperate with desire, and straddled my chest, his strong buttocks resting lightly against my breasts. His large, thick cock was now poised level with my mouth. Without being ordered to do so, my lips had parted and my tongue snaked out, desperate for his beautiful penis. He eased forward slowly, until just the head was resting lightly against my lips. I eagerly began to lick and kiss the satiny, smooth skin, trying to suck him further into my mouth.

'Remy, Remy.' He laughed, his South Carolina accent rich like dark honey. 'You are such a little slut. But I forgive you, this one time, because I want this too bad to stop and punish you for not waiting for permission to kiss me. You will learn, darling. You will learn.'

He eased the cock further in now, and slowly glided the shaft until it was lodged just into my throat. I opened to him, accepting it all, sucking, licking, adoring that cock as he began slowly, sensually, to fuck my face. I could see the image of us in the mirror on the wall, my legs and arms spread wide, tied to the bed, my reddened ass exposed, and gorgeous Eric straddling me with his strong legs across me, his broad back leaning over me as he arched and thrust into my mouth.

'Are you mine, Remy?' he asked, his voice husky with lust. I nodded, unable to speak, his cock stuffed down my throat. 'Will you do whatever I want? Are you ready to suffer for me, to take what I give you, to learn grace and true submission?'

Yes, a thousand times yes, I would have screamed, had I been able. I was so deeply excited by this man, by his total and confident control, by his ability to arouse me so completely and so easily. And he wanted me! He wanted me for his slave girl! He wanted to use me till I dropped, to torture me until I cried, to love me until I died from pleasure.

The room was thick with the smell of sex, raw sex. I could smell his spicy, musky scent, mingling with our sweat, and my own wanton pussy juices. I was aching with need and I could feel the juice from my pussy actually tricking down my thigh. I was too far gone with lust to be modest about it. For the first time, I didn't long to slam my legs shut, to hide my obvious desire. I just wanted him to come, to spurt his lovely hot jism down my throat. And I wanted him to fuck me, hard and fast, to give me at last the release I craved.

Eric moaned, thrusting harder, holding my head still with a hand on each side, gripping my hair. I was ready, ready for the sweet, salty tang of his release, but before he went too far, he stopped and pulled out, his penis shiny with my saliva and his own precum. I forgot my now-aching arms and legs as he began to kiss me again, on my lips, my neck, my nipples, his hands running sensually up and down my body.

At last, he began to kiss and suckle my aching, needy pussy. My body jerked convulsively; I couldn't control the spasms of pleasure that wracked me. It was impossible to stay still as he had earlier commanded me, but luckily I was granted a reprieve as he said, 'You may move, my darling. Let go and give in to me totally. Come for me.'

I did, arching into him as far as I was able, bound spread-eagle as I was. 'Oh, God!' I screamed, and then, remembering my place, said, 'Please, Eric, please may I come?' The last word was drawn out, as my poor, undisciplined body had already succumbed totally to his touch. I couldn't have stopped that orgasm if I had wanted to.

He didn't answer, but continued to kiss me fervently, fiercely, as I came and came, my body hot from the cropping and my own exertions. Before the spasms had totally subsided, he climbed astride my body again, this time kneeling over me so that his hard cock slid smoothly into my spread and sopping pussy. I was longing to close my legs around him, to take him fully into me as deeply as possible, but as he had reminded me earlier, I wasn't the one running the show.

He began slowly to ease his rigid member in and out of my pussy, slowly, teasingly building the tension until I was literally whimpering with need for his thrust. Faster and faster, he began to fuck me hard now, slamming into me, our bodies slick with sweat, our breathing shallow and fast. I could feel from his rhythm that he was about to come and, as he did, he opened his beautiful, sea-green eyes and looked straight into mine. Our gazes held as he pumped his precious seed into me. It sent me over the edge and again I begged, 'Please, oh please, can I come?'

'Yes,' he whispered.

* * *

246

From passion and romance to schoolbooks and olive drab. The transition was a difficult one, and I could barely concentrate at school. I was still a member of the Hard Corps, but for me the pleasure was gone. And the need.

I'd done what Amelia had asked, and given it one more try. The pony thing, while very odd, had been an interesting experience. And even though I had even managed to come, it was more a physical reaction to stimulation than any real sensual experience. My heart just wasn't in it any longer. Someone had stolen that heart and I knew now with certainty that all I wanted to do was fall into Eric's arms and kneel at his feet. It was as if the Corps had been a practice drill, a dry run. This was the real thing, and I wanted it and only it.

I told Amelia I was ready to talk things over with her again. As soon as we both were free, we met again in the SCU building for our final talk. I think she knew before I started what I was going to say, but she waited patiently for me to begin. I decided to dive right in.

'Well. I don't quite know how to say this. I've never thought of myself as a quitter. But I want out. Out of the Slave Corps. Maybe even out of Stewart.'

Amelia's eyes widened in disbelief. 'Out of Stewart? But this is your life! You told me you wanted to be an officer since you were a kid! And you're halfway there. Why would you want to throw that away?'

'Well, I haven't decided that part for sure yet. But I've been doing a lot of thinking. I think I always wanted a military career because both my parents were in the army and that was what I knew. What I was comfortable with. What I thought I admired. I guess I never really examined my own motives. I just kind of decided back when I was a kid that this was what I would do, and then just stayed doggedly on the path without ever considering any options.

'But like I said, I'm not yet absolutely sure that I want to leave the Academy. But I do want to leave the Corps.'

Amelia looked resigned, but sad. 'I know the Corps isn't for everyone. It certainly isn't a substitute for romance, but it does have its own special offering: the chance to submit safely and in a variety of ways.'

'I have nothing against the Corps, Amelia. Really I don't. I guess I just can't reconcile it with who I'm becoming. I find that I have lost the yearning, the flush of desire, and need to submit to strangers. I want something more. I can't do it with sincerity. I would be betraying the Corps by staying in it when I feel like this. Surely you can see that.'

'I do, I guess, though I can't really relate, never having been in love myself.'

I went on, compelled to explain further. 'I guess I'm seeing things in a different way. The Corps isn't bad in itself. I think it's great, as far as it goes. I've learned a tremendous amount about myself and about D/s. But somehow it isn't enough anymore. No. It goes beyond that. It isn't right anymore. Not for me.'

As much because I was dying to share it with someone, as to explain myself to her, I told Amelia everything. About meeting Eric, and what it felt like to add love into the equation of submission and SM. How it took things to a different plane. How it made the Corps seem like too much of a game for me now. And sometimes a game whose rules I didn't like at all.

Amelia listened, rapt, sighing, and asking the occasional question. When I was done, she nodded, still looking a little sad. 'I understand, Remy. You've found something I could only dream of. True love.'

'Why do you say that? Why is that only a dream?'

'Oh, come on. It's me, Amelia. The fat girl with a nice personality. I love the Corps because here I'm treated like a total sex object. No one seems to mind if I don't have a perfect figure. They still want to strip me and beat me and use me like the slut girl I am.' Her eyes sparkled as she said this, and I couldn't help but smile back. But she was way off the mark.

'You are so wrong, Amelia. First of all, you aren't fat. And you seem to be slimmer every time I see you. Not only that, you have such natural grace, such obvious sensual submissiveness. My God, who wouldn't want to use you!'

Amelia blushed and looked down. 'Remy, do you really think so?' She spoke in almost a whisper, as if a sudden sound might make me admit that I was only kidding.

'Of course I mean it. And when you get out of the Corps and give yourself permission to find someone, you'll see. They'll be knocking the doors down.'

'Oh, I don't want to leave the Corps. I feel safe here. Safe and in constant demand. A perfect combination for a girl like me.'

'Well, I'm glad. I really am. I mean, that you should have this wonderful haven to explore your sexuality. It has been terrific for me, too. I just think

249

it's time for me to move on now. To continue would be to betray what I feel for Eric.'

'Did he tell you to quit?'

'No. Not once has he put the slightest pressure on me. So different from Jacob. It's like he really cares about me. About me, not just about our shared passion for SM. He told me he would wait for me. A thousand years, he said, if that was what it took. Isn't that romantic?'

Amelia giggled and then sighed. 'Is it ever,' she breathed. 'Well, we better get down to business.' She pulled out a stack of papers, all very formal and businesslike, from the folder she kept locked in a filing cabinet in the little room. 'You just need to read these, and sign these contracts where the Xs are. It's all pretty clear. Take your time. Read it all. I have to get to class, but just leave the stuff here and lock the door when you go. Don't forget to return your key. I'll be back later and I'll get it to the right people. Don't you worry. You aren't the first person to quit the Corps. You won't be the last.'

'Thanks, Amelia. I can't tell you what a terrific support you've been through all this.'

'Oh, Remy. I like to think we're friends. Not just here in the Corps, but in "real life" if you know what I mean. I hope you don't transfer out of Stewart. I would miss you terribly.'

'Well, if I do, I won't be going far. Just over to Columbia, South Carolina. It's only a few hours away. You can come out on breaks and visit. Who knows what might develop?' I grinned at her and she reached over and hugged me impulsively. Then she said goodbye and was gone. I sat down, fingering the little gold key I had worn for so long, and was now giving up voluntarily. Reading the pages set before me, I attended to the business of setting myself free.

Things happened rather quickly after that. It was weird to just go to class and PT, knowing there were no special assignments waiting in my mailbox to send me off, naked and vulnerable, to be whipped and used by some master or mistress in the Corps. Other Corps members seemed to avoid me. I was off limits somehow. I had left the secret life, but still knew of its existence. It felt very lonely.

Eric and I talked on the phone every night. One day I asked him to look into what it would take to transfer to the University of South Carolina. 'Oh, Remy! Do you really mean it? You would consider coming out here? To be with me? Oh, Remy! My heart is pounding.'

I laughed, delighted at his outspoken enthusiasm and pleasure. I was again reminded of the stark contrast between open, effusive Eric and tight-lipped, cautious Jacob. Everything seemed so easy with Eric, so right. With a few phone calls and a meeting with a guidance counsellor, I found it was very easy to change the entire path of my life. I was going to leave the Army I thought was in my bones and embark on something new with someone new.

During this process, I got a call from Dr Wellington. She had heard I was leaving, she said, and she wanted me to visit her in her office when I could get away. I went to see her, pleased that she wanted to see me, but prepared to object if she tried to talk me into staying at Stewart.

As I went into the chemistry building, with its constant vague, not entirely unpleasant smell of chemicals wafting from the student labs, and up to

251

her small office, I smiled, remembering how very nervous I had been that first time I had gone for an assignment with her and the then-hated Ms Dillon. How things had changed! Now Jean and I were friends, and I had discovered a definite bisexual streak in myself that I was looking forward to exploring with my master to guide me. I felt comfortable at last with my own body and my orientation as a submissive.

I knocked lightly on her slightly ajar door and the professor beckoned me to come in. 'Remy, how nice to see you. I hear you're leaving us!'

I smiled, a little nervously, and said yes, I was. I was transferring at the end of the term.

'So what happened, darling? Nothing in the Corps that ran you off, I hope –'

'Oh, no, Dr Wellington –'

'Please, Remy, call me Amanda. What is the point of such formality now? We are like old friends, after all.' She smiled impishly, reminding me without speaking that I had licked her shaven pussy until she came in my face, and that she had watched me be whipped and then made love to by another woman. We were certainly 'friends', and intimate ones at that.

'OK, Amanda, then. It has nothing to do with the Corps. At least not directly.'

'A man, isn't it? I see it in your face. You are in love.'

I felt myself blushing, and giggled, unable to suppress the little flutter of joy bubbling up through me. 'I guess that's true, though I can hardly believe myself that I would do something like this "for a man". Definitely doesn't fit my image of myself, or at least the one I used to have! But it isn't really like

252

that, anyway. I'm doing this for myself, not anyone else. I think I probably would have ended up leaving the Academy, and certainly the Corps, even if I hadn't met someone.'

'Tell me,' she said, leaning back in her chair, her eyes inviting me to continue. No reproach, no attempt to change my mind. I relaxed.

'Well, for a long time the Corps was very exciting to me, and you of all people know how much I wanted to get into it. But maybe the nickname, the Hard Corps, is really apt. It's a tough kind of place, just like this army gig. It isn't about warmth, or loving. It's about submission, but in a very limited way, for an hour here, an hour there, with virtual strangers. It was enough, more than enough, for me for a while, but not any longer.'

Amanda laughed. 'Yes, I can see that. I saw from the beginning a passion in you that isn't easily satisfied. I should have known we wouldn't get to keep you for long. I only wish you and I had had more of a chance together.' She looked down, almost shy.

'Could I ask you something, Dr, um, Amanda?'

'Anything you like.'

'Why are you here, at Stewart, and why the Slave Corps? You seem too romantic, and definitely not "regular army".'

'Well, Remy, the "army" part really doesn't affect me. I am a chemistry professor, and I teach chemistry to interested students. The fact that they also receive military training is of no interest or consequence to me, except maybe that the cadets are generally very respectful, more so than at the average college campus. The pay here is very competitive and the students are bright and ready to learn.

So really, as an academic, I find the life very satisfying.

'Now, as to the Corps. I got involved rather by accident. I had actually been working here for several years, blithely unaware of this secret society seething all around me, when I met someone here after hours at a party that was to change my life.

'You see,' she went on, warming to her story, 'I've been involved in BDSM for a long time, but would never dream of mixing work and pleasure. I've always had a dominant streak, but it didn't assert itself sexually until I got married.'

I lifted my eyebrows. I was not aware that she was married.

Answering my unspoken question she said, 'Oh, I'm divorced now, but I was married for six years to a lovely man named Howard Wellington. I kept the name because I like how it sounds. Much better than Weygant. But it just didn't work out between us. We got married too young, I think. But as I was saying, my dominance didn't become sexual until my husband got up his courage to confide in me that he was submissive, and longed for someone to control and use him. I was shocked at first, but very intrigued, and we began to experiment with the dominant/submissive lifestyle. I loved it, but nothing seemed to be enough for Howie.

'He wanted me to keep him bound and in chains at all times when at home. He got his cock and nipples pierced, and wanted me to brand him with my initials, something I could never quite get up the nerve to do.

'Well, we were at this party one night, this SM play party. I was in full dominatrix gear, all black leather and stiletto heels, with my Howie on his knees at my feet, cock and balls in a cage, ball gag in his mouth. And who should I see but my colleague, John Clements, all in black leather, his wife in cuffs and a corset, trailing along behind him! We both must have blushed a hundred shades of red, but then we laughed about what a small world it was when you were a pervert. We became friends as couples, and would meet on a regular basis to play. That is, until Howie left me.'

'Oh! I'm sorry,' I said, thinking how I would feel if Eric left me.

'Oh, it's ancient history now.' She smiled a little ruefully. 'I just wasn't enough for him, I guess. He needed more than I could offer. He wanted to be humiliated constantly. To be embarrassed in public, to be made to sleep naked outside, covered in filth, to be whipped until his skin was raw and bleeding. I just couldn't do it. The romance wasn't there for me. I wanted a partner, at least some of the time. He needed a sterner taskmaster than I could be for him. But I did love him. And I think he loved me, but, as I say, it just didn't work out.' She sighed, and was quiet for a moment. I tried to gently change the subject, to wipe that sad look from her eyes.

'And the Slave Corps? Where did that come in?'

'Oh, the Corps. Yes. Well, John knew I was pretty broken up about the divorce, and he mentioned that maybe I needed some distraction. He told me about the Corps, and invited me to join. I guess I have rank,' she said, smiling, 'because I didn't have to audition. Just John's recommendation was enough to get me mistress status right off the bat.

'Well, for these past four years I've found it a great distraction indeed! I get to indulge my sadistic fantasies and pleasures, with no strings attached. I

255

have my pick of lots of gorgeous boys and girls and use and abuse for as long as I like and then dismiss I like sleeping alone, and this way I get to, without explanation or apology.'

I smiled at her, but couldn't help thinking that it sounded like a rather lonely, if active lifestyle.

Again she read my mind. 'It is kind of lonely sometimes. But I do have friends, very dear friends both in and out of the Corps. And who knows maybe one day I'll get lucky and find my own true love, just like you seem to have done. I'm only thirty-four, after all, and there are lots of sweet little submissive boys in the sea.' She laughed, that wonderful, deep throaty laugh, and I couldn't help but laugh with her.

'Anyway, Remy, let's keep in touch. Here, take my card. It has my address and home phone number on it too. I'd love to meet your lover, too, and who knows what fun we might have?'

To use her words, who knew, indeed?

To my surprise, my parents didn't object too strenuously to my decision. They said it was my life, and I had the right, even the duty, to do whatever it took to be happy. If that didn't include a career in the military, they didn't mind. They said they were glad I was thinking of transferring to Columbia since we had family there.

Next came Aunt Salome, who was all excitement and support. Once the applications were submitted and things were in progress, she confided in me 'Remy, I never really thought that you were cut out to be a military gal. You have always had your head in the clouds, seems to me. Too romantic for all that heel-snapping saluting business, if you ask me.'

I finished out the year at Stewart, doing well in all courses. Eric and I met for weekends as often as we could, and our passion continued to startle and delight us both. I couldn't wait to move there permanently and take my place by his side and at his feet.

Surprisingly, though I'd been at Stewart for two years, I realised I wouldn't miss too many people when I left. I had held myself rather aloof, as I tended to do all my life. But for Amelia there would always be a special place. I got her to promise to come out to visit as soon as she could this summer. We were sharing a last few minutes on our favourite bench by the fountain when I said, 'You know, Amelia. I have some ideas for when I graduate. I want to start something. Something special for people like you and me. Not a Slave Corps. Not a civilian repeat of what we have here. Because when you think about it, the Slave Corps really isn't for the slaves at all. It's for the masters. I mean, as far as it goes, you can learn to submit within the Corps, but it's really up to what is inside of you. There isn't a nurturing, constant relationship where you can really develop as a submissive.

'Mostly, it's about how to look and act appealingly for the doms. It's about fulfilling their sexual fantasies without our own being at all considered. No. What I have in mind is something expressly for the submissive, man or woman.

'Maybe we could call it the Freedom Club. Freedom to submit with grace and sensuality. We could teach people to understand and accept their submissive natures. Help them to revel in the joy of their particular brand of sensuality, without shame and without compromise.'

257

Amelia's eyes were glowing. 'Yes!' she almost shouted. 'We could teach them all the technical stuff. How to take a whipping, how to swallow a cock to the hilt without a tremor of resistance. And we could add the poetry, the beauty, of true submission. We could even go further! We could train dominants to understand not only the power of their positions, but the responsibility.'

I interjected, my excitement growing as I saw her shared enthusiasm, 'We could teach them about the strength of true submission. We could show them how to whip without damaging, how to bind without marking, how to control without crushing the spirit of the one they control.'

'And don't forget,' said Amelia, laughing, a glint in her eye, 'we can have fun!'

We both laughed, out of breath, excited at our shared vision.

'Oh, Amelia! You have to come out to see us. Just as soon as you can. We can start work on this idea now. This could really be something important, something for us.'

She nodded, happily. At last we stood and embraced.

'See you soon, Amelia.'

She raised her arm in a gesture of triumph. 'Here's to the Freedom Club!'

BLACK LACE NEW BOOKS

Published in March

FIRE AND ICE
Laura Hamilton
£5.99

Nina is known as the Ice Queen at work, where her frosty demeanour makes people think she's equally cold in bed. But what her colleagues don't know is that Nina spends her after-work hours locked into fiery games with her boyfriend Andrew, ones in which she acts out her deepest fantasy – being a prostitute. Nina finds herself being drawn deeper and deeper into London's seedy underworld, where everything is for sale and nothing is what it seems.

ISBN 0 352 33486 X

MORE WICKED WORDS
Various. Ed. by Kerri Sharp
£5.99

Black Lace anthologies have proved to be extremely popular. Following on from the success of the *Pandora's Box* and *Sugar and Spice* compilations, this second *Wicked Words* collection continues to push the erotic envelope. The accent is once again on contemporary settings with a transgressive feel – and the writing is fresh, upbeat in style and hot. This is an ideal introduction to the Black Lace series.

ISBN 0 352 33487 8

GOTHIC BLUE
Portia Da Costa
£5.99

Stranded at a remote Gothic priory, Belinda Seward is suddenly prey to sexual forces she can neither understand nor control. She is drawn into a world of decadence and debauchery by the mysterious aristocrat André von Kastel. He has plans for Belinda which will take her into the realms of obsessive love and the erotic paranormal. This is a Black Lace special reprint.

ISBN 0 352 33075 9

Published in April

SAUCE FOR THE GOOSE
Mary Rose Maxwell
£5.99

Sauce for the Goose is a riotous and sometimes humorous celebration of the rich variety of human sexuality. Imaginative and colourful, each story explores a different theme or fantasy, and the result is a fabulously bawdy mélange of cheeky sensuality and hot thrills. A lively array of characters display an uninhibited and lusty energy for boundary-breaking pleasure. This is a decidedly X-rated collection of stories designed to be enjoyed and indulged in.

ISBN 0 352 33492 4

HARD CORPS
Claire Thompson
£5.99

Remy Harris, a bright young army cadet at a prestigious military college, hopes to become an officer. She understands that she will have to endure all the usual trials of military life, including boot-camp discipline and rigorous exercise. She's ready for the challenge – that is until she meets Jacob, who recognises her true sexuality and initiates her into the Hard Corps – a secret society within the barracks.

ISBN 0 352 33491 6

To be published in May

INTENSE BLUE
Lyn Wood
£5.99

When Nan and Megan attend a residential art course as a 40th birthday present to themselves, they are plunged into a claustrophobic world of bizarre events and eccentric characters. There is a strong sexual under-current to the place, and it seems that many of the tutors are having affairs with their students – and each other. Nan gets caught up in a mystery she has to solve, but playing amateur detective only leads her into increasingly strange and sexual situations in this sometimes hilar-ious story of two women on a mission to discover what they really want in their lives.

ISBN 0 352 33496 7

THE NAKED TRUTH
Natasha Rostova
£5.99

Callie feels trapped living among the 'old money' socialites of the Savannah district. Her husband Logan is remote, cold and repressed – even if he does have an endless supply of money. One day she leaves him. Determined to change her life she hides out at her sister's place. Meanwhile Logan has hired a detective and is determined to get his wife back. But she is now treading a path of self-expression, and even getting into the ancient art of Voodoo. Will he want her back when he finds her? And what will she do when she learns the naked truth about Logan's shady past?

ISBN 0 352 33497 5

If you would like a complete list of plot summaries of Black Lace titles, or would like to receive information on other publications available, please send a stamped addressed envelope to:

Black Lace, Thames Wharf Studios,
Rainville Road, London W6 9HA

BLACK LACE BOOKLIST

All books are priced £5.99 unless another price is given.

Black Lace books with a contemporary setting

RIVER OF SECRETS £4.99	Saskia Hope & Georgia Angelis ISBN 0 352 32925 4	☐
THE NAME OF AN ANGEL £6.99	Laura Thornton ISBN 0 352 33205 0	☐
BONDED £4.99	Fleur Reynolds ISBN 0 352 33192 5	☐
CONTEST OF WILLS	Louisa Francis ISBN 0 352 33223 9	☐
FEMININE WILES £7.99	Karina Moore ISBN 0 352 33235 2	☐
DARK OBSESSION £7.99	Fredrica Alleyn ISBN 0 352 33281 6	☐
COOKING UP A STORM £7.99	Emma Holly ISBN 0 352 33258 1	☐
THE TOP OF HER GAME	Emma Holly ISBN 0 352 33337 5	☐
VILLAGE OF SECRETS	Mercedes Kelly ISBN 0 352 33344 8	☐
PACKING HEAT	Karina Moore ISBN 0 352 33356 1	☐
TAKING LIBERTIES	Susie Raymond ISBN 0 352 33357 X	☐
LIKE MOTHER, LIKE DAUGHTER	Georgina Brown ISBN 0 352 33422 3	☐
ASKING FOR TROUBLE	Kristina Lloyd ISBN 0 352 33362 6	☐
A DANGEROUS GAME	Lucinda Carrington ISBN 0 352 33432 0	☐
THE TIES THAT BIND	Tesni Morgan ISBN 0 352 33438 X	☐
IN THE DARK	Zoe le Verdier ISBN 0 352 33439 8	☐
BOUND BY CONTRACT	Helena Ravenscroft ISBN 0 352 33447 9	☐

Black Lace books with an historical setting

Black Lace anthologies

Black Lace non-fiction

------✂------------------------

Please send me the books I have ticked above.

Name   ....

Address   ....

              ....

              ....

              .... Post Code ....

Send to: **Cash Sales, Black Lace Books, Thames Wharf Studios, Rainville Road, London W6 9HA.**

US customers: for prices and details of how to order books for delivery by mail, call 1-800-805-1083.

Please enclose a cheque or postal order, made payable to **Virgin Publishing Ltd**, to the value of the books you have ordered plus postage and packing costs as follows:
    UK and BFPO – £1.00 for the first book, 50p for each subsequent book.
    Overseas (including Republic of Ireland) – £2.00 for the first book, £1.00 for each subsequent book.

If you would prefer to pay by VISA, ACCESS/MASTER-CARD, DINERS CLUB, AMEX or SWITCH, please write your card number and expiry date here:

....

Please allow up to 28 days for delivery.

Signature ....

------✂------------------------